HAUNTED BY YOUR TOUCH

JEANIENE FROST

SHAYLA BLACK

SHARIE KOHLER

POCKET STAR BOOKS

New York   London   Toronto   Sydney

Pocket Star Books
A Division of Simon & Schuster, Inc.
1230 Avenue of the Americas
New York, NY 10020

This book is a work of fiction. Names, characters, places, and incidents either are products of the authors' imagination or are used fictitiously. Any resemblance to actual events or locales or persons, living or dead, is entirely coincidental.

Night's Darkest Embrace Copyright © 2010 by Jeaniene Frost
Darkest Temptation Copyright © 2010 by Sharie Kohler
Mated Copyright © 2010 by Shelley Bradley, LLC

First Pocket Star Books paperback edition November 2010

POCKET STAR BOOKS and colophon are registered trademarks of Simon & Schuster, Inc.

For information about special discounts for bulk purchases, please contact Simon & Schuster Special Sales at 1-866-506-1949 or business@simonandschuster.com.

The Simon & Schuster Speakers Bureau can bring authors to your live event. For more information or to book an event contact the Simon & Schuster Speakers Bureau at 1-866-248-3049 or visit our website at www.simonspeakers.com.

Cover design by Juliana Kolesova
Cover illustration by Gene Mollica

Manufactured in the United States of America

10 9 8 7 6 5 4 3 2 1

ISBN 978-1-4391-6676-5
ISBN 978-1-4391-6679-6 (ebook)

Contents

HAUNTED BY YOUR TOUCH

Night's Darkest Embrace

Jeaniene Frost

Chapter One

The sun's rays slipped further behind the Bed Bath & Beyond sign across the parking lot. Soon it would be dark. All I had to do was *not* be stupid until dark, less than ten minutes from now.

I wasn't going to make it.

Shoppers drove in and out of the complex. If they noticed me, they chose to mind their own business instead of asking why I was pacing like a crazy person in the back of the parking lot by a Dumpster. If my father were here, he'd urge me to follow their example and mind my own business, too. But the raspberry shimmer in front of the Dumpster called to me. Even the wafting stench of garbage wasn't enough to slow my pulse as I stared at it. This had to be the smelliest gateway this side of the Mississippi, but I was looking at the only known entrance into Nocturna.

For a few more minutes, anyway. The gateway was only active between dusk and dark.

The shimmer in front of the Dumpster started to fade even as the lights in the parking lot turned on, signaling the arrival of evening. If I let the gateway disappear, I'd do the same thing I'd done every night for the past month—go back to my apartment and try not to think about what lay on the other side of that fading raspberry veil.

Don't go back there, Mara. Please.

My father's plea replayed in my mind, but it wouldn't sway me this time. There were worse things than danger. Like guilt, or doing nothing and risking more people you loved being picked off.

I backed up several feet before flinging myself toward the Dumpster. Only the faintest haze remained in front of it now. My sneakers thudded on the pavement as I picked up speed, running right at the center of the smelly container, streamlining my body into a dive . . .

I barreled not into the metal Dumpster but into Nocturna, making it through the gateway before the veil closed into itself. I rolled when I hit the earth, the putrid stench of garbage instantly replaced with a heady, wood-smoke-scented air. Darkness also replaced the previous glow from the parking lot lights. It was always night in Nocturna. A few blinks later and my eyes adjusted, revealing a man on horseback galloping toward me.

"Back again, eh, Mara?" a familiar voice called out when the rider drew near enough for me to see the silver streak in his otherwise dark hair.

I brushed myself off as I stood. My backpack shifted with my movements but I shoved it into place, adjusting the straps until they were straight. Landing on my ass inside another dimension tended to jostle things.

"You're the best patrolman here, Jack, you know that?" I replied, not bothering to answer his question. Obviously I was back or we wouldn't be talking. "Most of the others don't find out if anyone's crossed over unless the person yells for them to give 'em a ride."

"People can pop up anywhere along the barrier, and that runs for miles," Jack said, still with an undercurrent of amusement. "And you said you weren't coming back the last time I saw you."

I didn't look at him but continued to brush my jeans, as though getting every last bit of dirt from them was extremely important. "Can't a girl change her mind without getting hassled? I missed this place—"

"Horseshit," Jack interrupted, even as his mount snorted in what sounded like agreement. "You still think you can find the Pureblood who took Gloria, but you need to let go of that fantasy and get on with your life."

I stiffened, my head snapping up to meet Jack's blue gaze. "I am getting on with my life," I said, biting off every word.

Jack shook his head in a way that reminded me of my father. The two men even looked a little alike, with their lightly lined faces and wiry frames. Plus, Jack had never made a single pass at me, which was why I trusted him enough to stay at his place when I came here.

"Suit yourself," he grunted. "I'm not your baby-sitter. You're too old for one now, anyway. Go on. You can use my cabin to freshen up."

I thought I heard Jack add, "Like usual," but I chose to ignore that. Now that I was here, a feeling of peace washed over me. Maybe it was because traveling through dimensions was my birthright as a partial demon. Or because I'd determined to let nothing stop me on this trip. That wouldn't be easy—or safe—but I was old enough now that most of the Purebloods weren't interested in me. Twenty-two was almost middle-aged to them. They only liked children or, at most, older teenagers.

Like Gloria had been. *And my half sister now was.*

That, more than the guilt over Gloria that was so familiar as to feel normal, was why I'd had to break my promise and come back. An overheard conversation between my little sister and her friend about Nocturna had been enough to convince me that I couldn't stay away. I was the only living eyewitness. If I never came back to search for the Pureblood who'd taken Gloria, maybe next time it would be my sister who was doomed to die a horrible death. Damned if I'd let that happen, no matter my father's fears.

By the time I followed the line of mounted lanterns that took me to Jack's cabin, I was convinced that I'd made the right decision. I went inside the small lodge, noting that Jack had added a few more crossbows to his weapons cache, but aside from that, nothing else had changed. The mirror Jack used for shaving looked like it hadn't been cleaned since the last time I'd wiped it, and his floor probably hadn't been swept since then, either. If I didn't stay here occasionally, the dirt would be up to Jack's waist.

I pumped some water from the spigot and cleared away the dust from the mirror, frowning a little once I saw my reflection. Dirt smudged my cheek and I had bits of leaves in my hair. That wouldn't do.

A few more pumps of the spigot and I washed off the remaining traces of dirt from my face, using my fingers to comb bits from the forest floor out of my hair. At least I thought I got it all out; the dried leaves matched the deep brown color of my hair, so a few stragglers might have remained. Then I shrugged out of my backpack and took off my jeans, T-shirt, and sneakers to put on the long denim skirt, boots, and blouse that I'd folded up inside. The other clothes were more comfortable, but a little glimpse of cleavage or a flash of leg went a long way toward getting reluctant residents of Nocturna to spill information. Once I was finished, I put on my gun belt and then my leather jacket, giving my reflection another critical glance.

Lipstick would help, but I'd forgotten to slip some into my backpack. Lucky for me, my mouth was naturally full and reddish, so that, along with a clean face and somewhat tamed hair, would just have to do.

Multiple lights glowed in the distance as I left the lantern-strewn path and approached Nocturna's version of a metropolis. When I first came here, I thought it looked like a cross between the Victorian era and the Wild West. Tethered horses and carriages lined the narrow streets instead of cars, with candlelight the only brightness against the perpetual darkness. Music floated out from different bands, merging together to form a profusion of sounds that dulled out the laughter, shouts, and occasional gunshots from the town's many occupants.

And at the end of the mini-city, set apart from the grid of bars, whorehouses, hotels, and pawnshops, was Bonecrushers. Skulls lit up like jack-o'-lanterns illuminated the front of the bar, a warning that those seeking tamer fun should look elsewhere.

If only Gloria and I had heeded that warning several years ago, but to us, Bonecrushers had looked more exciting than frightening. Add that to the "You're not scared, are you?" challenge from our dates, and nothing would've stopped us from walking through those doors.

Nothing would stop me this time, but that wasn't because of teenage bravado anymore. Bonecrushers was my only link to the Pureblood who'd taken Gloria, so just like all the previous times I'd come here over the past two years, once again, that's where I was headed.

I took a deep breath, then strode into the town, not pausing to look at the various people on the sidewalks. My quick pace—plus the guns holstered on my belt—said I wasn't in a mood to buy something, get laid, or get robbed, which meant I was of no use to most of Nocturna's residents. Rafael kept a loose form of law, but "accidents" were common. No surprise, considering everyone here was at least part demon, and the day people with demon blood could completely obey rules would be the day things got snowy in hell.

Not that I'd seen hell to know if it snowed there or not. Only Pureblood demons could travel through the gravitational layers separating the first few realms from each other. Beyond that, only the original race of fallen angels could make it all the way through the rest of them to the mythical Sheol.

That was the story, anyhow. No one I knew had ever met a Fallen and lived to tell about it. Pureblood demons fed off the life essence of partial demons like me, but the Fallen fed on Purebloods, leaving the predators in the unfamiliar position of being prey. In my opinion, it was poetic justice.

"Mara."

I jerked my head toward the sound of my name, cursing myself for dropping my attention from my surroundings. In Nocturna, that was a good way to end up hurt — or worse.

"Hiya, Billy," I said in a casual tone, pretending I'd spotted the brawny Halfie all along. "What's new?"

Billy grinned, showing sparkling white teeth that contrasted with his unkempt appearance and tattered leathers. "I guess what's new is that you're *not* gone for good," he noted with amusement.

All those farewells would bite me in the ass now. In my defense, I'd meant it at the time. I just hadn't counted on how heavy my guilt would get if I officially gave up on avenging someone I'd already let down in the worst way.

"Who could live without Bonecrushers's famous warm beer?" I asked flippantly. "Bars serve it watered down and chilled on the other side. Couldn't stomach it."

Billy laughed, his bald head gleaming in the reflection of the lit skulls around him. "Sure. But just in case that's not the only thing you came for, thought you should know: He'll be here soon."

Before I could stop myself, I glanced behind Billy to the open doorway of Bonecrushers. The sensible part of me warned that I could still leave, it wasn't too late . . . but my determination slapped that down. One-quarter reckless demon in my genetic makeup was enough to overcome three-fourths of cautious human any day.

"He who?" I asked, as if I didn't know.

Billy laughed, his deep voice making it sound like his vocal cords were grinding together. "Right. Come on, Mara. I'll buy you a brew, since you came all the way through a dimension for it."

His tone said he wasn't fooled. For a second I hesitated, despair competing with resolve in me. Billy knew I was here for more than Bonecrushers's heated, throat-searing beer. But did he also know, as Jack did, that I'd been drawn back to Nocturna for more reasons than its darkly alluring ruler?

No need to wonder about that waiting out here. I swept out my hand.

"First round's on you? Lead the way, my friend."

Billy shouldered past the crowd by the door and I followed him inside. The open fire pit in the middle of the bar, combined with oil lanterns hung in various locations and the close proximity of numerous people, raised the temperature about twenty degrees from Nocturna's natural chilliness. I took off my leather jacket, tying it around my waist instead of holding it. It had been several months since I'd needed to shoot anyone, but just in case, I wanted both my hands free.

Several sets of male eyes wandered over me as I passed by. I nodded to the people I recognized and gave cool stares to those I didn't. Acting coy would have been like begging for those stares to turn into Bonecrushers's version of being hit on, which frequently consisted of being tongue-kissed before introductions were even exchanged. Shame to end my no-shooting streak on such a silly thing as an unwary flirter.

"Hank," Billy called out once he reached the bar. "Two brews."

The band began playing something that might

have been Nirvana's "Smells Like Teen Spirit." The music here tended to be at least a decade behind the times, and the band's look was something from a former era, too. The musicians were pale even by Nocturna's standards, with dark circles under their eyes and clothes that hung off bony frames. The lead singer had no microphone, electricity seldom working in this realm, but he managed to keep his voice louder than the chatter or the continual smashes of drink glasses into the fire pit.

"Someone should tell those guys that the 'heroin chic' look went out in the nineties," I noted to Billy when I made it next to him at the bar.

He grinned, handing me a beer the bartender thunked on the counter. "Help 'em out. Bring some new *Rolling Stone* magazines next time you come over."

Better to let him think I was indecisive than tip him off to my goal. "Maybe there won't be a next time. I like sunshine, cars, electric toothbrushes, iPhones . . . all those things Nocturna will never have."

Billy's smile turned sly. "Some people can't live without those. But you, Mara, you can't live without your kind."

"Except for my stepmother, my family's all part demon." I took a swallow from my mug and savored the burn regular beer never left. "I've also got Partial friends on the other side, so I'm around lots of my kind."

"That's not what I meant. You're caged there, but here"—Billy raised his beer, indicating our general surroundings—"here we don't pretend to be so emotionless or controlled. Some Partials can shut that part of themselves off, but you're not one of them. Neither am I."

Billy finished his beer in a single gulp, then sent the empty mug sailing into the fire pit. I took another drink, but slower, quietly acknowledging the truth in his words. My part-demon heritage meant I often did feel stifled living in the normal world, but at least there, I didn't have to worry about Purebloods snatching up younger members of my family.

Or wonder which people around me might be helping them get away with it.

I scanned the faces in the crowd more out of habit than the thought that I could spot a Pureblood demon. Partials, Purebloods . . . all of us looked the same. Stand us next to humans and you couldn't spot the supernaturals unless you caught the tiny lights that occasionally appeared in our eyes. Even Fallen were supposed to look normal until their hidden wings made an appearance, but if you saw those, it was already too late to run.

A hand appeared next to my arm, fingers long and masculine, with an ancient knot adorning the index finger and a simple ebony band encircling the thumb. Even if I hadn't recognized those rings, I'd have known who was behind me for one simple reason—my heart had sped up, like something inside me had known he was close before the rest of me registered it.

"Rafael," I said, not turning around.

That hand slid along my arm in the lightest of caresses, belying strength that had bested even a Pureblood in a fight. Beside me, Billy inclined his head.

"Rafe," Billy rumbled. Then he got up and winked at me. "See ya later."

I didn't protest Billy's departure. Acting flustered would have been the same as slapping a sign on my forehead that said Too Damned Interested For My Own Good.

I tipped my mug at the man as he slid into Billy's seat, admiring Rafael out of the corner of my eye. He moved with a beautiful, controlled fluidity, each gesture full of grace and purpose. His long jacket was open, revealing the trademark black leather vest studded with thin knives over a dark blue shirt. Only Rafael could make post-apocalyptic fashions look sexy.

"You've been away a long time," Rafael said, his voice soft compared to the gaze he lasered on me.

I shrugged, glancing back to the scarred wooden bar instead of his vibrant blue eyes. "Technically, with how it's always the same endless night here, I haven't been gone at all—"

"Weeks," he cut me off as his tone hardened. "Tell me I'm wrong."

I took another swallow of my beer, but not even supernatural liquor could suppress my shiver as I turned to stare fully at Rafael. His golden-red hair and cobalt eyes accentuated high cheekbones and a face that could make angels weep with jealousy. If it wasn't for his deadliness, Rafael's ethereal looks might invite constant challenges to his being ruler. But the three-quarter demon was as ruthless as he was dazzling, enabling him to stay in control of Nocturna for the past two hundred years. He could rule for the next two hundred if he could hold off future challengers. Time froze in Nocturna. Night didn't turn into day, seasons didn't change, and even aging stopped—one of the big lures of living in a secondary dimension versus the modernized world.

And I had to stop letting Rafael get to me, especially when I wasn't sure if he was helping Purebloods shuttle Partials from this realm to the next.

"What, you missed me?" I asked with a softly challenging grunt.

"And if I did?" Rafael caressed his words while tiny lights began to gleam in his eyes. He leaned closer, warm breath falling against my skin with his next words. "Would you like that?"

Truthfully, *yes*. For many reasons, not least of which was the secret crush I'd had on him since I was fifteen. But Rafael knew more about what had happened to Gloria than he'd let on. All the information I'd gathered in the past two years of poking around Nocturna implicated him either directly or indirectly. Plus, he'd never really explained why he'd been there that night, so conveniently close when the Pureblood had tried to pull me through the barrier. . . .

"Speechless, Mara?" he asked, a hint of a smile curving his lips.

I took another long sip of my beer — and started to choke as I sucked in a breath instead of swallowing. The bar and its surrounding seats were two steep steps up from the rest of Bonecrushers, giving me an elevated view of its occupants even while seated. And for the briefest moment, my gaze locked with that of a young man who was just ducking out the front door.

One glance was all I needed to recognize him. After all, his face had been burned on my memory for the past seven years. *Ashton.*

Chapter Two

I vaulted to my feet, still choking, beer leaking out of my mouth and nose as I charged into the crowd after the Pureblood. Rafael tried to grab my arm but I shoved him aside, already pulling out one of my guns. Several large bodies blocked me, giving me annoyed glances as I shouldered past them, still coughing and spewing beer, but even though my eyes watered from the burn in my lungs, I didn't slow down. I *knew* one day he'd come back!

"Mara, wait!" Rafael commanded.

I didn't look back but continued to plow my way toward the front, barreling into Billy, who lounged by the door. He grabbed me at a shouted word from Rafael, making me curse as I attempted to wrest away. Only our friendship kept me from shooting him on the spot.

"Let me go!" I tried to scream, but it came out in a gasping cough that splattered more beer. Even if Billy understood, he ignored me, holding my arms in a hard grip and nimbly avoiding the kicks I aimed at his legs.

Firm pounding began on my back a moment later, helping me expel the liquid in my lungs all over the front of Billy's shirt. Through my watering vision, I saw him give a disgusted grimace, but since he wouldn't budge from his position, I couldn't see past him to find out which direction Ashton had taken.

A few more measured whacks on my back later and I could breathe enough to talk, but that didn't make me less furious.

"Let me go or I'll blast a hole right through you!"

Billy released me at the same time that strong hands grasped my shoulders and spun me around. Rafael backed me out of the door while managing to block the gun I tried to raise at him.

"Cranky when you choke, aren't you?" he noted without the slightest hint of anger.

"Damn you, he's getting *away*," I snapped, looking over his shoulder and trying to jerk free at the same time.

Rafael frowned, glancing behind me. "Who?"

"The Pureblood who kidnapped Gloria!" I all but roared, so frustrated that I didn't care who overheard me.

Rafael let me go so abruptly that I stumbled. My gun went off when I instinctively reached out with it to break my fall. For a sickening second, I wasn't sure if I'd shot someone. Then I jumped to my feet, determining to apologize later, if that was the case, but I had to find Ashton *now*.

When I glanced around, Rafael was nowhere to be seen. I didn't pause to wonder where he'd gone but ran to the back, behind Bonecrushers. This was where the sneaky Pureblood would go instead of heading into the more well-lit areas of town. Behind the bar was an expanse of dark fields that stretched for miles until they met woods that reached all the way to the end of Nocturna—and the gateway leading to the next realm. But with these high, swaying grasses, I couldn't see if Ashton was in them, and even at my best run, I couldn't catch up with him. I needed a horse.

I spun around, hating the necessity of heading in the opposite direction from where I *knew* Ashton had run, but having no choice. Once in front of Bonecrushers, I grabbed the reins of the first horse I saw, tensing for the blasting pain from a gunshot if its owner saw me. *One bullet won't kill you*, I reminded myself as I swung up into the saddle, whirling the horse toward the back of the bar and that cloaking darkness. It would take two shots to be lethal to a Partial like me, though one would do damage, that was for sure.

Luckily for me, no gunshots tore into my back. I spurred the horse into a gallop, one hand on the reins and the other grasping my gun. The horse charged through the tall grass like it knew exactly where we needed to go, to my relief. To stop a Pureblood, I'd need to land at least three good shots, and I needed to be close in order to see Ashton. *Let me get him in my sights*, I prayed. No way would I miss.

Gloria's smile flashed in my memory, as bright and mischievous as her personality had been. *Mara, this is Drew and Ashton. They're Partials, too, and guess what—they know how to get into Nocturna!*

I remembered the thrill those words had elicited. Our parents had strictly forbidden us from going into any realms and had refused to tell us where the gateways were, so that had made Drew and Ashton irresistible. It helped that they'd been hot, too, and since our parents had thought we'd been seeing a double movie, our evening had been wide open. So I'd cheerfully gone with my cousin and her two new friends to the smelly Dumpster at the back of Bed Bath & Beyond without a single protest, thinking this would be the most exciting night ever.

And I'd been the only one to come back through that gateway, hating myself as I'd told my aunt and uncle they would never see their daughter again. They'd eventually forgiven me, but I hadn't forgiven myself. How could I? If I'd refused to go with Gloria, or told our parents, or even *once* tried to stop her, Ashton wouldn't have taken her where none of us could follow to save her.

And now, just like I'd anticipated, he was back. Probably trolling for more young Partials to snatch away and feed on. What if my sister decided to wander into Nocturna with some friends one night, knowing the dangers but drawn toward the wild realm, like Gloria and I had been? No drinking age and an entire dimension to party in was a powerful lure for a lot of teen Partials, because of course bad things happened to *other* people, not them. If my sister ran into Ashton, she'd never know what he was until it was too late.

My hand tightened on the gun and I ducked closer to the horse's neck to urge the animal faster. *Where are you?*

Even with the rush of wind and pounding hooves, I thought I heard a whoosh above me. Startled, I looked up, but the town's lights didn't reach this deep into the field. No moon brightened Nocturna's sky to provide contrast against the endless darkness, either. The moon didn't exist on this side of the realm. Only the stars prevented the field from being swallowed up by impenetrable blackness, and somehow, plant life here managed to renew itself in a reverse sort of photosynthesis with starlight instead of sunlight.

I snapped my attention back to the barely visible grass in front of me. Did I hear scrambling off to the left? I kneed the horse in that direction, straining my eyes against the breeze and the darkness. It was so hard to see, and being enveloped in blackness with the pounding of the horse's hooves, wind, and my drumming heartbeat brought back awful memories.

My nose was stuffy from crying, but the duct tape plastered across my mouth meant those clogged inhala-

tions were the only things keeping me alive. Grass blades slashed at my face like whips, burning my cheeks, until we entered the forest. Then the grass was gone, but the trees blocked out most of the starlight. I couldn't see Gloria anymore. Last I'd glimpsed, she was slung over Ashton's horse just like I was slung over Drew's. Neither rider slowed his pace, however. I prayed the horses would stumble, or that something would stop them from taking us deeper into the woods, but nothing happened. The Purebloods must be able to see in the dark.

Purebloods. My nose threatened to close completely with my fresh spurt of tears. Ashton and Drew were Purebloods, and every child of my race knew what would happen if we were ever taken by one of them. . . .

I slowed when the horse's rapid pace brought me to the end of the field. Once there, I trotted along the edge of the forest instead of entering it. Ashton could still be hiding somewhere in the tall grass. Or maybe he'd outpaced me and made it into the forest; it wasn't likely, but Purebloods *were* very fast runners. The barrier had to be where Ashton was heading. He'd seen me, and I didn't doubt that he'd recognized me, too.

Did I risk getting lost in the forest trying to beat him to the barrier, or should I continue combing the grasses? The forest offered more danger than just further reduced vision. Ashton might not be the only Pureblood in the area. Most residents of Nocturna avoided the forest. They knew that going into it might be the last thing they ever did.

If only batteries didn't always fry when crossing through the gateway! What I wouldn't give for a high-powered flashlight right now, or some night-vision goggles. Sure, I had my guns, but without visibility they didn't do me much good. Ashton could be waiting to ambush me from above in a tree, and I wouldn't even see him until he knocked me off my horse.

I muttered a curse before swinging the horse around and backtracking through the waist-high grasses. Maybe Ashton was somewhere close, hiding. Waiting to see if I was rash enough to go into the forest and give him the advantage. The other thought was too frustrating to contemplate. *Maybe he was already in the forest, running toward the barrier, and I was letting him get away.*

I led the horse in a brisk trot down the length of the field parallel to the tree line, cursing the darkness and the high grasses the entire time. Ashton could be fifty yards away, but if he was stealthy, odds were I wouldn't spot him. This field was large, too. Five miles square, easily.

Ashton had all the time in the world if he chose to wait me out.

Something stirred the grass ahead, about thirty feet in the distance. I didn't charge right toward it but did a wide circle, not wanting to startle my target into hiding.

Yes. A definite disturbance in the grass. I tightened my grip on my gun until my hand ached. *Come out, Ashton, where I can see you.*

My heart began to hammer as a tall form stood up where that disturbance was, revealing himself from the concealment of the grass.

Thank you! I sighted down the barrel and—

"Mara."

I jerked the gun up just in time. That silhouette strode toward me, starlight faintly reflecting off golden-crimson hair as he drew near.

Rafael. He'd been out here searching, too.

"Did you see anyone?" I demanded in a low voice, half wondering if he'd tell me the truth if he had.

"I saw no one."

Something in his tone made me narrow my eyes. "He's out here," I said crisply when I diagnosed what that tone was. *Doubt.* "He might have headed into the woods."

Rafael turned to consider the tall, forbidding forest ahead of us. "Go on," he said finally. "I'll watch out for you."

I shouldn't have found that reassuring, but for an inexplicable reason, I did. Maybe it was because I hoped I was wrong about Rafael's involvement with Purebloods, even if the cynical part of me doubted I was wrong. Or perhaps it was my frustration at the thought of Ashton skipping through the woods, chortling to himself over how I was too chicken to follow. Caution urged me not to trust Rafael, but desire for revenge had me spurring the horse into the ancient forest with a firm kick.

Just like before, three-quarters cautious human was no match for one-quarter reckless demon.

I bent close to the horse's neck as I navigated the woods, trusting the animal when he side-stepped over dips in the ground I couldn't see. I'd only gone a couple hundred yards before I realized my chances of finding Ashton in this pitch-black maze had gone from bad to worse. The trees towered above, shutting out most of the light and making only the immediate area in front of me faintly visible. If I'd been human, I couldn't have seen my hand in front of my face, but I didn't have enough demon in me to see as clearly as Ashton could. Still, I kept going, hoping he'd be arrogant enough to show himself or try something.

Of course, if Ashton was in league with Rafael, these darkened woods would end up being my tomb. I didn't like the idea of rotting here forever, so I discarded that thought. I'd chosen to trust Rafael—for the moment. So for the moment, I'd believe that if Ashton tried to ambush me, Rafael would step in long enough for me to get off a few good shots.

Then, *oh, then*, I'd make the Pureblood pay for what he'd done to Gloria.

But as my internal clock told me that more than an hour had ticked by since I'd first glimpsed Ashton at Bonecrushers, even my dim hopes of catching him waned. There simply were too many places he could hide in these woods. I kept my senses as sharp as possible, straining to hear the slightest sound that wasn't a natural part of the woods, but nothing stood out. No telltale footfalls, no snapping branches, no indication of the Pureblood who'd gotten away for far too long.

Still, I didn't stop but kept steering the horse grimly in the direction that I hoped was the right one. Getting lost here would be easy, with no real way to identify landmarks, and forget about navigating by the stars. I only caught the barest glimpses of them through spaces in the canopy of leaves above me.

Just when I thought that I was indeed hopelessly lost, something loomed ahead, as black as a snapshot into oblivion. My pulse picked up as I realized what it was. The barrier. I hadn't been going in circles; I'd steered the horse right to the end of Nocturna and the wall that marked the boundary between it and the next realm.

That wall loomed above the trees, disappearing from my vision into the sky. I ignored the thumping of my heart and went nearer, thinking that although it wasn't made up of rock, it looked like the sheer face of a cliff. Once we were only a dozen feet from it, my horse sidestepped away with a nervous neigh. Truth be told, I was rattled by the sight of it, too. I hadn't seen it since that night, when I'd stared in horror as a section of it had parted to let Ashton — still clutching Gloria — through. If not for Rafael, I would've been next to vanish into its surface, never to be seen again.

Physicists had an explanation for barriers that separated the multiverses from one another. They called it M theory, hypothesizing that the membranes dividing up the dimensions were invisible. In that, they were close to right. They *were* invisible, but only to humans. If you had demon blood in you, you could see them plain as day, and this one was huge.

I climbed off the horse, still holding the reins so the animal couldn't bolt away, to walk over and trace my hand over the cool surface of the barrier. If I'd been a Pureblood, I could have parted this with my power, pulling me and anyone I had a hold of through the gravitational field separating the realms. But if I were a Pureblood, then I would have been a ruthless predator like Ashton, snatching away Partials to feed off of. Making sure my victims were young, because the life essence from youth had more power to nourish me. *Bastard.*

Some powers would never be worth their price.

"Get away from that."

At the first syllable, I whirled, aiming my gun, but then I recognized Rafael's voice and froze instead of squeezing the trigger. Damn it, that was twice I'd almost shot him tonight! This time, not a single twig had snapped, nor had any other noise preceded him to warn of his presence. He was so silent that if I hadn't been staring right at him, I'd have sworn no one was there.

"You think something's on the other side, just waiting to pull me through?" I asked, very softly.

I couldn't see his features, but I could make out the pinpoints of light in his eyes, like specks of stardust in the dark.

"You never know."

I stared at him as I moved away from the barrier. Rafael looked more like a compilation of shadows in the almost nonexistent light. Him, the barrier, the woods . . . it all served to make the rest of that memory come roaring back.

Something big crashed into us, driving me and Drew off the horse onto the ground. For a second, I was stunned, and dirt lodged up my nose, making it even harder to breathe. Hard, heavy forms tumbled over me before rolling away. Over the furious sounds of a struggle, I heard Ashton's shout.

"Drew! What's going on?"

Couldn't breathe! I rubbed my nose with my bound hands, trying to dislodge the dirt from it. My chest burned with a pain that made every other ache fade into insig-

nificance. One nostril cleared and I took in a staggered breath that wasn't enough, not nearly enough. Lights began exploding in my vision as a rushing noise filled my ears. Ashton shouted something else, but I couldn't make it out this time. Through my narrowing vision, my eyes focused enough to see him. Ashton's back was against what looked like an enormous wall, holding up a lantern with his other arm tight around Gloria.

And then a slit appeared in that wall behind him. Ashton melted into it, still clutching Gloria, both of them disappearing even as I screamed into my gag. A hard grip seized me, flipping me around, crushing me to the ground as I tried to scramble away. Then air— luscious, beautiful air!—filled my lungs as the duct tape was torn from my mouth and I sucked in a breath that ended on a sob.

"Gloria!"

"Why were you there that night, Rafael?" I asked, staring at the man who'd killed Drew and saved me. "What were you doing in the woods at just the right moment?"

Silence, then his shoulder moved in what might have been a shrug. "I told you before; something about those two boys struck me as odd when I noticed them at the bar. So I decided to patrol the barrier just in case and heard the horses."

Plausible, but I didn't believe him. Rafael was the ruler here. It would've made more sense if he'd sent someone to check the barrier instead of going himself.

Just like it didn't make sense that he'd come here now, by himself. Was he really trying to help me catch Ashton . . . or was he helping the Pureblood escape instead?

"Everyone says you're a three-quarter demon," I began in as casual a tone as I could manage. I was about to stomp on thin ice, but if Rafael meant me harm, I was screwed anyway. "That means one of your parents was a Pureblood. With a Pureblood for a parent, you must not hate them like the rest of us do. In fact, I've often wondered—what do you feed on? Regular food, or something else?" *Like Partials*, my tone implied.

A derisive snort escaped him. "I don't feed on what you're thinking, my sweet, or I would've eaten my fill of you years ago."

"Maybe I'm not your type," I murmured.

This time, laughter floated over to me before the caress of his words. "Oh, you're exactly my type, Mara."

A tremor ran through me. He'd projected only stern aloofness the night we'd met, telling

me who he was and forbidding me from returning to Nocturna while I was still a teenager.
Once I'd returned at twenty to backtrack over
my family's long-cold search for Gloria's kid-
napper, however, Rafael had made his interest
clear. I'd managed to hold him at arm's length
despite my attraction, but maybe I'd been going
about this all wrong. What if all the answers I
sought about Ashton and trafficking Purebloods
could be found by going *through* Rafael, instead
of *around* him?

"I'm cold," I said, deliberately giving a light
shudder. It was true; my jacket had come untangled from my waist sometime during my wild
ride, and my sleeveless blouse and denim skirt
weren't proper outdoor wear for these tempera-
tures.

"I don't think the two of us can find him, so will
you send a patrol out?" I continued. "Right now
I want nothing more than to go back to Bonecrushers and have a tall mug of hot beer."

He came closer, almost near enough for me to
see the faultless hollows and contours of his face.
"I'll send a patrol, but they might be looking for
a ghost. Are you *sure* you saw the same boy from
that night?"

Ashton's face flashed in my mind; black hair cut close, slightly crooked nose, brown eyes, and an easy smile. I'd only glimpsed him for a second, but I had no doubt. It was him. He wasn't a ghost born out of my guilty conscience.

"If I'm wrong, your patrol spends a boring several hours stomping through the woods. If I'm right, you might catch a Pureblood. What's to lose?"

He inclined his head. "Very true."

Then Rafael leapt onto the back of my horse, the animal's grunt the only noise from his movement. "Climb up," he said, holding out his hand. "We'll ride back together, and then I'll send some men out."

I slid my hand into his even as my plan finalized in my mind. It was far-fetched, yes, and it might get me killed, but if I succeeded . . . I'd find out exactly where the ruler of Nocturna stood regarding Purebloods.

"Hurry," I told Rafael after he pulled me up and I settled myself against his chest.

His arms tightened around me as he spurred the horse forward at a brisk pace. I said nothing, grimly noting what had escaped me back when I was a terrified teen and I'd thought Rafael was the demon version of a knight in shining armor.

He could see well enough in the dark that he didn't need to take the horse at a walk through the forest, like I had. The only other people I'd met who could see that well were Drew and Ashton. What if Rafael was more than a three-quarter demon? People only had his word that he wasn't a Pureblood, but to my knowledge, no one had met either of Rafael's parents to know for sure. He'd saved me from Drew several years ago, but maybe because Drew and Ashton had been hunting here without his permission, not because he bore the same animosity for Purebloods that all other Partials did.

If I was right, what I intended to do was akin to covering myself in meat before jumping into a lion's den, but it also might be the quickest way to get to Ashton. All I had going for me was the hope that this lion wouldn't see me coming.

Or that he'd turn out to be a vegetarian.

Chapter Three

Rafael might prove to be a Pureblood in Partial's clothing, but at least he saved me from a nasty confrontation with the owner of the horse I'd commandeered. When we rode up to Bonecrushers, a very beefy, very pissed-off Partial was describing to a group of onlookers all the different ways he'd beat the shit out of whoever had taken his ride. I'd have been forced to either shoot him to defend myself or take that beating, which, since I'd stolen his horse, most people in Nocturna would agree I deserved. But Beefy Angry Man went so abruptly silent when he saw Rafael astride his mount that it was all I could do not to laugh.

"Thanks for the loan," Rafael said pleasantly as he climbed off, lifting me and setting me on my feet before I could jump off as well.

"Well . . . since it's you. . . ," the man sputtered. The onlookers, who'd hung around expecting to see an ass kicking, wisely decided to go back inside.

Who said demons couldn't be civilized?

"Why don't you get your beer and I'll meet you after I've spoken to my men?" Rafael offered, still in the same pleasant tone with its I-dare-you-to-disagree undercurrent.

Since I'd said that was all I wanted, I was stuck now.

"Sure. I'll, ah, see you at the bar."

Ten minutes later, I pretended to be enraptured with my beer, but in reality, I strained to hear what Rafael was saying to Billy and several other of his men. Between the band and the noisy crowd, I probably only caught every fifth word. For all I knew, he could have been directing them to patrol the forest for Ashton . . . or telling them to gather up some extra firewood.

Didn't matter. This might have been a half-assed plan, but it was the best I'd come up with, so I was seeing it through.

I was on my second pint when Rafael came over. The alcohol warmed away the chill from the past two hours; what's more, it gave me an additional shot of courage. He only had to glance at the man on the stool next to me before the Partial dropped some coins on the bar and left. Rafael sat down, ordered another beer from the suddenly attentive bartender, and gave me a measuring look.

"The patrols have instructions to apprehend anyone they find in the woods and bring them to me."

"Good," I said, trying to sound appropriately grateful.

A small smile touched his mouth. "You don't trust me, do you?"

That was more direct than I had been prepared for. I paused, casting about for a response.

"I'd like to," I settled on at last, "but you didn't seem to believe me when I told you I'd seen the Pureblood, so you could just be humoring me about the patrols."

There. Just enough truth mixed in to—hopefully—get him to buy it.

Rafael lifted a shoulder in an elegant shrug. "You pointed out that I have nothing to lose by believing you. If you don't trust in my honor, Mara, at least trust in my practicality."

"And you should trust that I can *see*," I muttered before reminding myself that I wanted him to drop this topic. "Earlier you asked if I'd wanted you to miss me when I was gone. The answer is yes, I did."

His brows went up at my abrupt change of subject, but then a dusting of lights appeared in his eyes. For once, I didn't suppress the attraction I felt for him but let it rise to the surface, steeling myself for what I had to do. Then I stared into his dazzling cobalt gaze with a slow, inviting smile.

"Speechless?" I asked softly, echoing his teasing question from before.

Rafael's hand slid across the bar to cover mine, those strong fingers stroking with smooth, sure touches.

"Perhaps."

I didn't believe him, but I wasn't being honest, either, so who was I to criticize?

"That's all right, we don't need to talk," I offered, trying to make my tone sound throaty and enticing. "But maybe we could go back to your house and you can show me what you're thinking?"

According to everything I'd heard, Rafael didn't bring women back to his home. Instead, he had a fancy little room set up at the Plaza de

Souls for romantic trysts. It was all I could do not to hold my breath while I waited to see if my previous refusals would pay off and he'd break his routine to take me up on my offer.

The lights in his eyes began to brighten, like stars about to go supernova. Thanks to the genuine attraction I had to Rafael, I knew mine were probably also gleaming with tiny specks of brilliance. Humans didn't know that the expression "eyes lighting up" originally referred to demons, or they might hesitate to use the phrase themselves.

"What's behind your sudden change of heart?" Rafael asked, his voice low but filled with a tantalizing undercurrent.

I let my fingers twine with his, stroking over those ancient rings.

"I'm sick of being patient."

That was the truth, even though Rafael didn't know I wasn't talking about jumping into bed with him. Either way, it seemed to be enough. His hand tightened on mine, pulling me to my feet, and then he began leading me toward the door. The crowd around us reacted by pulling back slightly, deference this rough bunch showed to no one except Rafael. By the time we reached the entrance to Bonecrushers, his black-and-gold carriage was already out in front, the driver staring ahead impassively.

One day I'd have to ask Rafael how he always managed to have his ride waiting for him, but tonight, that was last on my list of things I intended to find out.

"You're sure?" he asked, drawing me close to whisper the question against my ear.

All those years of guilt-infused wondering, waiting, and wishing I would've acted differently were about to come to an end.

"Hell yes."

He opened the door and I climbed up into the interior of the carriage. A single gas lantern provided dim lighting when Rafael shut the door behind him. He hadn't taken a seat before the carriage lurched forward, but he managed to stay perfectly balanced even as my head thumped against the cushioned seat. The horses seemed to be as impatient as I was, but to my relief, the carriage didn't turn around and head toward the Plaza de Souls. It went straight, the direction of Rafael's home.

Part one of my plan accomplished.

Yet now that I'd put the first step in motion, some of my bravado faltered. Odds were I wouldn't be able to pull this off without paying a price. Gloria's face flashed in my mind, followed by my sister's. Both images firmed my resolve. Whatever the cost, I'd see this through.

Besides, I was already in over my head; all I had left to find out was whether I could tread enough water to survive.

Rafael sat next to me instead of taking the bench across from mine. The single flame kept most of his face in shadows, but it highlighted the richness of his red-gold hair. Being this close to him, knowing what would come next, made my heart speed up. I took in a steadying breath and an enticing scent teased my nostrils. Odd, I'd never noticed before that Rafael wore cologne. Probably because there had always been so many people around every other time I'd been near him, except for the two instances when we'd been on the back of a smelly horse.

"Mara." His voice was no louder than a sigh, but it raised goose bumps across my skin with its intensity. "Come to me."

I licked my suddenly dry lips. Many times over the past several years, I'd wondered what it would be like to kiss Rafael, even, if I was honest, going so far as closing my eyes and pretending former boyfriends were him during intimate moments. But this situation was nothing like how I'd fantasized. I had an agenda to accomplish, not a desire to fulfill.

Very slowly, I slid my hands up his vest, over his shirt, and to the collar of his jacket. Even through the layers of material, I could feel his heat and the firmness of his flesh. The lights in his eyes shone brighter while his mouth parted in the most sensual of smiles. Despite my unromantic intentions, tingling warmth swept over me. Rafael might have been a means to an end—and a treacherous one at that—but the reckless part of me still thrilled as he lowered his head. It was in my blood to find danger tempting, after all.

His mouth seared across mine, surprising me at the rush of sensations the contact caused. Before I could regroup and remind myself this was just a kiss, his tongue flicked along my lips, seeking entry. I opened my mouth, accepting the warm flesh that explored inside with knowing, sensual thoroughness. He tasted like spices and honey, a heady combination that incited me to draw on his tongue even though it was more than my act required.

He let out a muffled groan and pulled me closer,

the pressure of his mouth increasing. Each stroke, flick, and probe of his tongue seemed designed to raze my detachment, centering me in the feel of him instead of my reasons for being there. His hand kneaded my neck, making it so easy to tilt my head back and let his arm support me. Then his kiss deepened even further, becoming more intense, until I began to feel dizzy. Need built inside me with no regard for my suspicions. I'd only meant to get a *little* turned on, but the throb that had taken up cadence below my waist was no half-hearted act. Maybe that was a good thing. No way would he believe I didn't want him, not with how I couldn't stop myself from pressing closer and moaning at the rough deliciousness of his kiss.

His arms almost crushed me to him when I slid my mouth down to his jaw and then to his throat. I couldn't help it; his skin was unlike anything I'd felt. So smooth and silky, in such contrast to the hard, rippling muscles it covered. With his layers of clothes, I could see only the smallest bits of flesh peeking out from his face and neck. Naked, would his skin look as incredible all over his body? Have the same luscious suppleness on his arms, chest, stomach—and lower?

At the thought, that throb below my waist

began to increase until it thrummed like a gong. As if he could sense it, Rafael yanked me onto his lap, the large, heated bulge in his pants pressing right against that demanding ache. Not even my gun belt jabbing me in the hip could distract me from the bomb of sensation that resulted, especially with the jostling carriage providing enough friction to throw gasoline onto the blaze of my desire. I was so caught up in the explosion of need that I didn't notice he'd raised my skirt until it was well past my thigh.

Oh crap. I'd let *this* get out of hand in a hurry.

"Rafael," I managed. "Wait."

His hand dropped from my thigh, but he leaned back, still holding me to him with the other arm. I wasn't even on the bench anymore; my body was draped over his instead of the cushioned seat. I sucked in a choked breath when he began to unbutton his vest and then his shirt, revealing inch by inch that his skin was just as gorgeous as I'd imagined.

Get focused, Mara, you're blowing this! I railed at myself. If only the carriage didn't keep rocking me against him in the most damningly intimate way, making it even harder to concentrate than it had been when I'd kissed him.

"Wait," I said again once his shirt hung open and he reached for the buttons on my blouse.

"What's wrong?" His voice was rougher, but whether that was lust or anger at my objection, I wasn't sure.

I took in a deep breath, trying not to stare at the muscled beauty that was his chest. Even in the low lighting, he was the most stunning thing I'd ever seen.

"Not here," I said, giving my head a slight shake for lucidity. "Unless I'm not good enough to have sex with in a bed?" I added, managing to sound both hurt and offended, if a bit breathless.

Rafael let out a husky laugh before gathering me close. "Fear not, my sweet. I won't be finished with foreplay before we arrive."

His mouth covered mine again, taking my breath away with the raw hunger in his kiss. He didn't pause to tease my lips this time but delved past them with commanding purpose. Those hot, skillful flicks of his tongue made that buzzing return in my head, as if his mouth had the ability to intoxicate me. I didn't protest this time when he began to unbutton my blouse, telling myself I didn't want to make him suspicious, but the truth was that I burned to feel his hands on my skin.

Every adolescent imagining I'd ever had was left in the dust at the reality of how incredible it felt to touch him, taste him. Feel the slide of his flesh as his mouth erotically ravished mine, hinting at what a few hundred years of experience could do.

That scorching mouth dipped to my neck at the same moment his palms cupped my breasts, brushing aside my bra. My head fell back as a harsh groan came out of me. He sucked my throat while his thumbs seared across my nipples in the same relentless rhythm as the friction of our lower bodies. I couldn't think anymore, and I couldn't keep my hands from traveling up his chest and over his shoulders. The feel of his skin was addictive, each flex and bunch of his muscles flaring even more heat through my core. Some stubborn bit of conscience nagged that I should stop, but I ignored it. So what if things went further than I'd originally intended? I'd still do what needed to be done when the time came.

"Mara," he breathed, suddenly ceasing his unbelievable stroking of my breasts to catch my hands. "Stop."

"Why?" I burst out before recalling that stopping would be a *good* thing.

"I can keep from taking you here, now, as long

as you don't touch me like that," he replied in a tight voice.

Like what? I'd only been caressing his shoulders, not usually the spot of no return for a man. But then Rafael kissed me, sitting up to press his body against mine, and my thoughts reeled at the contact of his hard flesh against my sensitive breasts.

He pulled my free leg around him, the other one trapped under the tangle of my skirt, to rock me against his hips while his chest flattened my breasts. That hard bulge raked against my most sensitive part, the pressure building with each strong, undulating stroke, until finally I cried out as rapture shattered within me.

It spread from my loins into what felt like every vein, filling my body with hot, silken throbs. I couldn't stop the gasps that Rafael absorbed between deep, branding kisses as I shuddered, those throbs turning into waves of sweetness. I felt like I was melting, sinking into his skin with each ripple of ecstasy, and if he wouldn't have held me, I'd have tumbled onto the carriage floor.

"This is what I've waited for," he muttered thickly when I tore my mouth from his to take in gulps of air. He stroked my hair away from my face, still holding me with his other arm, the flickering candlelight revealing a look of triumph and possessiveness on his face.

Confusion and embarrassment competed with euphoria from the spine-tingling orgasm. So much for "acting" with Rafael! Ten minutes into making out and he'd blown away anything my two former lovers had made me feel—all without taking off his pants or kissing me below the neck. If this was what he could do to me with foreplay, I might die from pleasure overload if I actually had sex with him.

But these circumstances weren't real. Oh, if only they were, I'd be giddy instead of fighting off a stab of guilt. Yet despite how I wished to do anything except what lay ahead, chances were Rafael was using me for even more sinister purposes than what I had planned. I might *want* to believe his interest was genuine, his passion without ulterior motive, but then I'd be ignoring the pile of evidence that suggested he was involved with Purebloods. Rafael might have been the man of my dreams since I was fifteen, but that didn't change the fact that he had a dark cloud hanging over his activities.

Otherwise, hell, I might have even been

tempted to move to Nocturna to be closer to him. Electricity was overrated, plus cell phones and gas fumes were bad for my health. But here, I could be with Rafael and neither of us would even age. I wouldn't be saying good-bye to my family, either. They could still visit me and I could go back to see them. . . .

I gave my head another shake, harder this time. One orgasm and I was mentally picking out wallpaper to redecorate Rafael's home with. So much for moonlighting as a tough undercover Partial operative. The word *pathetic* applied to me right now.

With relief, I felt the carriage shudder and sway as it went over a particularly bumpy stretch of road. We had to be on the drawbridge outside Rafael's home. *That* was an obvious indicator that the person whose arms I was still curled inside had nefarious connections. Rafael lived in a castle surrounded by a *moat*, for Pete's sake. Even for a demon ruler, that was piling on the creepiness.

"We're here," he said, giving me a kiss that still incited shivers even though I'd managed to patch up most of my tattered self-control.

"Good. I-I want to finish things," I stammered when he lifted his head.

His smile was dark, wicked, and tempting. "Oh, we shall. As soon as we're inside."

I shifted to unseat myself from his lap, feeling suddenly clumsy and awkward as I buttoned my blouse without bothering to rehook my bra. The bumps from the carriage kept swaying me into him, hampering my progress. He lifted me, setting me back onto the bench with his usual smooth, controlled movements, not even a grunt to show for it. The strength and grace I'd so often admired in Rafael would prove to be my biggest obstacle soon. I'd have just one chance to take him down or the jig would be up.

It's the only way, I reminded myself, forcing a smile as he leaned down to brush his lips across my temple. I knew it was true.

Yet if I knew that, why did it still feel so wrong?

Chapter Four

Rafael didn't bother buttoning his shirt or his vest. Both hung open, revealing the hard lines of his chest, with its impossibly smooth flesh. I tried not to stare as he jumped out of the carriage and held out his hands to me, his clothes gaping open even further with the action. I accepted his help down, determining then and there to make my move *before* he took off all his clothes. Otherwise I might be too busy drooling to do anything else.

The warm pressure of his body taunted me as we walked up a narrow outdoor corridor. I glanced around discreetly, noting the torches set up in various places along the high walls and the deep shadows between them. If he had guards, they were concealed in the various darkened recesses of this medieval castle knockoff. I kept taking mental notes as we walked further inside the stone behemoth. *Two lefts past the fancy sword display, a right at the ancient-looking tapestry, up two flights of stairs, then left at the flame-eyed gargoyle, up another flight of stairs, left at the blacked-out window, and then through the second wide door on the right.*

It opened up into a room that looked like a snapshot of a gothic fantasy. Candlelight made the dark gray walls appear welcoming, while the ceiling had to be twenty feet high, with designs carved into what looked like opaque glass. A large leather chair had a book perched on its arm, facedown and open to mark its place. Boots I'd seen Rafael wear before were carelessly tucked into an open alcove next to more pairs of masculine footwear. Another archway, a smaller one, opened to a dark space that I couldn't see inside but assumed must be a closet or bathroom.

And of course, in the center of the room was a large bed with sumptuous pillows and thick blankets in varying shades of indigo. A nearby fireplace cast low lights onto the bed, revealing that it was unmade, an indentation from a large body still visible in its surface.

Rafael's room. By all accounts, the place he never brought anyone back to.

His arms encircled me from behind, pulling me against him. For a moment, I closed my eyes, absorbing the feel of his body and the heat sinking into my back from the bare skin of his chest. If circumstances had been different, I'd have turned around, pressed my mouth to his, and tumbled us both onto that inviting navy bed.

Instead, I stroked his arm with one hand while I surreptitiously dipped the other one into my gun belt. He brushed aside the hair on the back of my neck with his mouth, tracing his tongue into the sensitive dip there. Erotic tremors broke out across my skin, increasing when he breathed my name into the same spot with a voice gone scratchy from desire.

Damn, damn, damn him for making me feel this way, when he might be involved with Purebloods!

I unfastened my belt, letting it drop to the floor with both guns still in their holsters. Then I turned around, wrapping my arms quickly around his neck. His mouth came down onto mine, scorching me with passion, while his hands tightened on my waist to bring our bodies closer.

Those hands clenched convulsively in the next moment. I froze, my heart rate tripling, braced for pain but unable to extricate myself from his embrace. He didn't strike out, though for the space of several heartbeats, I could tell he was lucid enough to. Then, slowly, his hands relaxed and he pulled away, a look on his face that I didn't want to name.

Finally, his legs buckled and he fell to the floor with more grace than someone unconscious had a right to. The end of an empty syringe still protruded from his neck, a little something I'd carried in my gun belt for months in the hopes that I'd get to use it on Ashton one day. I'd never thought I'd use it on Rafael, and certainly not like this.

It paid to have a Partial relative employed at an animal reserve. That needle had been filled with enough sedative to fell a small elephant—or the two-hundred-pound ruler of Nocturna, as it turned out. I stared down at Rafael, guilt once more swirling inside me, before pushing it back with all the ruthlessness of my supernatural heritage. I'd had to do it. Somewhere in this castle that few ever saw the inside of had to be a link to Rafael and Purebloods. He couldn't have ruled Nocturna for over two centuries without knowing far more than he claimed to about the kidnappings.

And I doubted that any of his people here would dare to disturb their master for the next several hours, at least. Not with what everyone had to assume we were doing. If I was stealthy enough, I could soon find out more about Rafael than anyone else had in decades. That information might mean the difference between life and death for some unlucky young Partials who ventured into Nocturna even though they, like me, knew the dangers.

Besides, once Rafael woke up, I'd better be long gone from here, or guilt would be the least of my problems with him.

After what had to be two hours of furtive searching, I was both frustrated and confused. I'd found nothing interesting except a lot of neat, barbaric antiques, and for all that the castle was large, so far I'd only come across four guards. Two of them seemed most interested in protecting the food in what I surmised was the kitchen, from the sounds of laughter, burping, and pots clanging together. The other guards were outside the castle, patrolling the perimeter and making sure no one snuck in by swimming the moat, I guessed. What I couldn't understand was why.

For all its size and impressive adornments, the place seemed strangely barren of people. It didn't make sense. Rafael was renowned for his fighting skills, true, but everyone had to sleep eventually, and he'd left himself virtually unprotected here.

The thought of Rafael and sleeping made another twinge of guilt flare in me. God, his *face* when he realized what I'd done! Even though I tried to push the image aside, it rose in my mind anyway. He'd looked shocked, which I'd expected, but there had been more to it than that.

He looked betrayed, my human conscience whispered.

I had no choice, the demon in me snarled back.

There are always *choices*, my conscience countered ruthlessly.

Not this time. I'd asked Rafael repeatedly why he had been there the night Ashton had taken Gloria, and every time he answered, some part of me *knew* he was lying. Why would he lie if he hadn't been in on it somehow? Add that to the whispers about Rafael that Gloria's parents had uncovered during their previous searches here, plus the things I'd heard about how he was always conveniently close by when Purebloods were sighted, and it all added up to one thing: guilty. My not wanting it to be true because of a long-held infatuation didn't change that.

So, if I were the guilty ruler of a large dimension populated by Partials who would descend on me en masse if they found out about my involvement, where would I hide evidence of that guilt? What would I consider to be the least likely place where someone could stumble across some form of damning clue that would tie me to Purebloods? Somewhere in this house, obviously. For the average Partial, it was harder to get inside Rafael's castle than it was for a typical American to get a private audience with the president. But this place was huge. Damn it, if only I had more time to search! There could be hidden catacombs beneath the foundations, tunnels, vaults, secret rooms —

Rooms. An image of Rafael's bedroom flashed in my mind. It was his private sanctuary, the place he never brought anyone back into. . . .

Holy shit, I was so *stupid*! I'd spent all this time looking around the castle when I should've been concentrating on turning his bedroom upside down. I spun around, hugging the wall as I made my way back toward the main part of the castle.

It took several agonizingly stretched-out minutes during which I was sure I'd be discovered, but eventually, I made it close enough to recognize where Rafael and I had first come in.

Now, where had we gone from there again?

Two lefts past the fancy sword display, I began to chant to myself, easing past the corner before ducking out into the open hallway. *Then right at the ancient-looking tapestry...*

By the time I passed the blacked-out window on the third floor, I was sweating even though the castle corridors were chilly *and* drafty. Then, once I reached Rafael's wide bedroom door, that sweat turned cold on my skin. Logic said he should still be out like a light, but what if I was wrong? I'd never tranqued a three-quarter demon—or possible *Pureblood*—before; how did I know how long the sedative would keep him out?

Only one way to find out. I took a deep breath, then gingerly opened the door, muscles bunched to run if I heard the slightest sound of movement within. When nothing but deep, rhythmic breathing met my ears, I dared to go all the way inside before closing the door quietly behind me.

Rafael lay right where I'd left him, his big body still in that elegant sprawl. Guilt flared in me once again, but I squashed it. If I was wrong, I'd wait for him to wake up and then offer the most sincere apology of my *life*, but until then, I had a job to do. I stepped around him, one hand on my gun just in case he'd been faking sleep to lunge at me. When he still didn't move, I began my search.

I owed my animal reserve relative huge for this one.

Nothing was under the bed or in the three closets that artistically blended into the room. Of course. That would have been too obvious. I tapped along all the walls, feeling for any inconsistency in the stone that might mean a barrier. Then I piled pieces of furniture on top of each other to make a precarious ladder that I fell from twice before ascertaining that the opaque glass with the odd designs was *not* a gateway to another dimension.

Finally, prodded by a pinch from my bladder, I went into the bathroom. The tub was sunken, made of highly polished stone, and looked like it had a real faucet, too. When I was done using the toilet, it flushed just like a normal one. Rafael must have had a clever pumping system inside the castle to have pulled *that* off. The bathroom was pretty nice for one belonging to a bachelor, with towels neatly stacked on a stand by the tub, a stone sink with another authentic faucet, and even a faux picture-frame window with one of the plush drapes pulled back for artistic effect.

Who'd have thought a potentially evil demon ruler would have good decorating taste? Too bad there wasn't anything in the bathroom that looked like it might be a barrier, though. Despair pricked me. What if all my efforts tonight were a waste, and all I'd succeeded in doing was tipping my hand to a powerful demon who was going to be so *pissed* when he woke up?

I left the bathroom, determined to search more of the castle again, when something nagged at me. I spun around, heading back into the bathroom, to run my hands over the fake window. It couldn't be here. Not right out in the open like this . . .

When my hand slipped under the drapery to touch the wall behind it, I froze. Very slowly, I pulled away the entire drapery to reveal the wall, and a harsh sound escaped me.

This wasn't a wall. It was a dimensional barrier. *Two* of them, in fact.

I traced my hand along the barriers, noting

the difference in feel between them. The one on my left felt completely rigid, even colder than the stone wall around it, but the one on my right . . . ah. That felt pliant. Cautiously, I pressed against it, surprised when my entire hand slid through. I jerked back at once, seeing water clinging to my fingers before dripping onto the floor.

The one on the left was a barrier I couldn't cross, which meant it must lead to a Pureblood dimension. Right here, under everyone's noses, Rafael had hidden two gateways into the other side, and there was no innocent reason he would've done that. This discovery made me want to go over to Rafael's supine form and start kicking him. All of my worst suspicions were confirmed. Rafael was in league with Purebloods, and no one had caught him because no one knew he had his very own private access in his *bathroom*, of all places. No wonder he didn't keep a lot of people on staff in his house. He must not have wanted to increase the odds of anyone finding this and telling others.

Yet he'd brought me back here. For a second, I was confused. Why would he do that and risk my finding this barrier? But then, like a hot poker to my heart, I understood.

Rafael had had no intention of letting me leave. He hadn't brought me back to his house because I was more special to him than any other girl; he'd brought me back because he'd been planning to give me a personal tour of the barrier when he pulled me through and delivered me up to some Purebloods! Maybe my spotting Ashton earlier had spooked him. Maybe he was just sick of me poking around asking questions. Whatever the reason, it was clear that he'd intended to eliminate the problem once and for all.

Jab, jab, jab! went that poker in my heart. What a fool I'd been.

I shook my head, disgusted to find my vision blurred. Rafael wasn't worth my tears, and neither were my hurt feelings. If I should be crying for anyone, it should be Gloria and all the other Partials who'd suffered because of what lay in front of me. Grimly, I forced myself to focus, pressing again on the barrier to the right. My hand slipped inside just as easily as before, coming out dripping water once more. I could penetrate it, so this gateway had to lead back to my world.

My stomach roiled with nausea. Did Rafael allow Purebloods to go back and forth shuttling

Partials through these two barriers? How easy that would be, and how private. Even if one of his people found traces that had been left after each passage, who'd think twice about water being splashed on a bathroom floor? No one, that's who.

I left the bathroom, my fingers trembling with the urge for revenge as they curled around my gun. But when I stomped over to Rafael and stared down at him, despair replaced the rage seething in me. He deserved to be killed in his sleep for all he'd done, but even as I raised the gun, my hand wavered. Rafael looked almost angelic lying there, with golden russet hair draped over part of his face and his mouth slightly open. His beauty shouldn't have mattered to me, nor should the memory of how I'd felt in his arms, but even though he deserved it, I knew, deep down, that I couldn't pull the trigger.

My Partial side might have been howling at me to shoot and avenge my people, but killing Rafael felt wrong in every fiber of the rest of me. For once, the three-quarters of my humanity were stronger than even the urgings from one-quarter's worth of seething, vengeful demon.

I lowered the gun and spun back around, heading into the bathroom. Maybe I couldn't kill Rafael, but I could warn people about him. I wasn't so weak that I couldn't do *that*.

I stared at the barrier to the right. Wherever it opened up to, it was somewhere wet, so I'd better take some deep breaths first.

Chapter Five

I didn't wait for Lena to put the car in park before I jumped into the passenger seat. My younger half sister gave my sodden clothes a disbelieving look before rubbing her nose.

"What is that *smell*?"

"You don't want to know," I replied shortly. Rafael's portal had indeed opened up somewhere underwater. No wonder the location of the other gateway had remained hidden on this side for so long. What Partial in their right mind would go for an exploratory dive in the waters of a sewage treatment facility to stumble across it?

"Guess now I know why you told me to bring you a change of clothes. I would've brought a bucket of water and some bleach, too, if I'd known how much you'd stink—"

"Drive," I cut Lena off in exasperation. "We

don't have much time. You don't even know the shit that's about to hit the fan."

"You found something out about Gloria?" she asked, losing the mocking tone at once. To my relief, she also hit the gas, lurching the car forward with the carelessness of a teenager who'd only recently learned how to drive.

"Did you get ahold of Dad?" I replied, not answering that. If I could avoid involving my little sister in this, I would.

"Left a message, but you know his cell has crappy reception in the Bahamas. Bet that's why they go there every year for their anniversary, so it's harder for us to bug them."

I agreed with her reasoning. Normally I wouldn't begrudge my father or my stepmother their private time together, but it was more than an inconvenience now. Of course, his being out of town was why I'd chosen *this* weekend to break my promise by going back to Nocturna. I knew he'd never even realize I was gone, and Lena was fine staying home alone. She was more mature at sixteen than I'd been at that age.

"Aunt Nancy and Uncle David?" I asked next.

Lena shook her head. "At the movies. They're supposed to go out to eat afterward, too."

Damn it! It figured everyone would be un-
available when I had the most important news of
my life to relay.

That left Lena. I gave her a hard look that she
didn't see as she concentrated on the road. *More
mature than I was at her age, for sure.* And I had to
tell *someone* before I went back. Just in case I
didn't return.

"Rafael's involved in shuttling Partials out of
Nocturna and into the next realm. He has two
secret barriers in the bathroom of his castle."

Lena swerved, narrowly avoiding another car
before easing back into our lane to the tune of
angry horns blaring.

Yeah, guess I should've had her pull over before I blurted that out.

"You're shitting me!" she exclaimed.

I didn't criticize her language, though my
father would have, had he heard her use that
word.

"I wish I were," I said glumly while another
tiny, invisible spear jabbed me in the heart.

"You saw the barriers yourself?" she went on,
glancing at me.

"Maybe we should talk about this when you're
not driving—"

"I'm fine," she cut me off, looking back at the road with a clenched jaw. "Go on."

"I went through one of them to get here. It opens in the sewage facility a few miles back; that's why I stink," I said. "All I know about the other one is that it doesn't lead to anything on this side, so I give you three guesses as to where it *does* go."

Lena was silent as she absorbed this, getting onto the freeway. We were several cities away from the Bed Bath & Beyond gateway, and it was already afternoon. I had to get back to that gateway before dark or risk giving Rafael a whole day to think up a way to stop me from telling others what I'd discovered. He'd know I'd found the barriers. The puddle of water I'd probably left on his bathroom floor crossing over would be enough to let a smart bastard like him figure it out.

And if I gave him time, he might decide to come after more than just me. I glanced at Lena again. Maybe it was a good thing my father was out of town. In fact, Lena, my cousin, and my aunt and uncle should all follow suit.

"When you drop me off at the mall, I want you to go straight to tell Aunt Nancy and Uncle David what's going on. I'll tell everyone I can over in Nocturna. Maybe Jack'll believe me, he's a friend. Billy . . . I don't know, but I'll try. But even if not everyone believes me, I should be able to get enough of them riled up to demand to see that bathroom for themselves. Once they do, Rafael's finished."

Damn the little needles of pain those words caused me. What was the matter with me, still getting upset over the well-deserved fate of a murderer?

"Are you going to be all right?" Lena asked softly. "I know you've always had a thing for Rafael. . . ."

"I'm fine," I said briskly, echoing her words from before. I didn't want to talk about it, let alone think about it. "Got any paper towels in here?" I went on, changing the subject.

She pointed to the glove box. I opened it, relieved to see a travel pack of tissues *and* a tiny bottle of hand sanitizer. I should have just squirted the entire bottle all over me, but even that wouldn't have been enough. Instead, I dabbed some on a tissue and flipped the vanity mirror down, determined to get the nasty grime off my face and hands, at least.

But one good look at my reflection made a

scream escape me. Lena didn't swerve again, though she yelled, "What the hell!" at the top of her lungs.

Words failed me. I squeezed my eyes shut, sending a fervent prayer to any god listening that I hadn't seen what I had. Then, very slowly, I opened my eyes.

The five pinpoints of light around my pupils were still there, taunting me. I'd seen them before in other Partials' eyes, such as my father's when my real mother was alive. These weren't the temporary flickers of illumination that happened during the heat of the moment. They were the mark of claiming for my kind, more intimate than a wedding ring and far harder to get rid of.

Despite my suspicions before, and what I'd found out afterward, at some point when I'd been in Rafael's arms, the demon in me had decided I was his—and marked my eyes so everyone else would know it, too.

The lot's exterior lights, set to switch on at the same time every evening, lit up right as Lena pulled into the Bed Bath & Beyond shopping complex. As if we needed reminding that we were almost out of time. She hit the gas as she swung the car around to the back and headed toward the Dumpster. My fingers had been drumming impatiently on the dashboard for the past ten minutes, but now I yanked the straps of my new backpack tighter on my shoulders. It had cost me a couple extra hours to fill it with the necessary contents, but no way was I going back into Nocturna unprepared.

Once Lena screeched to a stop by the Dumpster, I gave her a last, tight smile.

"Go straight to Aunt Nancy and Uncle David's," I reminded her.

"I will." She grabbed me in a fierce, one-armed hug. "You come back, Mara," she said, low and vehemently.

I nodded as I jumped out of the car. "I intend to."

Then I ran at the Dumpster, seeing the faint shimmer around it grow dimmer. Adrenaline made my legs pump faster as I closed the scant distance. *I'm going to make it, I'm going to make it!* I chanted, as if willpower could force that gateway open for a few seconds longer. Then I leapt for the shimmer that surrounded the metal container right as it disappeared, bracing myself for the probable impact of slamming into it instead of Nocturna.

But in the next instant, my body hit soft earth instead of hard metal. Out of habit, I rolled to lessen the impact, feeling a split second of overwhelming relief that I hadn't been too late. Then my survival instincts kicked in and I came up from my roll with both guns pointed.

No one right in front of me waiting to pounce, good. That didn't mean I was off the hook for long. I heard multiple sets of hoofbeats, and they weren't far from my location. I scrambled for a bush—the nearest cover I could find—and crouched there while I swiftly unhooked the backpack from my shoulders and dug through it. Two Glocks went into my gun belt, two more went into the homemade straps I'd fashioned at thigh level on my black jeans, and several extra clips of ammunition were tucked into my pockets. In addition to that—and in homage to Rafael—I put away several knives into homemade sheaths on the vest I wore over my fitted black shirt. Too bad I hadn't been able to risk bringing grenades over, but I'd heard stories about the gateway activating the pins, which had never ended well for the carrier.

I might not have had time to wash the stink off me, but I'd managed to gather up as many weapons as I could carry. That was more important than smelling nice.

Once I emptied the backpack, I dug a shallow hole with my hands and covered it up with dirt. I had no use for the backpack anymore, and it would be unwieldy during a fight, but I didn't want to leave an obvious sign of my presence. Then I waited for the space of a few heartbeats before easing out from behind the bush, my gaze darting around for the first sign of attack.

Those hoofbeats sounded closer, but I couldn't see anyone yet. Of course, that meant they couldn't see me, either. One good thing about Nocturna's perpetual darkness and lack of electricity and batteries meant that hiding was a lot more efficient. Torchlight only went so far, after all.

Though if Rafael was out here, he might be able to see me in the dark. I still wasn't sure if his increased vision meant he was a Pureblood himself, or if he just offered those gateways in his bathroom to Purebloods for profit. Didn't really matter; either way, he was a murderer, and soon all of me would accept that and those damned lights in my eyes would go away. Until then, I'd treat them as a reminder of what happened when I ignored my suspicions about a man.

"Checking the south side again," I heard a familiar voice call out, then the sound of hooves headed in my direction.

My heart leapt. *Jack*. Could I get him to listen to me before he sounded the alarm to the rest of the guards? We were friends, but he'd been employed by Rafael a lot longer than he'd known me.

I ran into a thicker part of the woods, weighing the decision. From the amount of extra hoofbeats, I could surmise that Rafael had woken up. He'd obviously sent more guards to watch the barrier, but not so many as to draw undue attention. Once again, he was being crafty. The only thing I had in my favor was the fact that the gateway spit people out anywhere along a ten-mile stretch on this side. Otherwise, I probably would have tumbled right into a steel cage with Rafael dangling the key just out of my reach.

Rafael. I cursed him as I continued to dart between the trees. How amused he must have been to see those five points of lights in my eyes. He must've thought I was the most gullible Partial in the world. Well, I'd shown him when I'd dropped him like a stone with that tranquilizer, though oddly enough, the memory of the look on his face didn't bring the satisfaction it should have. Only hollowness and echoes of pain.

You'll get over it, I reminded myself bleakly. If I lived long enough, that was.

About fifty yards away, I heard Jack's horse clamber through a patch of bushes. He was close to the same place I'd crouched in upon entering Nocturna. Jack always did have a knack for being the first to find people who'd crossed over. Maybe I could use that to my advantage now.

Or I'd have to shoot him and take his horse before he recovered, which I really didn't want to do.

I went further ahead toward a denser part of the woods that would slow his horse down, deliberately cracking a twig or two along the way. It wasn't long before Jack took the bait, changing course. He rode in a roundabout path, not spurring on his horse or charging straight for those sounds but pursuing me subtly. If I hadn't been paying close attention—and stringing him along with those occasional twig snaps—I might not have been aware that he was onto me.

Best of Rafael's guards by far. Had to hope he was the smartest, too, and that he believed me.

Once he was close enough that his torch would soon reveal me to his sharp eyes, I quietly climbed up a tree, sitting myself in a crook of branches. The leaves provided better camouflage than the tree trunks would. Then, keeping my gun trained on him, I waited for Jack to draw nearer.

After he passed directly beneath me, so close I could almost count the strands of the wide silver streak in his dark hair, I cocked the gun. The sound made Jack spin his horse around, pointing his own gun, though not high enough to be a danger.

I aimed very carefully, the light from his torch helping me. Then I pulled the trigger.

Jack's gun blasted out of his hand with little more sound than a sharp cough. Silencers were a great invention, if you asked me. His horse reared, but Jack got it under control, wisely not reaching for one of his other weapons. Once his mount was still, he stared at his empty hand. Blood seeped out from some superficial cuts, but otherwise, he wasn't hurt.

"That you, Mara?" he asked with a grunt.

"Before you yell for the others or do anything

else," I said rapidly, "just *listen*. I could've shot you five times in the past ten minutes if I wanted to, so that ought to prove I'm not your enemy. But Rafael is. He may or may not be a Pureblood himself, but he's definitely in collusion with them. I know it sounds crazy, but I have proof."

In the flickering torchlight, I saw that Jack's mouth was hanging open. "Proof?" he asked at last. "What proof?"

"A set of secret gateways in his castle, one leading to my world, the other to a Pureblood realm," I replied, jumping down from my perch in a show of good faith. "I saw them. I went *through* one. It's true."

Before replying, Jack sent his dark blue gaze raking over me, taking in the various weapons I had strapped on. "You were in his castle?" He sounded doubtful.

I nodded. "Last night . . . er, or it would've been last night, if you had day and night here. Some people from Bonecrushers saw us leave together, and we didn't go to his hotel room, which you can confirm. I think Rafael brought me home because he intended to use that gateway to get rid of me permanently once he was done having fun with me."

"And you stopped him? Managed to get away from him?"

He still sounded doubtful, but at least he was listening instead of yelling for the other guards. "I tranqued him when he wasn't paying attention. He never even saw the needle coming."

To my surprise, Jack began to laugh, though he kept it from being loud enough to draw attention to us. "You got the drop on Rafael?" he said at last, quieting his chuckles. "He must be *beyond* pissed at you."

"I have no doubt," I replied dryly. "But that's not important. What is important is telling as many people here as we can so he's stopped. You have to help me, Jack. He's killing our kind, either directly or indirectly."

"Where are these gateways in the castle?"

I took it as a good sign that he was asking about their location instead of questioning their existence. "In the bathroom attached to his bedroom. I've never seen two barriers so close together before, but they're there. Trust me."

Jack seemed to mull this over, the lines of his face deepening as he frowned. I waited, hoping that all the time we'd spent together before would serve me well now.

"It's worth checking out," he said at last. "We need to avoid the other guards, though. Rafael's got a DOS out on you. If one of them sees you, he might take you back to Rafael no matter what you'd tell him."

DOS, *detain on sight*. I had no doubt that the other guards would be less likely to hear me out, let alone believe me, since I didn't know most of them.

"Get me to Bonecrushers. The more people who hear about this at the same time, the better. Not even Rafael can stand against a mob of pissed-off Partials."

"Climb up," Jack said, holding out his hand.

Despite the years I'd known him, I hesitated. What if Jack didn't believe me and was just pretending so I'd be in the vulnerable position of having my back to him? He could shoot me, pistol-whip the back of my head, or even stab me, and there wouldn't be much I could do about it.

"I'll get on behind you," I said, my hard tone letting him know that wasn't negotiable.

He let out another grunt. "Suit yourself, Mara."

Jack didn't seem at all uneasy about giving me that kind of advantage. I shook my head, feeling ashamed. Being duped by Rafael made me give everyone a suspicious eye now, even people who didn't deserve it.

"Sorry," I murmured as I accepted his hand and climbed up behind him.

Jack spurred his horse once I was settled, dropping his torch into the first brook we came across with a muttered "Don't need them seein' you up here with me." Instead of following close to the torch-strewn path that led into town, Jack went into the thicker part of the woods. After he gave up our only source of illumination and headed away from the path, the woods soon returned to their normal, almost impenetrable darkness. Jack seemed okay with it, though. He steered his horse confidently through the trees, making me wonder how many years he'd patrolled this particular section to get so familiar with it.

Very familiar with it, in fact, because he spurred his horse again even though I now couldn't see more than a dozen feet in front of me.

"Should you be going so fast?" I called out, stretching to be closer to his ear so he'd hear me.

"Aren't we in a hurry?" he countered, the words whistling by me as he kicked the horse to increase its pace even more.

Yes, I wanted to get to Bonecrushers as soon

as possible. Definitely before one of Rafael's guards spotted us, but riding at a gallop when you were mostly blind wasn't my idea of smart. Even if Jack knew these woods like the back of his hand, he was only a quarter demon like me. So if I couldn't see, then he couldn't see—

The truth hit me right between the eyes, but unfortunately, so did the large overhanging branch that Jack saw in time to duck from and I didn't.

My last thought before lights exploded in my mind was, *Pureblood...*

Chapter Six

*I*cy water splashed over me. I came back into consciousness with a jerk, my senses sluggish but instinct warning me of danger. Remembering what had happened before my eyes even opened, I reached for my weapons but realized my hands were bound.

"Yep, that woke her," Jack's familiar voice noted with an undercurrent of laughter.

My gaze swung around as I tried to orient myself. It was very dark, but I could make out Jack standing several feet away on the edge of a river. I was *in* that river, getting chilled to the bone from the frigid water, someone big holding me in a tight grip from behind.

Must be Rafael, I realized, the sinking sensation in my stomach increasing until it felt like my gut had descended to my knees. I hadn't told

Jack anything about Rafael that Jack hadn't already known, because Jack was a Pureblood, too. What if *all* the guards in Nocturna were Purebloods? Hell, what if half the population was, Partials being slowly weeded out under the watchful eye and instruction of its centuries-old ruler?

At least my family knows about Rafael, I thought with a pang. When I didn't come back, they'd tell other Partials, too. Enough that even Rafael and his people wouldn't be able to suppress them forever. It wasn't the most compelling legacy to leave behind, but it was all I had.

"Best patrolman in Nocturna, huh, Jack?" I said bitterly while Rafael dragged me deeper into the river. I tried not to panic, not to wonder if drowning hurt, because I wanted to die fighting, not begging. "No wonder you were always first to discover who crossed over. You could see in the dark, you filthy Pureblood."

"Aw, Mara, don't be pissy," Jack said in a chiding tone. "I told you to quit coming back looking for Ashton, but no, you just wouldn't listen."

"So it's *my* fault you're a murdering prick who devours the life essence out of *children*?" I spat, trying to kick even though my feet were bound, too.

I could barely see him now, but it looked like Jack shrugged. "I gotta eat just like you do. Can't help it if my food is Partials."

"All this talk of food is making me hungry," a voice I hadn't expected purred near my ear.

Every muscle in me stiffened. It wasn't Rafael yanking me deeper into the river but Ashton!

I looked around again, but all I saw was the two of them. "Where's Rafael?" I asked, my voice almost eerily calm.

Ugly laughter came from behind me. "Nowhere near here, baby. He doesn't even know about this barrier, but thanks to you, now we know where another one is, too. Once we get rid of Rafael, we'll have our choice of a few different barriers to play with. I can't wait."

"Get rid of Rafael . . . ," I repeated, my eyes closing in the agony of revelation. Whatever Rafael had been doing hiding those barriers, he hadn't been involved with Ashton. Or with Jack, or possibly with *any* other Pureblood.

And I'd used him, tricked him, drugged him, and now set him up with my family to take the fall. Drowning all of a sudden seemed too good an end for me. *What had I done?*

I didn't have long to wallow in revulsion over

my actions before Ashton's hand clamped over my mouth, pinching my nose at the same time. Before I could react, a horrible crushing sensation enveloped my entire body, squeezing me so hard that my organs ached. I would've screamed, but between the pressure of Ashton's hand and those merciless invisible bands compressing me, I couldn't even gasp.

Then I was on my back, looking up not at the ceiling of a dark underground dwelling but at a sky the most amazing shade of purple. For a moment, I stared, not moving. Was I dead? Was this the afterlife? If so, it didn't look all that bad—

"Get up," Ashton's voice snarled.

No, not dead. Unless this was hell and Ashton had arranged to personally greet me. I blinked, my eyes adjusting from the darkness of Nocturna to the new, hazy sort of sunset all around me. Ashton yanked on my bound hands, forcing me to my feet so abruptly that I stumbled into him. Yet I collided with him softly, as if something I couldn't see cushioned my impact. My body felt different, too. Lighter, like I'd suddenly lost thirty pounds.

A sick tremor ran up my spine. Ashton must have pulled me through a barrier in the river.

Now I was in the next realm, a place that I could never leave even if I did manage to get away from him.

"Like it here? This is where I took the girl you were with that night," Ashton murmured, hauling my face right up next to his. His brown eyes gleamed. "You know, I don't even remember her name—"

"Gloria," I interrupted him through gritted teeth. "Her name was Gloria, she was my cousin, and she was sixteen years old, you piece of *shit*."

He just smiled. "Whatever."

Then he began to drag me toward some tall slabs of rocklike formations. With the odd, buoyant feel to the air, it seemed like it took him less effort than it would have on Nocturna, or even in the normal world. Gravity must not be as strong here. Why I cared, I had no idea, but the analytical part of me was taking note of my surroundings in far more detail than the fatalistic part of me was.

Warmer here than Nocturna. Gravity might be a little off, but oxygen levels must be similar or I'd be dead already. Lots of big, whitish formations, like a crystal forest around us. Gray fog everywhere. Dark blue ground underneath us, similar to sand. . . .

"Stop right there," a hard voice thundered.

Ashton froze even as my heart constricted with a wild mixture of hope and disbelief. Rafael came out from behind one of those tall, smoky-colored pillars. His jacket, shirt, and vest were open, muscled arms crossed over his chest and leather-clad legs tucked inside knee-high boots. With the fog swirling around him, he looked like something out of a dream.

Or a hallucination. Maybe that's what Rafael was, a trick my subconscious had formulated as a way to buffer me from the horrors of my reality. Then, just as quickly, I discarded that thought. Rafael couldn't be a mirage, because it was clear that Ashton could see him, too.

"How did you get here?" Ashton demanded.

I wondered the same thing myself. I'd abandoned the idea that Rafael was a Pureblood after Jack and Ashton revealed he wasn't involved in any of their dirty workings. Yet here he was, and only Purebloods could cross the barrier—unless Rafael had somehow managed to get a Pureblood to pull him through?

"I'll give you one chance to die with your essence intact," Rafael replied, each word bitten off with palpable fury. "Let her go now, and I'll only take your life as punishment for what you intended to do to her."

My mouth dropped even as Ashton's grip on me tightened. Maybe the different atmosphere in this realm was messing with my mind, because Rafael *couldn't* mean what that sounded like. . . .

"You," Ashton said hoarsely. "That night, I couldn't see your face, but it was *you* — "

"Yes," Rafael cut him off, flinging aside his coat, shirt, and vest in one fluid movement. Then, as if out of a nightmare, I saw shadows begin to form behind him. Those shadows grew, darkening, solidifying . . . until a pair of charcoal-colored wings spread out in terrifying, magnificent formation, extending well past Rafael's shoulders with their lighter tips trailing all the way to his feet.

Not a Partial or a Pureblood. *Fallen*.

Ashton flung me away from him as he ran. With my hands and feet still bound, I landed face-first on the sandy indigo ground instead of catching myself. Something whooshed over me, punctuated by a scream from Ashton. It took a second or two of awkward twisting, but I finally managed to flop over — and then stared.

Rafael had Ashton in his arms. Between the fog

and the incredible span of his wings, I couldn't see everything clearly, but it looked like Rafael had his mouth pressed to Ashton's in a chilling parody of a kiss. Ashton bleated in terror, kicking and flailing against Rafael's ruthless embrace, but to no avail. After several long moments while I watched, transfixed, Ashton's movements slowed and his head fell back. When Rafael let go of him, he fell to the ground with a limpness that spoke of permanence.

Lights seemed to flicker in a spiderweb pattern over Rafael's skin before they faded, vanishing into his natural creamy skin tone. Part of me was howling that now would be a really good time to attempt *running*, bound feet or no, but I didn't move as Rafael turned and began to walk toward me.

"Am I next?" I rasped, mildly surprised that I could still talk after what I'd just witnessed.

Those unbelievable wings fluttered once before Rafael reached down, breaking through the duct tape around my wrists as though it were tissue paper. He did the same thing with my feet, until the sticky substance still clung to my skin but no longer restrained me.

"I told you before, Mara; if I wanted to eat

you, I would've done so years ago," he replied, no emotion in his tone or in his gaze. Then he hauled me into his arms, his grip unyielding, that lovely, killing mouth mere inches from my own.

I stared at him, barely able to breathe, thinking that if my heart beat any faster, it would burst.

"But now you know what I am, so you know what I *do* eat," he whispered before brushing his lips over mine.

Then the air exploded around us as his wings lifted and fell, vaulting us upward into that deep violet sky while Ashton's lifeless body lay below on the ground.

Chapter Seven

From the glimpses I caught when I wasn't fighting off nausea from the dizzying dips and ascents, this realm looked like a cross between Antarctica and the Grand Canyon, except in different colors. Rows of crystal formations—or their mineral counterparts—littered the ground, interspersed by streams, that bluish sand, and something that resembled a forest of tumbleweed trees, of all things. We seemed to be the only people in the sky, to my relief. If I'd seen swarms of flying Fallen, I might have passed out on the spot.

Rafael was a Fallen. The proof of that was winging us to who-knew-where, yet I still had a hard time reconciling the fact. Fallen were ancient beings supposedly so twisted that they were banished to the middle dimensions because neither the highest nor the lowest ones wanted them. They were said to remain small in number because they ate their young. I'd even heard that the Pureblood species had come about only because the Fallen were so promiscuous that they hadn't managed to destroy all their offspring before they'd interbred enough to form into their own race of demons. Purebloods interbreeding with humans later resulted in Partials, but by then, the bloodlines had been altered enough to make my race able to survive without feeding off the essence of others.

If the history of the Fallen was true, then I should have been paralyzed with terror right now. But, inexplicably, I wasn't. Rafael's arms were tight around me, but not with the careless, bruising force Ashton had used, and the knot of bitter despair that had resided in my gut since I'd woken up in the river had eased into a nervous fluttering. Rafael might take out some payback on me for drugging him, but I didn't feel in danger of being murdered. That had been my first thought when I'd seen his wings, true, but if Rafael wanted me dead, all he'd have to do was let go. At this height, I'd splatter on the ground in an indistinguishable pile of goo.

All of a sudden, Rafael swooped downward, causing my stomach to lift in a way that made me glad I hadn't eaten recently. Who knew how a Fallen would react to puke all over his wings? I might not be in imminent lethal danger, but I didn't want to push my luck, either. Through eyes narrowed into slits, I saw we were headed right for a big crystal mountain. As the seconds passed, I waited for Rafael to swerve, but he flew in a straight line, his wings cleaving the air to eat up the distance between us and that huge, solid obstacle.

"Rafael. . . ." I began, tapping on his chest.

His mouth curled, but he only flew faster. My tapping turned into a frantic pummeling as less than a hundred yards remained between us and that crystal tower of destruction. What was the matter with him? It wasn't like the mountain was going to swerve first!

"Rafael!" I screamed, bracing for the unavoidable impact—

At the last second, he tilted, flying us sideways into a fissure I didn't see until we were already in it. From then on, I kept my eyes shut, deciding that was the wiser course of action or he'd have more than puke to clean off his dark gray feathers.

After several more abrupt turns and swerves, all motion stopped, and I felt something solid beneath my feet. For a long moment, I just stood there, panting and trying to quiet my ominously rumbling stomach.

"Please tell me there's a gateway back to my world inside this mountain and that's why you brought us here," I said when I felt settled enough to talk.

"No."

I opened my eyes, meeting his hooded cobalt gaze. "No, there isn't a gateway? No, that isn't why you brought us here? Or no, you won't tell me?"

He shrugged, releasing me from his grip. "Either way, the answer is still no," he replied in an intractable tone.

That stiffened my spine. Okay, I owed him an apology—several, in fact, plus a huge thank-you for killing Ashton—but if he hadn't been sneaking around and lying to me in the first place, I wouldn't have jumped to all the wrong conclusions later.

"I need to get back to my realm," I said, trying to sound very reasonable. "There are some issues I have to clear up—"

"They'll wait," he said, both words spaced while his brow ticced up in challenge.

Recklessness made me forget that I should try a sweet, charming approach. I jabbed him in the chest, stepping forward until our toes were almost touching.

"I need to go back so I can help clear your name, damn it, so you might want to—oof!"

Rafael picked me up, throwing me over his shoulder like a sack of potatoes. I would have screamed, but he'd done it so suddenly that the breath had been knocked out of me.

"Put me down!" I managed, kicking him as best I could.

"No," he said calmly, keeping me steady with only one arm. "This way, I know you won't be going anywhere until I've said what I need to say."

From my position, with his wings cradled around me, I had a great view of his muscled legs as he strode down what looked like a long hallway. Then he stopped right as I caught a glimpse of another set of legs ahead, but these were distinctly feminine. I tried to angle myself upward to see whom those legs belonged to when Rafael began walking again, jostling me.

"Rafael," a clear voice demanded. "What do you think you're doing with that female?"

"Taking her to my room to ravish her, Mother," he replied shortly.

My jaw dropped, both at his words and at the ebony wings I caught a glimpse of when Rafael turned a corner and I saw more of the woman. Then nothing but walls met my vision when he rounded another bend.

Not just one Fallen but *two* to contend with. I was so screwed, and not just in the way Rafael had outlined.

"Eh, I'll see you afterward, then," she replied in a disinterested voice, adding credence to the harsh rumors I'd heard about their race.

Yet they couldn't all be cruel. Rafael had saved me. Twice. If I had to make a judgment now, Fallen would outrank Purebloods on a kindness scale, no matter their fearsome reputation.

As for the ravishment, I took that as sarcasm instead of nefarious intent. Rafael might have blown my mind by revealing that he was a Fallen, but I didn't believe he was a secret rapist, too. No, he was the type of man who relished sensual surrender instead of brute force, as he'd proved in the carriage. The memory of that, combined with how long it had been since I'd had sex, made the prospect of being alone with him more enticing than daunting, Fallen or no.

Rafael deposited me inside a large, triangular room with crystal walls forming a point at the high, high ceiling. Light glowed from some of those crystals, bathing the room with a soft bluish tinge. A pool of silver water took up one corner, an assortment of thick pillows was piled in another, and a desk that looked formed from the wall took up the final corner. I didn't wait for Rafael to speak but walked over to the shining pool, kneeling by it with a questioning look.

"Is this safe for Partials?"

"Yes, but there's no barrier in there, if that's what you're thinking," he replied in a silky voice.

I kicked off my shoes. "I'm thinking that I still smell like a sewer and I'd like to change that. You should be all for this idea. It'll make your whole ravishment plan a lot more palatable for you."

His mouth quirked, confirming my belief that he'd never intended that, before his expression became stern. "Don't try to joke your way out of this, Mara. I'm still very angry with you."

"I don't blame you." Spoken as I began to unbutton my shirt. Nothing put a man in a better mood than watching a woman strip, as Rafael's fading scowl proved. Jack and Ashton had already taken my vest, gun belt, and weapons, so I had less to take off than what I'd started out with.

He watched me, his wings shifting and then folding back in a compilation of movements that somehow shrank them until I couldn't see them anymore. How could he hide them so completely? True, I hadn't seen Rafael's bare back before, but he'd never looked like he'd had a large hump under his clothes.

"Turn around," I said, wondering if he'd refuse.

Slowly, he turned, revealing wide, muscled shoulders, a narrow waist, and a set of odd, slight ridges that ran along his spine from its base to his neck. Impossibly, that was all that remained of the wings that had reached from his head down to his feet.

"How?" I asked, my voice coming out throatier than before.

"Magic," he replied, facing me once more.

I swallowed at the intensity in his eyes, their vibrant blue shade already dusting over with tiny little lights. "I'm serious," I told him.

"So am I." He spread his arms, and those incredible wings unfurled again, their dark span reaching a foot past his fingertips and their breadth twice as wide as his body. Then he lowered his arms, and just as swiftly, those wings curled up, disappearing from sight.

"There's no scientific explanation for these," he went on, his tone making gooseflesh break out over my skin. "They defy reason and natural order. Fallen were made before those things even existed."

I stood there in my bra and black jeans, feeling somewhat awed by the man in front of me, wishing I hadn't thought that my taking a bath would distract him from being angry. It was too late to change my mind, though.

I unzipped my jeans and stepped out of them, feeling his gaze move over me despite the fact that I didn't meet his eyes. Then I quickly lowered myself into the pool without taking off my bra or panties. Good thing it wasn't cold, because my nipples were already hard from a mixture of excitement and nervousness. It was deep enough that I sank into the water up to my shoulders, noting that the shiny liquid felt different—thicker, like salt water but without the grittiness. Within moments, my skin began to tingle, but not in an unpleasant way.

"The water in that pool is similar to hydrogen peroxide, so the tickling you're feeling is it dissolving away dirt and bacteria," Rafael said, as if reading my mind. "And I'm not one of the original Fallen," he went on, lowering himself into a sinuous crouch only a dozen feet away. "My mother is, but my father was a Pureblood. So while I have wings like my mother's people and I feed on Purebloods, I'm not like the other Fallen you've heard of."

I swallowed at the faintly ominous way he said that last sentence. "Are the other Fallen, the original ones . . . are they anything like their reputations?"

"They're exactly like their reputations," he replied flatly, making me shudder at the blunt confirmation of all the terrible things I'd heard. "My mother let me live because my wings were a curiosity to her. Most mixed-blood children don't have those, though I've met a few others like me over the centuries. After I was born, she sent me to stay with my father in the normal world so I would age into a man. Once I had, she brought me to this realm and taught me how to hunt Purebloods."

I couldn't imagine such an upbringing. Partials

were raised differently than regular kids, yes, what with being able to see dimensional barriers and knowing the world was made up of many different realms. But we didn't grow up knowing we'd escaped being eaten by our parents only because of a genetic *fluke*. Or learning how to kill people—even if Purebloods deserved it.

"Your father? Is he here, too?" I asked, almost afraid to hear the answer.

A small, grim smile touched Rafael's mouth. "When I was still young and living in the normal world, my mother visited unexpectedly and caught my father with another woman. He did not survive her displeasure."

Holy crap, what a twisted family he came from! I'd be happy if that one brief glimpse of his mother was all I ever saw of her. Clearly, the woman was homicide on heels.

"If she's so evil," I said, making my voice very, very low, "then why do you have a room here, where she is?"

Rafael slid closer, until he could reach out and trail his fingers in the silvery water of the pool. "What do you think the biggest deterrent is for Purebloods looking to populate this realm as a permanent home? There aren't many Fallen left, but the presence of even one will make most Purebloods fear to enter. And if there are fewer Purebloods crossing through this realm to get to one where Partials are plentiful . . ."

His voice trailed off, but I could fill in the rest. Purebloods flocked to where their food sources were—dimensions that Partials could cross into, like Nocturna. Without a safe dimension to drag their prey back into, the Purebloods were putting themselves at risk. They might be stronger than Partials one on one, but get enough of us together and we could kick some Pureblood ass.

The old expression ran through my mind: *My enemy's enemy is my friend.* Fallen were Purebloods' enemy, so they were a friend to Partials like me . . . as long as we didn't get too close to them.

"And the barriers in your bathroom?" But now that I knew what Rafael was, I could already guess.

His shoulder lifted in a half shrug even as he pulled off his boots. "The ruler of Nocturna before me built the castle around them so that Purebloods wouldn't find out about them and use them. I kept them a secret for the same reason. They also made it easier for me to cross into this realm to hunt without being observed."

Right. Because if anyone saw Rafael cross through a barrier, they'd know he was more than a Partial. But would that necessarily be a bad thing?

"If your mother's presence keeps most Purebloods out of this realm, why haven't you revealed what you are in Nocturna? Wouldn't the sight of your wings keep more Purebloods away?"

"No one knows where my mother's home is located, aside from me, and if other Purebloods knew what I was, I wouldn't long be safe in Nocturna."

Of course. If Partials knew a Pureblood's home address, we'd show up with some friends to drop off a welcome basket filled with Rest In Peace. It stood to reason that Purebloods would do the same to a lone Fallen.

Which brought up another, very obvious question. "Why are you telling me all this? To convince me to keep your secret?"

Rafael leaned forward until only a foot of that silvery, tingling water separated his face from mine.

"I'm telling you because a demon should know everything about her mate," he said softly, but with enough resonance for the words to hit me like a sledgehammer.

In the midst of my shock over discovering that Rafael was a Fallen, I'd forgotten about those five points of light in my eyes marking me for all to see as a claimed demon. Absurdly, I looked away, as if that made them any less obvious.

"Look, I don't—"

"Do you want to know the real reason why I was in the woods that night when you were a teenager?" he interrupted.

That redirected my attention from what I'd been about to say, which was a lame rationalization, anyway. "You're finally going to tell me the truth?"

A thick lock of golden-red hair fell over his shoulder as he nodded. "When I was a boy, my mother told me that Fallen knew their mates by sight. I asked how, and she said because we recognized them. That didn't make sense at the time, and as only a half-Fallen, I didn't know if it was a trait I'd inherited or not. But that night I saw you at Bonecrushers, even though I'd never set eyes on you before . . . I *knew* you. It only took one glance to feel a part of me saying 'this is her, my mate, the person I've waited centuries for.'"

It felt like my heart stopped beating. Then it restarted in a rush when Rafael slid into the pool with me, not even pausing to take off his leather pants. The water barely rippled as it enveloped him up to his chest, and his gaze held mine captive as he reached out to stroke my cheek.

"I was in the woods because I was following you, even though I fought to stay away because you were barely more than a child. Still, I had to speak to you, at least once, before sending you back to your world. My delay coming after you ended up costing the life of your kinswoman, and for that, I am deeply sorry. But I was there that night for you, Mara, no other reason."

Emotions welled up in me, pulling my heart in different directions at the same time. I wanted to respond to his incredible declaration of me being his mate, but it was so beyond anything I'd allowed myself to consider that I tried to focus on what I could grasp.

"Gloria," I breathed unsteadily. "You could cross realms. Why didn't you go after her when Ashton pulled her through?"

"I did go after her, but only once I'd seen you safely back to your realm. I couldn't risk leaving you in the woods where Purebloods and other dangers lurked. I looked, but I never found her, Mara. I also looked for the Pureblood who'd taken her, but until today, I didn't find him, either."

Poor Gloria. Familiar sadness rose in me, comforted by the memory of Ashton's last, terrifying moments. At last, Gloria had been avenged, and the knowledge of that would soon soothe the rest of my family even as we'd always mourn her.

"Rafael . . ."

I didn't know what to say as I stared at him, feeling the impossibly strong, smooth touch of his hand on my cheek. His gaze was intense, eyes flashing with tiny diamonds of light around those dazzling blue irises—

Flashing. Not stationary, like those five points of light in my eyes. My heart sank while disillusionment coursed like vinegar through my veins. He might think I was the one for him, but his eyes didn't bear the mark of a claimed demon. Rafael was far closer in bloodlines to the source of our race; shouldn't this trait be even more apparent in him? Some Partials never displayed those star points in their gazes, and it wasn't out of lack of love but too much dilution of bloodlines.

"You're wrong about me, Rafael. Your eyes prove it."

I glanced away as I spoke so I wouldn't do

something humiliating, like cry. For a few seconds, I'd felt happier than I had ever been at the idea that the man I'd secretly longed for since I was a teenager was really mine. Now that happiness turned to crushing disappointment when I realized Rafael's very gaze proved that he wasn't.

A low laugh rumbled from his chest even as he pulled me into his arms.

"I see you were taught the innocent version of what prompts the claiming metamorphosis." His tongue traced my ear, making shivers break out over me. "Your eyes changed only *after* you climaxed with me. I haven't had the chance to share the same pleasure with you, but I intend to correct that. Now."

Chapter Eight

Any hesitation I'd had over him being a Fallen vanished at the surge of need his words elicited. I slid my arms around him, letting my head fall back under the insistent demand of his mouth. His tongue teased me, probing my galloping pulse, teeth gently nipping. I traced over the hard sinews of his shoulders to his back, fingers brushing over the unusual ridges as I brought our bodies closer.

He arched and a groan came from him that sounded almost pained. Startled, I snatched my hands back, pulling away to look at him.

"Did I hurt you?"

"No." His voice was hoarse. "Those are . . . very sensitive."

Then he kissed me, backing me against the side of the pool to press his body fully along mine. His arms caged me while his warm, muscular chest, stomach, and legs lined up with my own, the delicious hardness of his erection prodding me even through his soaked leather pants. I moaned into his mouth as I arched against him, feeling my loins greedily clench at the increased contact, the buoyancy of the water allowing me to curl my legs around his waist as I did it again.

His hands traveled down my back to my ass, firmly kneading and pulling me tighter against him. Each twist and rub sent shocks of aching pleasure through me, building in intensity, until I hazily realized that I'd come if he didn't stop now.

"Not like this again," I gasped, tearing my mouth away. "I want you inside me. No, make that I *need* you inside me."

His mouth curled into a sensual smile as he unhooked my bra. "I've waited a long time for you, Mara. Too long to rush this."

My loins twisted in protest at the thought of delaying. How could he expect me to be patient when that bulge in his pants clearly showed he wanted me as much as I burned for him? He looked even more staggeringly gorgeous, too, with beads of silver water clinging to his body and making his skin silkier to the touch. Wait? What idiot invented *that* concept?

I slid my hands beneath the water to his pants, enjoying his intake of breath as I unzipped them. His mouth crushed over mine when I reached inside to clasp him, more heat slamming through me as his length filled my hands.

Oh *hell* no was I waiting, no matter that he wanted to take things slow.

"Mara," he moaned against my mouth when I began to stroke him with firm pumps, each slide of his flesh making that tightening in my loins almost painful. He might have enough control for extended foreplay, but I didn't. What was that he'd said in the carriage? That he could keep from taking me right then, as long as I didn't keep doing what?

That's right, touching his *back*, because he had all those "sensitive" ridges running on either side of his spine. Triumph flared in me. *You're mine now!*

His mouth slid down to my breast, closing over a nipple with enough passionate intensity to clear my head of all thought. A cry wrenched out of me even as I tried to ignore the continued sharp throbs of pleasure that sought to undo my intentions with mindless bliss. Before I got lost in the sensations, I let go of his amazing hardness to run my hands almost roughly down the ridges in his back.

His response was electric. Rafael jerked like I'd struck him, his eyes closing and a pure animalistic groan tearing out of him. He tried to grab my arms, but the water helped me wriggle away as I whipped around him to rub my bare body against those ridges next.

Something between a growl and a shout reverberated across the room. The muscles in his back bunched and rippled in spasms while those ridges grew, rasping my skin. I only had a split second to wonder if I'd pushed him too far when he spun around, the water seeming to explode as he vaulted us out of the pool, ripping away his pants and my panties with the same savage swipe. Then nothing registered except the crush of his mouth on mine, until a rush of movement made me open my eyes even as I felt something soft at my back.

Rafael was on top of me, his wings extended and rising like a dark canopy above us. Their ends curled downward to rest on either side of him, the soft edges of his feathers teasing my sides. Somehow, the framework in his wings supported him enough that his hands were free. He grasped my thigh and my neck at the same time, his mouth claiming mine in a burning kiss while he raised my hips.

"Yes," I choked as I felt the thick, blunt head of him pushing at my center. Then I gasped at the hard cleaving of his flesh into mine, his heat filling me with a thrust that sheathed him in one stroke. His mouth muffled the cry I made as he began to move, that deep inner friction turning the burn of my desire into an inferno. I dug my fingers into his back beneath his wings, loving the fierce rhythm of his thrusts, arching to take him deeper even as I wondered if I could stand it.

He reached down, cupping my breast and pinching my nipple with sensual roughness while his other hand held my thigh in a grip that I didn't want him to loosen. The hard silkiness of his skin, those deep, incredible thrusts, the throbs in my nipple, the demanding ardor of his mouth . . . all of it was too much. Quivers of rapture turned into shudders as I cried out, my loins seizing with an ecstasy that each continued thrust only intensified, until I was shaking with the force of my climax.

His hand left my breast and he gripped my hips with both hands, his thrusts becoming faster, harder. I broke our kiss to gasp in breaths that ended in moans at his intensity. Almost blindly, I reached past the smoothness of his back, finding those ridges between the new, wide stretches of flesh that supported the magnificence of his wings.

Rafael arched, throwing his head back while moving even faster. Our voices rose in a series of groans, his sharper than mine as he increased his pace even more. I was beyond thought, lost in the minefield of sensations that sent more and more bursts of pleasure along my nerve endings, until at last, he gave a guttural shout. His body stiffened while pulses of heat filled my loins, making me cry out as well. More deep thrusts followed, extending the pleasurable waves within me until finally Rafael stilled, his head dropping against my breasts while he took in ragged breaths.

My eyes fluttered shut while I continued to pant, bliss still tingling through me. After a few minutes, Rafael dragged his mouth up to my jaw, kissing it, his hands caressing me even as the last of the tremors subsided within me. He shifted slightly, but I didn't want him to pull away yet, so I hooked my leg around his hip with a noise of protest.

His laugh tickled my neck as his mouth slid there next. "Greedy, aren't you? I love it."

"I need you like this . . . just a little longer," I managed, the words spaced because I was still out of breath.

"Mara." His hands slid up to cup my face. "You're my mate. I'll be with you this way for a very, very long time."

Even in the midst of my reveling over those words, fear snaked up my spine. I wanted so badly for it to be just like he said, but what if when I opened my eyes, his were exactly the same as they had been? No pinpoints of light marking him as claimed because he'd been wrong about me? I'd rather face a horde of Purebloods than see that. My heart wouldn't be able to stand it.

Something wet slid down the side of my temple and I caught my breath as I felt him wipe it away.

"Mara." His voice was hoarse. "Don't doubt me for a moment longer. Open your eyes."

I took in a choppy breath. "Rafael, if it's not—"

"I'm yours," he cut me off, brushing a kiss across my lips. "I'm more sure of that than I've been of anything. Now, open your eyes so you can be sure of it, too."

Very slowly, I did, his dark wings the first

things I saw. Then, my heart pounding, I met his unblinking sapphire gaze.

Tears immediately overflowed my eyes, blurring his features, but it didn't matter. I'd seen enough. A laugh bubbled out of me even as my arms tightened around him until I must have been half strangling him.

"I told you," he murmured, squeezing me back but far more gently.

I pushed him away after a moment, blinking to clear my gaze so I could see those five pinpoints of lights in his eyes again. To me, they were more beautiful than a basket full of diamonds.

"I'm going to make you so happy," I promised in a voice gone scratchy from emotion.

His laugh became huskier while his hands began to travel down my back.

"I intend to make you happy as well, but slower this time."

I lay stretched across Rafael's chest, his wings gone except for those ridges decorating his spine, when his voice broke the peaceful silence.

"Tranquilizer shot. Very clever."

Inwardly I cringed, but in reality, my muscles

didn't even twitch. My body felt like it was in a permanent state of euphoric lethargy after the past couple hours.

"Sorry. With everything I'd heard and how I knew you were lying to me about certain things, I thought you might be a Pureblood. Fallen never even crossed my mind."

He dropped a kiss onto my shoulder. "It doesn't with most people. That's how I've managed to hide what I am for this long."

I rolled over to look at him. "I told my family horrible things about you. Among other important actions, I need to clear that up with them right away. I don't want them shooting their future son-in-law on sight."

A hint of a grin tugged at his mouth. "No, that wouldn't do." Then his expression sobered. "I've already surmised that you went back to Nocturna intending to tell everyone what you thought you'd discovered about me. What happened? Did Ashton catch you unawares in the forest?"

"No, Jack set me up," I said, cursing to myself at the memory. "I trusted him, so I told him about you, thinking if I had his support, other Partials would be more likely to believe me. But he knocked me out, and I woke up with him snickering as Ashton dragged me into a river where another barrier was."

Rafael's mouth curled downward. "Jack," he repeated bitterly. "He hid what he was well over the past century. Out of my men, I suspected him the least."

"Which others of your men did you suspect?" If Billy was also a Pureblood, I'd never trust my judgment in people again.

He listed a few people that, thankfully, I wasn't friends with. Then again, that didn't mean they were guilty and Billy was innocent. Or that any of them were guilty, for that matter. Wouldn't it be a relief if all of them were innocent?

"What if Jack is the only Pureblood hiding in Nocturna?" I offered.

Rafael gave me a dark look. "There are at least two more. Every time the barriers are breached, I can feel it as a Fallen. That is why I knew to come to this realm looking for you. I felt one person enter Nocturna, and then soon after, two people cross over to this side. I correctly feared one of them was a Pureblood and the other was you."

I shook off the suffocating, squeezing memory of being pulled through the dimensions. "So while you can't tell if someone's a Partial or Pureblood when the first barrier into Nocturna is breached, if the second one's parted, you know you've got at least one Pureblood wandering around."

"Exactly."

And I'd thought that as ruler of Nocturna, Rafael had his hands full just keeping a bunch of partial demons in line. Little had I realized that was the least of his concerns.

"We need to get Jack to tell us who the other Purebloods are, fast. Before they escape through the second barrier, which you know will be the first place they'll run once you take Jack into custody."

"If they do, I'll follow them," he replied with deadly emphasis.

"And blow your cover?" I reminded him. "If someone catches you crossing those barriers, your masquerade as a Partial is over. Plus, even if you do follow them, you might not catch them. I haven't seen all of it, but this realm looks huge. I'm beyond lucky you found me in time, but with a little head start, those Purebloods might get away permanently."

There was also the other, uncomfortable possibility, that because of me, Jack had turned the opinions of Nocturna's residents against Rafael. I'd told Jack where the other barriers were, and I'd told my family that Rafael was in league with Purebloods. At least several hours had passed since I left my sister in the Bed Bath & Beyond parking lot. Who knew how many other Partials she might have repeated my former, erroneous beliefs about Rafael to? Combined with Jack's support, that meant Rafael could be slaughtered on sight.

"You can't go back until we know who the others are," I said, steeling myself for the fight I knew would come with my next words. "Because of what I told people, it's too risky for you. I'm the one who has to catch Jack and get him to talk."

Rafael sat up, crossing his arms over the sculpted beauty of his chest. "That is too dangerous—"

"I got the drop on Jack before," I interrupted, my tone hardening. "This time, I won't give him a chance to take advantage of my trust. Besides, I'm the *last* person Jack will expect to come after him. He might be on the lookout for you, but

Jack thinks I'm nice and dead with my essence keeping Ashton's tummy warm."

Rafael still had a look of utter objection on his face. I sighed, reaching out to smooth my hand across his clenched jaw.

"I owe Jack for what he did to me, and for what he helped Ashton do to Gloria. You'll have your own battles in the future that I won't be able to fight for you, even though I'll want to, but this one? It's *mine*, and if you respect me as your mate, you'll let me fight it."

Rafael didn't say anything for a long moment. I waited, my stomach churning. His response would either strengthen our relationship, setting a foundation that we could grow on despite our differences in age, race, and abilities, or fracture our new bond under the weight of stubbornness and chauvinism disguised as chivalry.

"Once you've secured Jack," Rafael said slowly, to the accompanying burst of joy in my heart, "you'll need help to get him to talk."

I hugged him, feeling his fierce answering embrace and promising silently that I'd be the best damn mate in the history of demonkind. Then I let him go before the hard, sensuous feel of his body led to less planning and more time spent on the cushions.

"I know Jack's got to rat out his kinsmen quick, before anyone gets word of what's going on. I like the idea of sticking him with some hot pokers to get him to talk, but even that might take too much time."

"I'll show him what I am," Rafael said in a quiet, frightening voice. "That should get him to talking."

It no doubt would, but that presented its own set of problems. If Rafael flashed those incredible wings at Jack, then we'd have to kill him right away so Jack didn't report what Rafael was to anyone else. No, it was better if Jack was left alive so his guilt could be shown to all the Partials in Nocturna, clearing Rafael's name against anything Jack—or I—had said against him.

A wild idea formed in my mind. I stood up, ignoring the flare of heat that rippled through me when Rafael's gaze lingered over my body.

"There *are* gateways back to Nocturna in this mountain, aren't there?"

Rafael inclined his head toward the large crystal desk in the corner. "Inside that is the gateway that opens in my castle."

He could travel between realms straight from one bedroom into another? Talk about convenient, and that worked out even better for what I had in mind.

I gave Rafael a wicked smile. "I know we're not going to have a conventional relationship, but I'm going to ask my new mother-in-law for a wedding present anyway."

Chapter Nine

I ran through the woods, close enough to the main lighted path of lanterns that I wasn't worried about colliding with a tree, but far enough away that I shouldn't have been easily visible to the mounted patrols. Of course, at least one guard didn't need lanterns to see, but I wasn't worried about Jack. He wasn't patrolling the woods. He was up ahead by the barrier, ready to be the first to greet—and size up—any new entrants into Nocturna.

Still, I slowed down when I was within a hundred yards of the clearing that skirted the barrier and picked my way more cautiously through the trees. No need to screw things up by being impatient. Then, once I was close to the cross section that marked the beginning of the lighted path before the clearing, I hunkered down on all fours, digging quietly.

When I was satisfied with the shallow ditch I'd created, I crawled into it, covering myself back up with dirt and some nearby fallen leaves. Only my hands and my face were left exposed, and I'd already camouflaged my skin to blend more with the forest floor. My dark brown hair didn't need any additional help to blend in, so with my new nest and the darkness, I should have been nearly invisible.

Long minutes ticked by. I was glad no watches worked in this realm, or I would have been checking the time incessantly. Instead, I sought to stem my edginess by thinking back over everything that had led me to this moment. Gloria's excited smile flashed in my mind from that afternoon so long ago at the movie theater. *Mara, this is Drew and Ashton. They're Partials, too, and guess what— they know how to get into Nocturna!*

So many things had happened as a consequence of our stupid decision to go with two strangers into a realm we'd been warned about, but now that memory didn't bring only pain. A part of me would never get over losing my cousin, but another memory flashed in my mind, showing the good that had come out of such tragedy.

Large hands smoothed the hair back from my face, their gentleness a welcome balm after the brutal force Drew had used when he'd bound me and thrown me over his horse. I tried to squelch my sobs, vaguely embarrassed that I'd been smearing tears and a runny nose all over the chest of my unknown savior. But he'd taken me in his arms without hesitation when I'd collapsed after the shock of watching Gloria being yanked through that barrier, and he whispered that he wouldn't let anyone hurt me . . . and I believed him. Without even seeing his face, some part of me knew that he meant every word, and with that knowledge came a sense of peace that I shouldn't have felt under these horrible circumstances.

Then he let me go, standing and awing me with his height as I stared up at him. A scraping sound preceded the sudden flare of a match, making me gasp as I got my first real look at him. He was staggeringly beautiful, with hair the same reddish gold of the flame, a strong jaw, wide mouth, and eyes the most incredible shade of blue. It took me a second before I could even register that he'd spoken.

"Do not fear. My name is Rafael, and I am ruler here. . . ."

No wonder I'd thought he looked like an angel

that night. I'd been close to right; Rafael was the son of an angel, albeit a fallen one. I'd dreamed of him for the next several years, stricken whenever I'd heard my aunt and uncle report that his name had been linked with Purebloods. The night after I turned twenty—the end of the embargo Rafael had sternly outlined when he'd taken me back to the barrier—I'd returned to Nocturna, expecting my adolescent longings to vanish under the reality of seeing him again.

Instead, they'd grown stronger, until even the suspicions I'd had hadn't totally been able to harden my heart against him. Now that I knew what he'd been hiding—why he was so often close by when Purebloods were captured, and that both our bloodlines marked us for each other—I was filled with joy and determination.

Only a few things stood in the way of Rafael and me starting our lives together, and I was going to tear those things *down*.

Hoofbeats thudded in the distance, growing closer. After a few tense moments, I smiled. Someone was headed right this way. I cocked my gun and waited, straining my eyes for the first hint of the rider.

That hint came in the shock of white running

through the crown of the rider's hair. I smiled wider as I sighted down the barrel, taking my time, careful to compensate with my aim for the rolling gait of his horse so I wouldn't accidentally shoot the young girl Jack had in front of him. All the training and target practice I'd done over the years boiled down to the next few seconds. No way would I miss. No way.

And then I pulled the trigger. Not once, but three times, sending out a trio of staccato coughs that didn't even startle the horse. Jack slumped in his saddle, moaning. The girl grabbed him and the reins at the same time, steering the horse toward my position with a quietly authoritative "Yah!"

Atta girl, Lena. You are SO much more mature than I was at your age!

I rose up from my shallow ditch, waving so she could see me and ripping off pieces of duct tape from one of the two rolls I'd stuck into my pants. In the seconds it took for my sister to make it over, Jack tried to go for his gun, but she yanked it from his belt and threw it near my feet. Then I had the duct tape slapped over Jack's mouth before he could even gasp in shock at seeing me.

"Best patrolman in the realm, aren't you,

Jack?" I purred nastily at him. "I knew you'd
be the first to make a young teen feel welcome
here. You were so kind to me and Gloria that
night when we were kids, and you were the first
to welcome me so many other times when I came
back. . . ."

Jack's eyes bugged even as he made furious
muffled sounds behind the gag. I ignored him,
yanking him from his horse and handing off another roll of duct tape to Lena, who began to
wind it around his wrists.

"I think you punctured a lung," she said, giving one of the bleeding holes in Jack's torso a
critical look. Her coolness surprised me. I'd been
worried about including her in my trap to take
Jack down, concerned that Lena wouldn't be
able to handle being so close to Jack when I shot
him, but she insisted on being involved. She did
make the perfect bait for Jack, and contrary to
my prior apprehension, she seemed to be downright blasé about his wounds now.

At my gape, Lena shrugged. "What? I've studied anatomy already. Besides, dissecting a dead
pig last year was *much* grosser than this, let me
tell you!"

"Little sis, sometimes you scare me," I muttered, securing Jack's feet. Then, once he was bound just like he'd bound me, I hefted him sideways over the horse, enjoying the pained "Oomph!" he made against his gag. Three bullets wouldn't kill a Pureblood, but they would hurt like hell, and Jack had so had that coming. That, and a whole lot more.

"Okay, we're going to double back very quietly to the barrier and then you go straight back through to our realm like we agreed," I said, glad her part in this was over.

Lena shook her head. "There are too many other riders around the barrier. We passed two on our way here, and I heard more aside from them. You'll have to take me with you."

I chewed my lip. The plan had been for her to lure Jack into picking her up so he could bring her this way, where I'd shoot him. That had succeeded, but then Lena was supposed to go right back through the barrier afterward so she'd be safe—and wouldn't see what else I had in store for Jack. But if any of those other guards caught her with me *and* a trussed-up, shot patrolman, who knew what might happen? They might shoot first and ask Lena's age later. I also couldn't send my little sister off alone to walk back to the barrier. Not when there were still Purebloods roaming around.

"You know you don't have a choice," Lena pointed out logically. "So quit wasting time gnawing on your lip and let's get going."

My father and stepmother were going to kick my ass for this, but . . .

"All right," I whispered. "Get up there and make sure he doesn't fall off. I'll walk so I can keep my hands free."

After all, I drew the line at having Lena shoot someone, if it could be avoided. Yes, she'd had a gun concealed in her jacket just in case Jack tried anything before I had him in my sights, but even though Lena knew how to shoot, I hoped she wouldn't need to.

Lena kept one hand on Jack and the other on the reins as she directed the horse to follow me. I didn't need to stay close to the light from the nearby path as I made my way toward Jack's cabin. I'd taken this route dozens of times before, lulled into a false sense of security by the guard who had seemed so friendly and compassionate. Lies, lies, lies. If not for Rafael forbidding me to return while I was a teen—an order that, coupled with what had happened to Gloria, had held more weight than all the urgings my father had previously given me — I might have ended up as Jack's lunch one day.

I glanced back at my sister, perched on Jack's horse, her eyes wide as she took in Nocturna for the first time. Who knew if Jack had even intended to take her into town like she'd asked him to? For all I knew, he'd been heading to his cabin with Lena, intending to get in a little snack before he went back out patrolling.

Well, that snack turned out to bite back, didn't it?

I led us around the back of the cabin, tying Jack's horse out of sight by his shed instead of in its usual stall, where someone might see it. Then, with Lena's help, I dragged Jack inside his cabin, not being particularly gentle about it. Once inside, I lit only one candle, then sat him up in his favorite rocking chair, winding more duct tape around him until he looked like a bug caught in a spider's web.

"Lena, hand me that crossbow on the wall," I directed, smiling at Jack as I looked around. "All these nice weapons you have. I always liked how you decorated the walls with them. Now they come in awfully handy, don't they?"

Jack's blue eyes burned with hatred at me. I accepted the crossbow from Lena and jerked my head toward the back of the cabin.

"Go in the bedroom."

"But I don't want to!" Lena burst out.

I rolled my eyes. It was debatable whether it was the rebellious teenager or the one-eighth demon behind her protesting, but it didn't matter.

"Go. Or I'll tell Dad about you skipping school last week."

"Bitch," she muttered, but then went into the bedroom as directed.

I pulled out a small pocketknife as I approached Jack, making a small slit lengthwise in his gag. Jack sucked in a deep breath, but I dug the tip of that blade against his crotch before he released it.

"Scream and I cut your balls off. Understand?"

Jack let out that breath in a furious, but quiet, puff. "How'd you get away from Ashton and get back here?" he growled, the words somewhat garbled from the remaining tape.

I smiled. "Call me lucky, but that's not what we're going to talk about. You're going to tell me who the other Purebloods are here, and you're going to do it *right now*."

His mouth twisted in a gruesome parody of a grin. "Or what? You'll kill me? We both know you're gonna do that anyway. Or you'll have someone else do it, if you don't have the guts. You've got nothing to threaten me with, Mara, and even if you do cut off my balls for not talking, dead men don't need balls anyway."

I set the crossbow down to clap my hands. "Bravo! You're a brave man, even for a filthy Pureblood. So brave that I guessed threatening you with death or dismemberment wouldn't be enough to make you tell me what I want to know. But, see, I met a new friend while I was in the other realm, and I bet she can encourage you to talk."

Then I rose and opened the cabin door. "Oh, Rachael. . . ," I called out.

A rushing sound from the sky preceded my future mother-in-law's approach. She landed with an abrupt, predatory grace, those obsidian wings folding to allow her to pass through the doorway as she strode inside. Even though I'd expected her, the sight of the gorgeous Fallen still made me tighten my hand on my knife. Without her wings, Rachael might have looked like a normal, exquisite blond, but with those black wings trailing behind her and the aura of menace she exuded, Rafael's mother was more frightening than beautiful.

Jack must have agreed, because I had to slap my hand over his mouth to stifle his instant scream.

"Ah-ah-ah. We talked about screaming," I reminded him, wagging the knife.

Rachael's mouth curled as she looked between me and the Pureblood taped to the chair. "You amuse me, little Partial," she drawled.

Normally I'd have taken offense at the patronizing tone, but considering that amusement in her case was a good thing—it was novelty that had led Rachael to spare Rafael's life when he was born, after all—I wasn't going to complain. Hell, I hoped she found me downright *hilarious*, in fact.

"Jack, meet Rachael," I said. "She ate your friend Ashton, but you know women. Just not satisfied with one thing if they can have two. See, I promised Rachael that if she took me back here, I'd give her at least one more Pureblood to munch on, so you might want to rethink telling me about who the others are. Or I'll have no Purebloods to give her except you, and after I saw what happened to Ashton . . . you really, really don't want that. Trust me."

Jack stared at Rachael with the same horrified fascination with which I'd once stared at Drew and Ashton. I knew from experience what he was thinking: that he was trapped by a monster who could take far more than his life. Regular death still meant an afterlife, but Fallen fed from a Pureblood's supernatural essence—the same eternal imprint that would ensure existence after this life—and Rachael would take that, devouring Jack until there was truly nothing left.

Some things were more frightening than death, and oblivion was one of them. But since Jack had sentenced countless Partials to that same fate when he'd fed from them, I felt no pity for him.

Rachael smiled, revealing twin dimples that somehow lost their charm when her wings extended like a black cloud behind her.

"You test my patience, Pureblood," she said, her voice melodic and chilling at the same time.

Jack began to talk.

Chapter Ten

I rode down the main street of Nocturna, not acknowledging the various mutterings from Partials on the sidewalk as I passed by.

"... didn't I hear she was dead?"

"... Jack said Rafael killed her ..."

"... sure doesn't look dead, does she?"

But the lit skulls that marked the front of Bonecrushers were the only thing I focused my attention on. Every stride from the horse brought me closer, while a curious calm replaced my normal impatience. In so many ways, my journey for justice had started here, so it was fitting that it should end here.

I didn't bother tethering the horse when I reached the corral, instead jumping down and leaving it to wander at will. Its former owner wouldn't need it anymore, and soon someone else would claim it. Nothing valuable was wasted in Nocturna, and it was a fine horse.

"Heard you were dead, Mara," a cool voice noted behind me. "You sure stink like death, but I don't believe in zombies, so I guess Jack was full of shit about Rafael doing you in."

I turned to face Billy, noting the burly Halfie looked pissed. Not that I blamed him. Jack had told me all about how he'd spread the word that Rafael was a Pureblood. Had even added a nice touch about how he'd watched in horror as the ruler of Nocturna had dragged me through a barrier for munching on later. As Rafael's friend, Billy had a right to be mad, seeing me stroll around as though I hadn't been instrumental in smearing Rafael's name.

"I stink because I went through a sewage system, *again*, and if you want to help me catch some real Purebloods, I need you to do me a favor."

Billy tugged on the end of his tattered leather jacket. "This better be good. I'm in no mood for bullshit games."

I came nearer until we were close enough to kiss, but Billy didn't flinch. He just stared at me with hard brown eyes.

"Oh, it's good. I promise."

Then I whispered what I needed him to do, waiting until I got a nod of confirmation before walking through the double doors into Bonecrushers.

Several heads turned, and mutterings swept through the crowd. Even the singer on stage paused in his rendition of the Smashing Pumpkins' "Disarm" to stare at me. It seemed like everyone had heard the tale Jack had spread, but then again, such shocking charges against Rafael would travel at the speed of light. I was only relieved that my aunt and uncle hadn't had the chance to tell their Partial friends about my initial, mistaken belief about Rafael. If I hadn't used those gateways to cross back over right when I had, I would've been too late to stop the flow of information on that side.

I jumped onto the top of the nearest table, my new vantage point making it easy to see that the doors to Bonecrushers were now closed. Then, just in case anyone wasn't paying attention, I fired two rounds into the ceiling.

"People, we have Purebloods hiding in Nocturna," I called out loudly.

Various ominous rumblings sounded at that statement, punctuated by a few calls of "Rafael" and "Kill the fucking Pureblood!"

"I know what Jack told you about Rafael, but it's not true," I went on, still in that same ringing voice. "Rafael is *not* a Pureblood. Jack lied, and the reason he did is because he's a Pureblood himself."

An eruption of shouts followed this statement. I waited for the initial roar to die down before speaking again.

"In fact, there's more—"

"Don't believe her!" a voice screeched out. Heads swung toward the singer, who pointed his guitar at me. "She's lying to cover for Rafael, so she must be a Pureblood like him!" he continued emphatically. "Jack's been a trusted guard here for over a hundred years, but *she* just strolled in the past decade. You're going to believe her over him? She also just *happened* to survive a Pureblood attack, when everyone knows no one survives those!"

I was once again the center of attention—this time, with a wave of animosity from the crowd that was palpable. Bonecrushers catered to the toughest, wildest Partials in Nocturna. If this crowd charged me, I'd be toast, even with my guns.

"Yes, I'm new here," I called out, not showing the slightest sign of fear to incite them. "Yes,

Jack's been here for over a century, and yes, I survived a Pureblood attack when almost no one lives through those. In fact, I survived two of them. What are the odds of *that*, right? But let me prove who the real Purebloods are—"

The hole in the roof over the fire pit suddenly exploded with movement. Black wings fanned smoke and embers as Rachael burst through, dropping Jack's bound form onto the top of the crowd. He bobbled for a second on various heads and shoulders before thudding to the ground when people scrambled to get out of the Fallen's way as she landed beside him. A surge of patrons went for the doors, shouts ringing out when they found them blocked. *Thank you, Billy*, I said silently. I knew the Halfie could find a way to barricade them in time.

"Stop!" I yelled. "She's with me!"

It might have been sheer amazement that slowed the mad scramble for the door, although a few people still tried to claw their way out. I only had seconds to make my point before chaos took over, so I hurried to continue.

"We all know Fallen feed off Purebloods. *Purebloods, not Partials*. If Jack isn't a Pureblood, then that Fallen can't steal the essence out of him."

"Finally," Rachael muttered before snatching Jack up. She ripped the duct tape off his mouth, but Jack didn't even get the chance to scream before her lips sealed over his.

"Someone stop her!" the singer shouted.

No one moved toward Rachael. She had an empty circle around her that allowed for easier viewing as Jack thrashed in her arms, his eyes bulging in horror as she continued her deep, lethal kiss. After only a few seconds, he began to shudder, and then he went abruptly limp even as lights danced in an intricate pattern across Rachael's lovely skin. She dropped Jack's lifeless body to the floor as those lights on her skin ebbed, and then wiped her mouth almost daintily on a wing.

This was the second time I'd seen this in less than a day, so I wasn't shocked like most of the other onlookers. I spoke up in the sudden stunned quiet.

"Jack kidnapped me and handed me over to a Pureblood, who pulled me through to the next realm. Then Jack made up that story about Rafael to cover what he'd done and to get rid of Rafael. But when I was in the next realm, this Fallen came across the Pureblood and ate him.

She brought me back here because I promised to give her another Pureblood as payment. Earlier, Jack told me who the other Purebloods were. They're in this bar—"

A flash of metal caught my vision. I'd kept a wary eye on him and the other person I knew was a Pureblood, so I had time to lunge before the gunshot rang out, firing back even as white-hot pain blasted through me. My quick reaction meant the shot tore through my upper arm instead of my heart, so the impact spun me around, but I didn't collapse. Instead, I dropped to one knee and fired again, striking the shooter a second time. He tried to raise his gun at me again, but a large form barreled into him, knocking it away.

"Hold him," Rafael's stern voice commanded amidst the sudden pile of people jumping in to restrain Lance, the singer who'd shot me.

"She's lying! The bitch is lying!" Lance screamed.

"As you can guess," I rasped, raising my voice, "Lance is one of the two Purebloods here. Hank, our friendly neighborhood bartender, is the other."

Rafael reached me right as several people

hauled Hank over the wooden countertop. Rafael pulled me into his arms, shielding me from any other potential gunshots. Over the wide shoulders of my mate, I saw Hank disappear into the crowd of furious Partials. While Lance still shrieked and cursed me, Hank was oddly silent. He must have realized his fate had been sealed as soon as Rachael had dropped through that smoke hole.

Speaking of Rachael, she still stood in the center by the fire pit, watching the melee around her with a distinct little smirk.

"You Partials are more entertaining than I remembered," I heard her remark over Lance's screams and the rough cheers at whatever was being done to him and Hank. Then she caught my eye, nodded once, and flew back out the way she'd come in.

"Mara, your arm," Rafael muttered, setting me back to rip the sleeve off his jacket and tie it around me.

"It's just a flesh wound," I replied, wincing at the pressure from the makeshift bandage. "And *you* weren't supposed to come here until I convinced everyone that you're not a Pureblood."

He grunted. "I wasn't about to stay in the other

realm wondering if my mother would keep her word. I watched over you from the skies while you captured Jack. Then I stayed out of sight in the fields when you came in here, but once I heard the gunshots, I had to get to you."

I couldn't criticize. If it had been me outside hearing the gunshots, I wouldn't have stayed away either, danger or no danger. Luckily for us, by the time the shots had rung out, the people inside had seen enough to realize Jack had been lying.

And luckily for us, Rafael had put on his shirt and coat while waiting in the fields, so the markings on his back were concealed from any curious eyes.

His large hands stroked my face before he kissed me. The feel of his mouth, combined with the joy of wrapping my arms around him, even though one throbbed painfully, made the rough surroundings fade away. By the time he lifted his head, I didn't even notice the shouts around us as the Partials administered their own form of justice to the two Purebloods.

"Let's leave," Rafael murmured. "I have a doctor at my castle who can treat your arm."

"It can wait a little longer. We need to get my

sister back home. She's still at Jack's cabin, pouting because I wouldn't let her come with me."

Rafael shook his head with a snort. "Another stubborn Partial, eh?"

"It runs in the family," I whispered before kissing him again. Lena would be thrilled when I told her she could come here to visit me—and my father would be glad when I told him I'd only let her travel through the gateway in Rafael's castle, so she would avoid the town until she was older.

"Let's go, my mate," I said once we broke the kiss.

His smile took away even the pain in my arm. "Yes. First back to your world, and then back to our home."

I grinned at him. "Our home, huh? I'm glad you see it that way, because I intend to make a few changes."

A brow rose. "Changes?"

"We'll start with the front hall," I said, letting him lead me out of Bonecrushers. "Really, Rafael, 'medieval chic' is *so* last century. . . ."

Mated

Shayla Black

Chapter One

"Mathias attacked the Lowery estate and burned it to the ground. The family is dead."

Raiden Wolvesey staggered and fell against the nearby wall. Those terrible words repeated over and over in his head.

The *entire* family dead? Including Tabitha . . . and the child she'd been carrying? *His* child?

He'd never said good-bye, held her one last time.

The pain swept over him, fast and unmerciful, like a forest fire out of control. He struggled to stay upright, deny the news. Though he'd been witness to the aftermath of other such attacks, he refused to believe it until he saw her body himself.

After wreaking havoc on magickind for months, Mathias d'Arc, an evil wizard recently returned from exile, had been quiet for weeks, his indiscriminate raping and killing of magic-kind paused. He claimed to commit his crimes against the wizarding upper class, the Privileged, in the name of lifting the Deprived, magickind's lower class, to power.

Liberation based on blood and pain and torture? *Rubbish!* Raiden shook his head.

"I know what you're thinking, and you're not going alone," the bearer of the bad news said from the doorway.

Bram Rion. He led the Doomsday Brethren, a handful of warriors devoted to stopping Mathias. They'd taken to hiding in this series of caves like damn underground rodents scurrying for shelter. While others above them died. Like beautiful Tabitha.

Her fiery hair, her laughter, her hazel eyes . . . all gone?

Fury assailed him, and it was all he could do not to charge across the room and rip Bram's blond head off. "I'm going. I have to see if there's any way . . ."

Raiden raked a hand through his hair. He couldn't even talk about the possibility of Tabitha's death, much less accept it.

"The neighbors reported fires. When Caden and Ice"—Bram referenced two of the Doomsday Brethren's other members—"teleported over to investigate, they found no survivors. You won't solve anything by going there."

"If someone had attacked Emma's house, wouldn't you investigate personally?" Raiden snarled, referring to Bram's mysterious mate. She'd bonded with him, then disappeared after just one night.

Bram raised a brow. "It's different. Tabitha wasn't your mate. In fact, didn't you spend last night with another woman?"

Raiden steeled himself. Yes, he had. A human whose name he couldn't recall. And didn't he regret that now? While trying to avoid Tabitha so she could have a safer, better life, he'd left her to face Mathias alone.

Self-loathing ate his stomach like acid.

He shot Bram a menacing glare. "I'm going. I don't care if you come with me or not."

Forcing himself to concentrate, Raiden took a deep breath, centered his magic, and teleported to the Lowery estate.

The grand home lay in ruins, blackened, ransacked as if someone had searched it high and low. The devastation was absolute—and like a fist in his gut. Bodies were strewn on the lawn. Her mother, father, two brothers.

No Tabitha.

Raiden prowled through the charred remains of the house, which still smoldered with the aftereffects of the fire. No one in the foyer, the sitting room, the bedrooms. Upstairs—or what was left of it—downstairs, servants' quarters . . . all empty. With every step, his fear for Tabitha burned hotter. Panic rose.

He could think of only two reasons Tabitha's body wasn't among the dead: either she'd miraculously escaped, or Mathias had taken her with him. If the latter, the bastard would torture the beautiful witch unmercifully before ending her life in a cataclysm of humiliation and pain.

Suddenly, he heard a little whooshing sound and he whirled, heart chugging, anticipating a fight. Hell, he welcomed one. Instead, he found Bram. Again.

"She's not here."

As Raiden could plainly see. But he wouldn't rest until he found her . . . one way or the other. "You didn't mention that."

"You didn't let me."

Fucking semantics. Raiden had no time for them. "I must keep searching. Maybe . . . she escaped and sought refuge elsewhere."

"Maybe."

Bram didn't sound convinced, and Raiden stifled the urge to rage at him. Doing so would make him feel better, but it wouldn't bring back Tabitha.

With a sigh, Bram clapped him on the shoulder. "I know she's expecting your child."

"Yes," Raiden choked.

God, yes. She wasn't very far along, three months at most. If any other woman had ever conceived by him, he'd know exactly when because he never spent more than a single night with any of them, never went back for seconds. No attachments, ever. For Tabitha, he'd broken that cardinal rule. Repeatedly. He'd been unable to stay away, no matter how much better her life would have been without him.

"Rightfully, you're concerned about the baby," Bram placated. "Children are difficult for magic-kind to conceive, and I—"

"Shut up." Not for anything would he confess his feelings about Tabitha to Bram. Hell, he barely understood them.

"Or is this about Tabitha herself? If you loved her, why didn't you mate with her?"

Raiden didn't want to have this discussion.

"I'm not wired like you or the others. You know my family was cursed so that we can't sense our mates. The mating instinct was bred out of us generations ago," he said, referring to the sixth sense that allowed a wizard to taste a woman and know if magic intended her for him.

Bram raised a golden brow, his blue eyes laser sharp. "That didn't stop your twin. Ronan looks quite settled with Kari. For months he hasn't looked at another woman."

Nearly two years, if Bram wanted the honest truth. Oh, prior to mating with the pretty human Kari, Ronan had bedded other women. Magic must be powered by a strong exchange of emotion, and sex always worked like a charm. Playful encounters with many partners were expected until one mated. But almost from the start, Ronan had fixated on Kari, finally mating with her, despite the fact that the rest of the Wolvesey family, eternal bachelors all, thought him mad.

Raiden understood. Meeting Tabitha had been almost surreal. His first thought had been that no witch could possibly be so lovely. Once he'd talked his way into her bed, his second thought had been that no witch could possibly be so sweet.

It had taken great effort to leave her that next morning, but he'd vowed never to return. She'd been too tempting, had felt too damn good once he'd sunk into and made love to her. But he'd been back again three days later, hungrier than ever. Then again, and again . . .

"I'm not like Ronan." He clenched his jaw so hard that he swore it would shatter.

Bram scoffed. "Exactly. He's smarter."

When Bram turned away to sift through the ruins, Raiden charged after him. "What the hell does that mean? I don't have the instinct!"

"But, in theory at least, you have a brain. And a heart. You knew that woman meant something to you, but . . ." Bram shrugged. "Well, water under the bridge if she's dead."

Raiden growled, "I refuse to believe that until I have proof."

"Chances are—"

"Finish that sentence, and I'll wring your bloody neck. Call Shock. Find out what he knows."

It went against everything in Raiden's body to suggest that Bram call the Doomsday Brethren's supposed double agent. No one liked the confrontational bastard. They trusted him even less. But he alone was close enough to Mathias. Maybe Shock knew the truth. Raiden closed his eyes and prayed.

"Are you mad? If Shock says Mathias has her, what will you do? Charge in like her white knight? You'll be signing your own death warrant."

If Mathias had Tabitha, Raiden would go after her. Period. No one deserved to die the way Mathias preferred to kill: shaving, branding, raping, then leaving the victim to bleed to death. She was the warmest woman, passionate beneath that shy exterior, so smart it roused him, so welcoming he'd lacked the strength to say no. She was, in a word, perfect.

Tabitha deserved a better father for her child. Her parents had insisted on it and found her a suitable mate, whom she would have joined with in mere days from now. Raiden had never imagined that finding the strength to walk away from her would lead to this.

"Call Shock," Raiden demanded. "Now!"

With a shrug, Bram pulled his phone from his pocket. "You're presuming the wanker will answer."

After pressing a few buttons, Bram handed him the phone.

Shock did answer . . . in his usual manner. "What the fuck do you want?"

"It's Raiden Wolvesey. Help me."

"We have nothing to say."

The hell they didn't. "I need information about the Lowery attack."

Shock said nothing for a long moment. "Why do you think I can help you? What's done is done."

"You *knew* about this? Knew Mathias would attack Tabitha's family?"

Shock remained silent for so long that Raiden wondered if the wizard had rung off. Finally Shock said, "If you were Mathias and you could obtain information you needed while bedding one of magickind's most renowned beauties, what would you do?"

"So he planned to take her and—" Raiden couldn't finish the sentence. The reality made him altogether ill. "Did he succeed? Does Mathias have her?"

"I wasn't present for the attack. It was sudden. Mathias had this mad idea last night. Wouldn't share it. Just said he'd solved his problem and needed information. I don't know why. I don't know who, if anyone, he took with him from the Lowery estate. But he's in a foul mood now. That's all I know."

There was a soft click in Raiden's ear as Shock ended the call. With a curse, Raiden thrust the phone back at Bram, trying to tamp down his growing fear and fury.

Mathias had wanted information? But was in a foul mood now? Then something had gone wrong. And Raiden prayed it was that Tabitha had escaped.

He clung to that glimmer of hope. He must continue looking for her.

"Shock knows almost nothing," he muttered.

"Or is willing to admit almost nothing. With him, who knows the truth?"

Who, indeed? Raiden wandered into what had once been Tabitha's bedroom. Amidst the rubble on the floor, he found the green glass heart necklace she'd been so fond of. His breath froze in his chest. She'd never taken it off, and the fact that it wasn't around her neck now . . . He resisted the urge to hurl the little glass pendant across the room. Instead, he shoved it in his pocket. It might be the only thing he had left of her. The thought was another stab in the heart.

Damn it! How could he be this grief-stricken for someone to whom he hadn't given his heart?

Chapter Two

"If Mathias had Tabitha in his grip," Bram mused, "he'd likely be taunting you with the knowledge."

Raiden clenched his fists. "Why? As you pointed out, she's not my mate."

"But she *is* the mother of your child. Her magical signature would tell him so," he said, referring to the aura around every witch and wizard that told others about their power and lineage. "He'd start with the idea that you'd do anything to protect your coming youngling."

A very good assumption.

The phone in Raiden's pocket rang. He withdrew it, peered at the display, and swore. His father. If Nathanial told him that he'd scored two sisters and to come home immediately to share them, as he had last week, Raiden swore he'd throttle the man.

"What?" he barked into the phone.

"Good evening to you, Son. Are you . . . busy?"

In other words, was he already shagging someone tonight? Raiden rolled his eyes. How could a grown wizard think so much like a fifteen-year-old boy? Raiden had tried more than once to explain that since he'd joined the Doomsday Brethren, finding a different woman every night no longer topped his priority list. Staying alive did. Granted, that was likely futile. Seven warriors stacked against the most evil wizard in history and his growing army? The odds weren't good. But his twin, Ronan, was committed to this war, and the cause was noble, so Raiden wouldn't leave his brother to fight alone.

"Yes, I'm busy, Father." *Looking for Tabitha.* The lie would dissuade Nathanial from calling for a few hours at least.

"Very well, I'll tell your encinta that."

His encinta. The woman carrying his baby. Raiden's heart stopped. "Tabitha is there?"

"Indeed. Unless there's another—"

"No. Is she all right?" Raiden demanded.

"Shaken and bleeding a bit from a small wound."

A relief stronger than he'd ever felt poured through Raiden. Something in him had died when he'd thought he might never see her again. Now it awakened with a vengeance.

"I'll be happy to take care of her," Nathanial said.

"Don't touch her." It was all Raiden could do not to crush the phone.

He'd never been possessive of a woman—until recently. Before Tabitha, females had been interchangeable. Since meeting her, Raiden had done his best to put on a good front, but he ached for her alone.

And now he might have the opportunity to hold her again.

No. Though she was alive, she was all but pledged to another. It was better that way.

"Well." His father sounded affronted. "You needn't yell."

"Keep Tabitha there. I'll be home in a moment."

He rang off and bent to her family's burned, bloody bodies. He lifted Tabitha's mother. Her ending had been violent but quick. Small blessing, but better than the alternative.

The woman had despised him for impregnating her only daughter. Had said the baby had ruined her chances of mating and that a notorious playboy like Raiden didn't deserve her. Naturally, they'd been relieved when Sean Blackbourne, nephew to the head of the magical Council, had stepped forward and agreed to mate with Tabitha.

Older and well-connected, Sean sought a companion and heir now that his mate had perished without breeding. He would be better for Tabitha and the child. To protest the match would have been selfish, so Raiden had swallowed his pride and wished her well. That had been the last time he'd seen her, over two months ago. God, how he'd love to turn back the clock. Even if he could, he didn't know what he'd do differently. Nothing changed the fact that her parents had been right.

Raiden turned to Bram. "Help me take her family to my house."

"Tabitha is there?" When Raiden nodded, Bram shook his head. "She's going to be too grief-stricken to see their bodies now."

Did Bram think Raiden was daft? "I didn't plan on displaying them. I'm going to take them to the gardens, prepare them for burial."

With a nod, Bram took her father and middle brother. Raiden lifted her eldest brother as well and closed his eyes, focusing on home. Moments later, he found himself in his gardens, freezing in the December chill. Carefully, they laid her family out inside the gazebo, protected from the elements.

"I keep wondering, why the Lowerys?" Bram murmured. "It seems so . . . random."

Impatience chafed at Raiden. He wanted to see Tabitha, but this question had crossed his mind as well. "I haven't a clue."

"Random is unlike Mathias. Lowery hadn't spoken publicly against Mathias, hadn't lifted a wand to fight. Tabitha was to be joined to Blackbourne, a family with ties to Mathias. I can't imagine what Mathias would have sought from Lowery. He was a bloody historian. The information he collected is public to all of magickind. But by the looks of the ruins, Mathias wanted something badly."

Indeed. And Raiden wanted to get to the bottom of that mystery—after he'd seen Tabitha.

His heart pounded overtime as he ran toward the house, each step bringing him closer to her, to seeing for himself that she was alive and well and the baby was still safe.

As he reached the back door and threw it open, Tabitha stood waiting, her long skirts torn, her pale cheeks sooty. The air left Raiden's body in a giant rush.

Her fiery hair, which he'd loved to spread across white pillows, had come loose from its usual upswept do. A tear in her soft cinnamon blouse bared her shoulder. Her hazel eyes looked wide and stricken.

She was the most beautiful sight he'd ever seen.

The moment she saw him, she ran toward him. For safety and comfort only, he knew. Still, Raiden opened his arms and wrapped them around her, clutching her small frame tightly.

"T-they came so quickly. I . . . I didn't know what to do. Father told me to run. Mathias made it impossible to teleport and—"

"Shh," he comforted her. "I know. I . . . saw. Take a deep breath."

Wildly, she shook her head, and more of her fiery hair escaped its knot. "He killed them, didn't he?"

Oh, God. She didn't know her entire family was dead? And he had to be the one to tell her. She already despised him for walking away. The pain of her hatred already hurt so damn bad. . . .

But she deserved to know. No one else would break it to her as gently.

Lifting her in his arms, he carried her to a nearby sitting room, shutting the door against his curious father. He set her on his lap, then used his magic to pour her a bit of water from the nearby bar and levitate it to her.

"Drink this."

"Answer me!" That temper of hers flashed hot and suddenly. "Are they dead?"

What the hell could he say? "Yes. I'm so sorry, Tabby."

Tears immediately flooded her eyes as pain crested over her face. "A-all of them?"

He nodded. "I brought them here for burial."

Her hazel eyes were twin wells of anguish, and Raiden didn't know what else to do but hold her as long as she needed him.

Tabitha buried her face in Raiden's neck and did the one thing she'd sworn never to do again: she clung to him. As always, he was solid. Hard body, substantial shoulders. His long golden hair pulled away from the masculine angles of his chiseled face. The sight comforted her.

Everything she'd ever known, everyone she'd ever loved—except Raiden—was dead. Now she was virtually alone in the world. Scarcely knowing her intended mate, she really had no one else to turn to. And certainly no one else who knew anything about fighting Mathias.

Sobs overwhelmed her. Raiden could be a real bastard, and she didn't expect him to do more than protect her now—likely more for the baby's safety than her own.

Still, she couldn't help sinking into him as he held her tightly, caressing her back, whispering assurances. No, it wasn't going to be all right. Since the attack just after dinner, she hadn't felt safe for a moment. Until now. This Raiden was the considerate lover who'd seduced her several months ago, not the unfeeling cad who'd broken her heart.

Tabitha shoved that thought aside. That no longer mattered, only the here and now did.

"I-it was terrible," she muttered. "So unexpected. We'd just finished eating. Mother was pouring wine, Father informed me that Sean would be over for dinner tomorrow, then . . ."

Raiden's hand tightened on her. "You don't have to say more if you don't wish."

But she did have to. The danger wasn't over.

"The windows crashed in. There were men

everywhere. Wizards and half-rotted human corpses." She shivered.

"The Anarki. Mathias's army."

She nodded. "I-I . . . they swarmed like locusts. Everyone scattered. My father grabbed my arm and whispered in my ear, then used his body to protect me as he shoved me through a hidden door in his office."

She shook with fresh sobs as grief wrenched her all the way to her core. God, she could remember that last look at his face, so frighteningly resigned. "I . . . ran until I was far enough from Mathias's power, then I teleported here."

"I'm sorry you went through that. And I'm sorry about your family, Tabby."

"I didn't know where else to come. I know you and your friends fight Mathias . . ."

"You did the right thing." He held her even tighter, and through her grief, Tabitha wondered why. Raiden didn't love her. When her parents had demanded that he leave and never come back, he'd complied easily enough. If this hadn't been a life-or-death prospect, Raiden would have been the last man she sought.

But only he could help her now.

"What did your father say before you ran?"

"I-I don't understand it, really. It makes no sense. Maybe I misunderstood . . ."

"What?" Gently, he wiped her tears away.

Tabitha replayed her father's voice, filled with forced calm, in her head. Then she frowned. "He told me to protect the secret tree."

Chapter Three

*T*he secret tree?" Raiden paused, his thoughts clearly churning. "Did you have such a thing on your property?"

"I've no idea what he was talking about."

"Do you know where he might have grown a secret tree? Or why it's so secret?"

Tabitha shook her head. Frustration warred with panic. She must figure out what her father wanted her to protect or his death would be in vain.

She sucked back her tears and forced herself to focus. "He never mentioned a secret tree previously."

"We will figure it out," Raiden soothed her, cradling her against him. "Had he behaved differently of late?"

"Since this business with Mathias began a few

months past, he'd become cautious with his historical documents. He removed some from the house, but I've no idea where he took them. The only other time I saw him relocate work was long ago. When I was a child, he brought me with him once to an office. Perhaps a Council building? But who knows if it's still in use."

"Do you recall where? Maybe the secret tree is there."

She could picture his large, modernish building in her mind, remembered the guards smiling at her and the labyrinth of stairwells, the colorful tiles. "That was years and years ago. The memories are hazy. I . . . Do you think Mathias was after something of my father's work?"

"Possibly. Or perhaps Mathias just wanted to cause terror and instigate violence. Drink up, love." Raiden pressed the glass to Tabitha's lips.

She hesitated, then took a delicate sip. "Thank you."

A soft smile curved his mouth. "Always so ladylike."

Raiden had this way of poking fun at her gentility . . . yet making her feel so much like a woman. Tabitha sent him a bittersweet smile.

When she'd first fallen in love with Raiden, the

feelings had rushed her like a hurricane—hard, fast, undeniable. She'd quickly learned that loving Raiden was like eating too much chocolate—scrumptious and incredible, but decidedly detrimental. "You've said that to me before."

Indeed. The first time he'd seduced her. And shown her the meaning of passion beyond words.

Best not to think of that now. After spending amazing days with Raiden and even more amazing nights, she'd awakened one morning to find her magical signature altered to reflect the fact that she now carried his child. Within twenty-four hours, he'd been gone from her life.

Tabitha shifted away from him, rising to pace the room. She had to focus. Her family was dead, killed for something she didn't understand and didn't know how to protect.

"Tabby," he murmured. "I see your mind working. We're more likely to solve this problem together. Talk to me."

She shook her head. "Too much nervous energy."

And being close to him was too dangerous to her fragile heart.

He rose. The heat in his eyes was unmistakable. He wanted her. Very much. Then again, he always had. Sex for him meant nothing. She'd learned that the hard way.

What surprised her was the genuine warmth and concern in his expression. So unlike the Raiden who had turned his back on her suddenly. That man had been cold as ice. Did he feel sorry for her? The thought made her choke.

Tabitha rounded the couch, moving away from him. He changed course and followed. Slow. Stalking.

Running from Raiden was never an option. When he wanted something, he went after it ruthlessly. He never made any move without purpose.

She whirled, faced him, planted a hand on his solid chest to keep him at bay. Beneath smooth skin and hard muscle, she felt the *beat, beat, beat* of his heart. That sound had been permanently embedded in her memory the first time he'd covered her body with his, kissed her neck, then slid deep inside her.

"What do you want?"

He sighed and placed a gentle hand on her shoulder. "You look scared and ready to collapse. I want you to rest."

Before she could respond, she felt his magic pulling her under, compelling her into a deep slumber. And she collapsed into his arms.

Damn him! She wouldn't stand for this.

That was her last thought.

Raiden settled Tabitha on his bed upstairs and tucked the covers around her. Dark circles shadowed her pretty eyes. Being an expectant mother naturally drained a great deal of her energy, and she'd just lost her whole family. She should have been in bed. Instead, Tabby had been pacing, trying to solve this dilemma on her own.

Not while there was still breath left in his body.

As he settled her against his pillows, she released a contented sigh.

Rising to his feet, Raiden started planning. First, he had to ensure her safety. To do that, he had to figure out this secret tree business. And somehow, he had to bring himself to deliver her to Sean Blackbourne. Lucky, undeserving bastard. But the other wizard would take care of her and the baby in a way Raiden couldn't.

Shoving the terrible thought aside, he reached for his mobile and dialed a familiar number. Bram picked up on the first ring.

"Is Tabitha all right?"

"Shaken. Distraught." And still so beautiful,

she haunted him. Raiden couldn't deny that his desire for her went dangerously deep.

Bram's voice sounded heavy. "That's to be expected. Her life has been forever changed."

Indeed, and Raiden ached for the grief she must be enduring. But his first item of business must be protecting her. "What do you know about a secret tree?"

"A what?" Bram sounded puzzled. "Never heard of such a thing."

That wasn't good news. "Can you search your grandfather's texts?" Raiden asked, referring to the tomes the great wizard Merlin had passed down to his family. "Or talk to your sister?"

Then he explained Lowery's last words to his daughter.

Bram sighed. "Bloody hell, I have no idea."

Not what Raiden wanted to hear. "When the sun rises, I'll be searching her family estate again. There are clues, I'm certain. Damn it, we're simply missing them."

Trying to shake off dark dreams of screaming, destruction, and death, Tabitha awakened with night still streaming through the windows. Panting, she opened her eyes, eager to shake off the nightmare.

But she saw only an unfamiliar bed in an unfamiliar room. Raiden's arms were curled around her. His blue eyes searched her, intent, concerned.

Reality crashed in on her. God, her worst torment wasn't a terrible dream. Her family *was* gone. She turned her face away, not wanting to show him her tears.

"I'm so sorry about your family." He caressed her long, loose hair gently.

She shoved it behind her shoulder self-consciously. Her mother, raised in another time, had always preached that wearing her hair down was a sign of wantonness. She'd let her hair down for Raiden, revealed her inner temptress. He'd broken her heart. She shouldn't read too much into his concern other than compassion.

"I'll be fine." She tried to pull away.

Raiden held firm. "Should we have someone out to look at the baby? You've been distraught . . ."

Such emotions weren't good for an expectant mother.

Tabitha took several deep breaths and willed herself to be calm. "No. There's nothing wrong."

His thumb caressed her cheek as his fingers curled around her nape. And those blue eyes of his looked through her. She shivered, recalling a thousand intimate moments between them—and foolishly wanting a thousand more.

"Have you been feeling well? Is the pregnancy normal? Any problems?"

She'd never heard his voice so gentle, and she didn't want to be warmed by the fact that he'd asked. "No problems."

That wasn't totally true, but he didn't need details.

"Tabby, until—"

"Don't call me that anymore." He'd called her that when he'd held her, kissed her, made love to her. He'd called her Tabitha as he'd left. Once he'd done that, he'd lost the right to use the more familiar name.

He ignored her. "I heard that you experienced sickness early on. That you nearly lost the baby."

She gasped. How could he have known that?

"You never told me." He actually looked hurt by that fact.

Tabitha shook off the covers and darted to her feet, horrified to discover that he'd stripped her down to her bra and knickers. Spearing him with an accusing stare, she grabbed the top blanket, wrapped it around her, and shoved her hair behind her again. "You no longer have the right to look at me this way, to touch me, to know about the baby. You made yourself very clear when you said you wanted nothing to do with mating and fatherhood."

"I am not good for you." He withdrew. "You know I'm not cut out for mating. My work is dangerous. I care very much, but I'm not capable of the devotion you sought. I'd rather see you happy and settled."

"And allowing my parents to pawn me off on Sean Blackbourne made your life much easier, didn't it? In days, he and I were to exchange the words that allowed you to go, guilt free, back to your warring and whoring."

Something cold settled over his face. "Exactly."

"I shouldn't be here." She shook her head. "I shouldn't have come."

Safety had been her first concern. Raiden would know how to protect her from Mathias, but perhaps she'd underestimated Sean. His family was powerful. Maybe he would know how to protect her equally well.

"You did the right thing."

Clearly not. "I'm going to Sean. Now."

"The hell you are! In my home, you can't teleport in or out without my permission." It was a common safety measure. "As far as I'm concerned, you're remaining here. I'll keep you safe, even if it takes my last breath, and you know that. What do you know about Sean?"

That he was going to man up to the responsibility Raiden had rejected.

Anger boiled up in her, morphing to a new realm of fury. She marched to him and slapped his face. He recoiled from the blow, a tic working in his jaw, but said nothing.

"I gave you everything," she shouted. "Everything! I revealed myself to you in a way I've never done with another lover. I opened my heart and body to you. Yes, I knew your reputation, but when you came back to me again and again, I allowed myself to hope that you cared. And you knew that," she snarled. "You knew how badly I wanted you for a mate, how totally I gave myself over and over. I think I willed your seed to take root, praying that you'd . . ."

God, it seemed so stupid now. So foolish and naive. She'd bedded down with one of the most notoriously carnal wizards ever and gotten what she'd deserved. Still, the pain staggered her.

"You're right. I took advantage. I . . . the way you revealed yourself slowly to me, unfurling each time, shedding your ladylike inhibitions to embrace the sizzle between us, how could I refuse when you kept tempting me?" He shrugged. "Sorry. Next time, don't offer."

Chapter Four

As the sun rose, Raiden left her.

How like him.

After dressing and repairing her hair, Tabitha wandered from room to room in the big house until she encountered a cozy library—and found another intimidating wizard inside.

"Hello, Tabitha." A mirror image of Raiden rose, except his hair was dark as night.

This must be Raiden's twin.

"Ronan, correct?"

He nodded, approaching her slowly. "I'm sorry we've not met before."

They hadn't because Raiden had tried hard not to incorporate her into his life.

Then why hadn't he simply dropped her in Sean Blackbourne's lap and washed his hands of her, especially when she'd demanded he do exactly that?

When Ronan stuck his hand out, she approached cautiously. His eyes showed nothing but concern. His signature proclaimed him mated. She put her hand in his, and he smiled.

"Nice to meet you." And it was. She'd known that Raiden had a twin but not how identical they were. In fact, she knew very little about Raiden's life other than his sexual one.

"I'm sorry we're meeting under these terrible circumstances, rather than a more auspicious one, like the coming youngling."

"Where is Raiden?"

Ronan paused, clearly deciding what to tell her. "He had an errand and asked me to keep you company."

Doublespeak. Raiden had left, avoiding emotional intimacy, as usual. Or perhaps doing something he considered to be for her own good without first consulting her. Both possibilities rubbed her the wrong way. "Does every male in your family have difficulty with open and honest discourse?"

"Indeed. My mate has tried to teach me. . . ." His smile was self-effacing.

"You wouldn't want to disappoint her, then. Let's try this again. Where is Raiden?"

"He said that you were beautiful but neglected to mention that you're a cunning little thing."

She cut him a killing glare. "Don't flatter me. I'm a woman who lost her entire family barely twelve hours ago. I'm aware that as his encinta I have no claim on him, and he may very well be out with another woman. I understand your reluctance to admit that to me, but—"

"No. Raiden is looking for clues regarding the secret tree your father mentioned, as well as taking care of some of the burial details for your family. He didn't want to trouble you."

Tabitha froze, stunned. Her family? Did he think her weak or incapable? "They are my responsibility. I'll take care of them. Why hide that from me?"

"We both feel it's too much, given your condition and recent loss." He sent her a probing stare. "Raiden suspected you would disagree."

And had done whatever the hell he'd wanted anyway. Lovely. "I'm pregnant, not hysterical."

Ronan looked as if he swallowed a smile. "He will come to you for the decisions regarding clothing, location, time, and such. He merely wanted to spare you the preparation of the bodies."

A physically arduous, emotionally trying

task—one usually reserved for family. If Raiden was truly protecting her, she ought to be glad. Instead, she couldn't help but ask why. And why spare her the bathing, preserving, and painting of her family's bodies? Merely to keep her from becoming overwrought and harming the baby? It was the most likely explanation . . . yet could his caring mean more?

Such hopes had landed her alone and pregnant. She had to stop wishing for some ridiculous fairy-tale ending now.

"Hmm. Would you like to tell me why he's so secretive and closed?"

Ronan peered at her with amused disbelief. "I'd sooner wrestle in a pit of angry cobras without my wand."

"Brilliant. Should have known you'd take his side."

He shrugged. "Any good brother keeps his twin's secrets. Though if he's half as much like me as I believe him to be, there will come a point he won't be able to keep anything from you."

That didn't sound like Raiden at all. "What point would that be, when I'm threatening his life or manhood?"

Ronan choked back laughter, then shook

his head. "When he stops denying what's in his heart."

Raiden entered his house with a curse on his lips. Nothing. Not a single goddamn clue that would help him protect Tabby or figure out this secret tree, whatever it was. Now what the devil was he supposed to do?

He entered the library moments later. Ronan sat in the room's cozy armchair, studying Tabitha like an intriguing puzzle. Raiden would have been jealous if he hadn't known how crazy his twin was about Kari, his mate. And since Ronan was ridiculously happy with Kari and believed every wizard should be thus, Raiden knew that Ronan was plotting his downfall into an equally harmonious state.

Matters weren't that simple for him and Tabby. Never would be.

"Did you find anything useful? Or would you like me to take over the duties with my family?" she asked as he stepped farther into the room.

Raiden sent a glare his brother's way. "So much for secrecy."

"She has the right to be involved. It concerns her." Ronan's gentle chiding chafed him.

Raiden hated when his slightly older brother was right. "You may go now."

"Looking forward to it. It's somewhat painful to sit here and watch you make an ass of yourself."

"Bugger off," Raiden said with mock cheer.

Ronan saluted, then teleported away.

"So?" she prompted.

"Let me worry about this. You're dealing with grief and—"

"And trying to figure out this puzzle so that my father's sacrifice won't be for naught takes my mind off my pain. Please."

Raiden shook his head. She wasn't going to bloody leave this alone. And he couldn't just let her ache.

"I found nothing. Just an update to *The Peers and People of Magickind* that should be published soon, outlining changes to every family's births, deaths, matings . . . all of it public knowledge, really. Why keep track of it at all?"

She shrugged. "The older generation cares about such things, you know. Father loved his work passionately, enjoyed marking the passing of time by recording every magical family's momentous occasions."

"I can't imagine sitting down to read page after page of someone's family tree."

His last word echoed around the room, and they both froze. Raiden's thoughts started whirling.

"Tree?" she choked. "Father kept family trees for a living. Maybe . . ."

". . . we're not dealing with a real tree." He rushed across the room and grabbed her shoulders—and tried to ignore the sting of desire that threatened to overwhelm him every time he touched her. "Do you know of any family tree that's kept secret?"

"No. He took care to correspond with all families, no matter how Privileged or Deprived. Most people volunteered their family changes. Deaths, while sad, were always promptly reported. Matings, usually happy occasions, as well. He didn't always hear of a mate breaking right away, but often within a few months."

"Can you think of any circumstances in which that wasn't the case?"

"No." She paused. "Wait! Just one. That same trip when my father took me to that mysterious office in London I mentioned. The evening before, he took me to a hospital. It was quite late, and we met with a human couple. The woman had just given birth. She held her daughter once, cried, then gave the child to other humans. Her husband pleaded with my father to strike the child's name from his books. I remember asking him who the family was, why he would ever record a human birth, and why they wanted to keep the baby a secret. He never answered except to say that I was never to repeat the incident to anyone. He never spoke of the humans again. That's the only secret I can recall."

Raiden paced the airy room. "You went to the hospital *before* he took you to the office?" At her nod, he went on. "We must find that building. Perhaps he left something there."

"But what?" She shrugged. "Why would Mathias have a sudden interest in a human baby girl born over twenty-five years ago?"

"I don't know. But if there's a connection, I'm going to find it. And deal with it. Mathias isn't coming near you ever again."

Chapter Five

Raiden made a call to Bram in low, secretive tones that infuriated her. This was about her family and her future. Did he really think he was going to keep her in the dark?

When he rang off and turned to leave, she grabbed him by the shirt. "I'm going with you."

He shook his head. "Too dangerous."

"That's what you've decided?" she asked tartly.

Raiden sent her a wary glance. "I have."

"Too bad for you, then. You're not my mate." She shrugged. "You've no right to decide anything for me."

His icy blue eyes narrowed. "The child you carry is mine. I have every right to care about your well-being."

"Care, yes. Decide, no. Either I go with you or

I resume this search alone. If Bram Rion knew that easily how to find the office my father most likely visited, then someone else will as well. Unlike you, I'm more likely to have privileges to enter, given that I'm his next of kin. What reason will you use to access his paperwork?"

Raiden clenched his jaw. "Bram is a member of the Council. I'm sure he can pull a few strings for me."

He was right, Tabitha realized. In fact, they both were. Between his connections and her familial relation, they should have no trouble viewing whatever her father might have kept in the building.

"Should we be wasting time arguing about this, or should we be working together? What could happen, really? It's a Council building in the middle of the day. Others should be there. We're doing nothing wrong."

Raiden hesitated, looking like he was about to refuse.

"Hello?" Nathanial Wolvesey called.

Tabitha shivered. Raiden's father had looked at her all too sexually, given that she carried his son's child.

Raiden watched her with an unblinking gaze.

"What's the matter? Did my father say something to you that made you uncomfortable?"

A ginger brow rose. "Merely that he understood why you desired me so much. Then he assured me the two of you had passed a woman or two between you over the decades."

He winced. "Bloody hell."

Tabitha didn't ask if Nathanial had been lying. The truth was all over Raiden's face, and pain bulldozed her. He *had* treated women like interchangeable playthings. Convenient energy sources. Likely still did.

"He said that you wouldn't mind if I allowed him to—"

"I mind. A great deal." He clenched his teeth but met her gaze without flinching. "I'm sorry."

Sorry for the behavior or sorry his father had revealed the truth to her? She shoved the thought away. "I politely refused, in case you're wondering. But I won't be alone with him again."

"Hello?" Nathanial's footsteps across the gleaming hardwood floors came closer.

Raiden didn't hesitate. He grabbed her hand. "Let's go."

As always with teleporting, a loud sucking noise filled her ears. Then eerie silence. Suddenly, she lost her balance, and a sense of tumbling through air overwhelmed her. The weightlessness, the not knowing which way was up and which was down, made her slightly ill.

A moment later, they stood outside a neo-modern office building. Built in the 1960s and topping off at about five stories, the concrete structure had been carved with magical runes between each tier of white-draped windows. There wasn't a soul in sight.

"It looks abandoned." Eerily so, in fact.

He frowned, grabbing her hand tighter. "Indeed. Bram speculated that the Council ministries no longer use this building. Apparently, it's been the source of human speculation, particularly the meaning of the runes."

"I recognize some of the symbols. Magic, mastery, truth, Fate. Death."

Raiden shrugged, his wide shoulders looking almost menacing in a dark trench. "We don't have time to decipher it now. I have an uneasy feeling. Let's move quickly. I don't want you out in the open where you're vulnerable to Mathias or any eyes he might have watching."

"He likely has no idea where I am."

He hustled her under the building's portico,

deep in shadow, and pinned her with a glare. "Do you really think it would take Mathias very long to figure out that your father had a daughter he hadn't managed to kill in the attack? And that the daughter carried my child? Once he pieces all the information together, he's going to be but a breath behind us."

Dear God, she'd never thought of that before, but her father would have recorded her own birth. There would be no mating listed in *The Peers and People of Magickind* because she'd never mated. The fact that she carried Raiden's child wouldn't be listed until the youngling's birth, but even so, a wizard with Mathias's cunning and resources could find that information. After all, he hadn't managed to outwit most of the Council and stay a step ahead of the Doomsday Brethren by being a half-wit.

"Fuck." Raiden ran a hand through his long, pale hair. "And once he starts pursuing us, I know where he'll look first. We can't go back to your house. Or mine."

"You're right."

"I'll tell Ronan to warn my father away until this is settled. He won't be happy, but if we can find what we're looking for now, then I can set all back to rights soon."

"Meaning your father can go home, and you can wash your hands of me by dumping me on Sean Blackbourne's doorstep?"

His face tightened, darkened. Raiden's temper wasn't a small thing, and she wondered if she'd crossed some line.

He cursed and turned away. "That would be for the best."

"For whom?" she challenged, furious to the bone with his oblique answers. "It would certainly be easiest for you. Then you could rid yourself of me, guilt-free and—"

Raiden grabbed her and pulled her close. "Listen to me. I have tried every way I know to spare you more heartache. I was a bastard to you, yes. I seduced you with every intention of walking out the door. I don't mate. I am my father's son."

"I refuse to believe that." Tabitha shook her head.

"I'm trying to do the right thing now. Instead of seducing you again, I'm warning you away. Which do you think I'd rather do?" He raised a golden brow, his hot gaze wandering down her body.

She flushed hot and tingly. "You held me with such tenderness. The way you made me feel so secure and whispered to me when we were together was—"

"Designed to separate a pretty female from her knickers." He forced himself to be brutally honest. "It's a skill I've spent decades perfecting. Your parents knew this when they threatened me out of your life."

She blinked, her hazel green eyes wide and astounded. "Threatened you?"

"To step aside or have the Council elder, your mate-to-be's uncle, censure and incarcerate me until you were happily mated."

That would have left the Doomsday Brethren fighting with one less warrior. Had Raiden allowed that to happen, he might as well have signed his own twin's death warrant—along with those of the other Doomsday Brethren. They'd already been woefully outmanned. He hadn't wanted to leave Tabby, though he hadn't believed for one moment that he would have made a genteel witch like her happy. His desires ran deep, dark. He'd barely begun to unleash his wants on her. Eventually, he would have shocked her, and she would have realized what her parents already knew: he wasn't good enough for her.

"You didn't fight for me at all." She didn't ask

because she knew the answer, but the hurt in her voice made Raiden bleed inside.

"No." In good conscience, how could he?

Tabby stepped back, a protective hand over the gentle swell of her belly. Shielding their baby from him. Pain at that realization gouged his chest and nearly took him to his knees. Raiden forced himself to swallow and send her a stare of cold challenge.

"Why are you helping me now? Because of the baby?" she asked.

God, she looked ready to break into a thousand pieces, and Raiden couldn't stand to heap more pain on her. His gaze softened. "I'm not cruel. You and the baby matter. It would devastate me to see Mathias hurt you. And if you remain near me, he'd certainly try. Besides, I'm simply not built for commitment. The sooner you accept that, the happier you'll be."

She stared at him as if he were a stranger, her eyes wary and tear-filled. "Then you're right. We should find whatever is in this building quickly so we can part ways."

Without another word, she tried the door. It didn't budge.

"Drat!"

Bram had given him the heads-up on accessing these buildings, once used by Council officials and their ministers. Raiden closed his eyes and chanted the spell Bram had provided, then coupled it with his own ability to sense other beings near.

Seconds later, the latch in Tabby's hand clicked. She blinked and pushed the door open. "How did you do that?"

He shook his head, sensing they weren't the only people here and praying Mathias wasn't already hot on their tails.

"Quiet. We're not alone," he whispered. "Let's go."

Raiden led them away from the nearby encroachers, tiptoeing up the stairs with Tabby's hand in his. Once they'd started up the stairs, she squeezed his hand. He turned to her.

"This is familiar," she whispered with an unblinking stare. "I remember being here."

He took her shoulders in his grasp. "Do you remember exactly how to reach your father's office?"

She frowned, as if trying to sort through her memories. "I'll try. I know we walked up several flights of stairs, through a big brown door.

There was a reception area with lots of colorful tiles . . ."

For all he knew, every floor looked that way, but he smiled encouragingly. "We'll keep going and see if anything looks right to you."

They ascended another flight of stairs. When they peered out the door from the stairwell to the offices, she shook her head. They repeated the process with the same results. On the fourth floor, she nodded emphatically.

"My father's office was on the other side of the fountain, near the tiles shaped like the rune for Truth, a giant Y-looking symbol."

She raced across the floor before he could stop her. Thankfully, the building's other occupants, whoever they were, hadn't come this way—yet. Raiden prayed it remained thus. He needed to keep Tabitha safe, help her protect the tree her father had been willing to die for, then get her out of his life. Because God help him, with every moment he stayed near her, Raiden wanted nothing more than to grab her, kiss her, remember every perfect, lush curve, retrace them with his hands, his mouth. Keep her close always.

She tiptoed across the tiled floor quietly, then reached for the door. Raiden closed the space between them with a blink and clapped his hand over hers, staying her.

"Let me," he demanded. He sensed no one inside . . . but he couldn't be too careful where Tabby was concerned.

She stepped aside. "Be careful. Please."

And just like that, she undid his good intentions of keeping his distance. Even when he was a bastard to her, she goddamn cared. How was a man who'd never known genuine feelings supposed to do without them once he'd found them? It would be like living without sunlight.

Was he doing the right thing in letting her go?

For a moment, Raiden closed his eyes and sorted through the cacophony in his head, which was clashing with all the clatter in his heart. But at the end of the day, he still didn't know if he was capable of caring for one woman for the rest of his life. Was it fair to risk her to try and learn to love? No. He'd be putting his own desire for her above her safety. Mathias or the Anarki could kill him tomorrow and leave her mateless and mourning. Or she could become a target in her own right.

He would have to accept that as much as he desired Tabby above all others, he would be doing her a disservice to let her believe they had a future.

"Is something wrong?" she asked. "Is someone inside?"

Her questions brought him out of his reverie. "No."

Raiden shoved the door open to reveal a fairly standard, if outdated, office. A clunky desk with a fake wood-grain top and chrome legs. A phone. Empty file folders. A picture frame. A plant, curiously alive.

"Does this look familiar?" he asked her.

But when he turned, she was rushing into the room and lifting the picture frame. Tears filled her eyes, ran down her cheeks. "Daddy and Mum. Winston and James. I can't believe they're truly gone."

Looking so lost and alone, Tabby met his gaze across the room. Raiden couldn't stand it; he closed the distance between them and grabbed her up in his arms.

Chapter Six

*T*abitha felt Raiden's strong arms encircle her protectively. Like a life preserver in a sea of drowning grief, he alone kept her afloat.

She shoved aside the ugly thought that he'd soon leave her.

Wiping her tears away with impatient hands, she pushed out of his embrace. "Sorry. I know we don't have time for this now. We should look in the desk—"

Raiden didn't let her move more than a meter away. "You've suffered an incredible loss, Tabby."

"Tabi*tha*," she reminded him through gritted teeth.

He stifled a curse. "And you've been so strong since the attack. If you need to lean on me, do."

And what, he would be here for her? She studied him, trying to discern the answer. But she couldn't. His face appeared like granite, ungiving. Yet his blue eyes radiated warmth, life. The picture of compassion. Would he be here for her today? If today, why not tomorrow?

Because he pitied her, not loved her. God, what a bitter pill to swallow.

"I'll be fine."

But she lied. Her hands shook as she set the picture down on the desk. She didn't quite manage to balance it, and the metal frame clattered onto the desktop. Sadness and frustration crashed down on her as the loss struck her all over again. Angry tears flooded her eyes, poured onto her cheeks.

Raiden cursed, grabbing her by the shoulders. "That's it. I admit that I've been a bastard, and I'm probably the last person in the world you want comforting you. But I'll be damned if I'm going to watch you bleed inside and do nothing. Don't shut me out if you need to cry."

She did need it. Tabitha hated to admit it, but shoving all her shock and grief down for the past day had finally caught up with her. But if she burdened him more, he'd only leave faster. He wanted nothing to do with emotion or commitment, and taking advantage of his momentary compassion would only hurt more when he left.

She looked down, tried to hide her crumbling expression from him. Raiden was having none of that.

As the first sob wracked her, he lifted her chin and stared into her tear-filled eyes. Tabitha averted her gaze, but she knew he saw right through her.

Raiden knew her so damn well. Knew her . . . and simply didn't love her the way she loved him.

With a curse, Raiden crushed her against his chest. The steady beat of his heart under her ear was both a joy and a sorrow. Needing Raiden too much to push him away, Tabitha clung to him, throwing her arms around his neck and burrowing closer.

"Raiden . . ."

A moment later, he brushed the tears from her face and cupped her cheeks, his blue gaze penetrating hers, open and full of a thousand emotions.

Tabitha caught her breath. She'd seen Raiden with many expressions, but in nearly every one, the windows to his soul had been closed to her. Hot, challenging, alluring, yes. But never revealing, stark. Haunted. Like now.

He lowered his head, slowly, so that she could stop him at any time. But stopping him was the last thing she wanted. Her heart thumped so hard that it threatened to beat out of her chest.

Raiden did this every time he touched her. She couldn't absorb the rush of feelings and sensations quickly enough. He always took her to a new place, and she knew, even without a wizard's mating instinct, that he was the mate of her heart.

Too bad that he lacked the instinct—or love—to believe she was his mate as well.

The first brush of his lips over hers pushed those thoughts aside. He lingered, breathed, urged her to open. Then he waited until she was breathless, on her tiptoes, silently begging as she grabbed his shoulders and pressed closer. Suddenly, he was deep inside her mouth, stealing her sanity, reclaiming her soul. That familiar taste of his haunted her, so male. So Raiden. So irresistible.

With a moan, she opened more to his kiss, and he sampled gently . . . yet took in that subtly commanding way of his.

Unable to remember why she shouldn't, Tabitha ran her fingers over the hard breadth of his shoulders, caressed her way across his chest.

Raiden gripped her hips and pressed closer, demanding. He was so solid—in every way. He was her something to hang on to. Her safe harbor in a raging sea.

"I'm here, Tabby," he murmured against her lips. "I'll help you. I'll keep you safe."

Before she could object, his lips lowered to her neck. She gasped at the electric sensation of his breath feathering over her sensitive skin, his lips claiming the flesh he'd claimed so many times before . . . but with a new urgency she'd never sensed. A new possessiveness. She rolled her head to the side, allowing him all the access to her that he craved.

One hand left her hip to caress its way up her waist, her rib cage, the sensitive side of her breast. When she gasped into his ear, he murmured, "That's it, Tabby. Don't do anything but feel me. Let me take your pain and give you pleasure."

Impossible. She'd be leaning on him too much. He wouldn't be here later when she needed him and realized that she'd never learned to cope with her grief on her own. But his thumb trailed over her puckered nipple. Her entire body pinged with tingles and need at that one touch, and she arched his way.

Suddenly, he was nuzzling that nipple right through her shirt . . . even as his hands rose to her buttons and began to undo them, one slow unfastening after another, measured with a seductive cadence. Mere seconds later, they were all open and the only thing between him and her breasts was a flimsy lace bra.

"Raiden . . . ," she breathed. "We shouldn't."

"There's no one on this side of the building. You need someone to hold you as much as I want to."

He didn't say another word, just pressed reverent kisses to the swells of her breasts, his lips hovering just above the scalloped lace. Fighting him was no use. The feel of his mouth on her, his hot breaths warming her skin . . . it was too much. She fisted her hands into the hair at his nape and let her head fall back, opening herself to him totally.

Raiden moaned his appreciation and pushed the cup of her bra aside, exposing one mound. His thumb scraped across the sensitive surface, bringing it back to screaming life, just before his mouth followed suit.

The sensations bombarding her were instantaneous. They sucked her under, into a world of pleasure. Tingles abounded. Her skin felt tight. She was itchy inside, restless, dying to get closer to Raiden.

After removing his trench, she attacked his sweater, pulling it over his head, baring the broad, ridged chest. The bronzed skin, brown male nipples, light dusting of pale hair, corrugated abdominals . . . he was pure male animal power, and Tabitha basked in the fact that she'd have him once again. All hers.

At least for now.

As his teeth scraped against her nipple, his free hand pushed her other bra cup aside. He took that nipple in his mouth as well and pinched the first with devilish fingers. The pleasure zinged from the sensitive points straight down, right between her legs, where she was wet and welcoming and so achy that she couldn't wait much longer.

Raiden did this to her. Every time. Yes, every witch or wizard relied on sex for the majority of their energy needs, so Tabitha hadn't made it through her thirty-six years without physical recharging. But she'd never basked in the sensations, never lingered over a lover, as she had with Raiden.

Today was no exception.

He ripped into the rest of her clothes and shoved them down her hips, falling to his knees so he could still worship her breasts whilst stripping her bare. And she let him, gladly.

Once he'd peeled away her skirts and knickers, he remained crouched, staring at the most secret part of her. He reached a finger through her slick flesh. She gasped.

"Always so wet and ready, Tabby. For me? Just for me?"

She didn't know how to answer that question. Yes, just for him. No lover had affected her so much. But to admit that . . . He already knew how much she loved him, and still he wasn't prepared to stay with her, raise their youngling together.

"Touch me," she said instead. "I want to feel you deep inside me."

"You will," he murmured, coming closer, closer . . .

A moment later, he lifted her leg with one powerful hand, opening her to him. He licked his lips, and Tabitha's heart stopped. As intimate as they'd ever been, Raiden had never indulged in the intimacy of tasting her. He'd kissed her, yes. But this sort of behavior was common among wizards sampling their mates . . . or so she'd heard.

Why was he doing this with her now?

Then his mouth latched onto her, and the answer didn't matter. Gently, he raked his tongue through her slit, sucked the sensitive bead above into his mouth. Gentle fingers caressed her hip with hypnotic rhythm.

It didn't take long for Tabitha's entire body to light up. Inside, she tightened, yet expanded. Burning as she hurtled toward climax. And Raiden's unrelenting mouth seemed hungry, insistent. Thought-robbing. The lash of his tongue against her clit generated the sort of pleasure that robbed her of sanity. Tabitha couldn't rub two thoughts together, couldn't find the will to do anything but plant her hands in his hair and try to absorb all the wanton sensations clawing through her.

As her body coiled up and the ache behind her little bud turned to fire, she burst out like a supernova, screaming through the most intense peak in memory. And Raiden's powerful hands held her in place as he murmured against her sensitive flesh and lapped at her in reward.

"Raiden . . ." She couldn't catch a breath, couldn't believe the stark inferno of pleasure his touch incited.

Suddenly, he raised his lips, pressing a series

of soft kisses against her abdomen, which was just beginning to show the bump of the growing baby inside. He smiled against her skin, his palm swiping a caress across her belly. And her heart melted. Yes, he could give her pleasure unlike any other, but he could also touch her heart. This big, proud warrior cared for her and their baby somewhere in that thick skull. He was capable of love and devotion. He had to be. Surely, he couldn't touch her like this and not be.

With that thought bouncing through her head, she let him back her onto the desk. Tabitha hissed at the feel of cold faux-wood, but didn't finish the sound before she felt the thick stalk of his flesh pressing at her swollen folds, tucking just inside her body. That hiss became a moan as he began to press in . . . in . . . in, until he was so deep that she felt deliciously stretched and filled with him. Completed.

"Oh, God," he moaned in her ear. "I've missed the feel of you."

She had missed him as well.

Raiden gripped her hips in his large hands and took control of their lovemaking. Swift, sure strokes deep into her heat . . . right into her heart. He filled her everywhere, rubbing against flesh still swooning from her last orgasm, he built another tsunami of ecstasy so quickly that Tabitha literally felt her head spin.

His fingers tightened on her. He began to pant. His pace picked up. Sweat popped out on his forehead, down his temples, across his back.

"What the hell do you do to me?" He breathed the words into her face, his eyes lost and angry, yet so focused on her.

His question was all it took. The earth shifted beneath her. Her body clamped down on him, convulsed, then careened into pleasure so strong that she cried out, clutching his shoulders for dear life.

"Look at me," he demanded.

No. If she looked at him, she'd be totally lost. Already, her heart was his. And even after this absolute exchange of pleasure, he'd leave her soon. And even if she mated with Sean Blackbourne, a part of her she'd never get back would be his forever. She shook her head.

"Tabby, now! Please . . ."

He moaned, all but begging, his hips pistoning in and out of her with rapid force and devastating pleasure, keeping the climax ravaging her endlessly. Though she wasn't looking at him, his gaze burned her. His plea resonated in her head. Her heart beat for him.

Tabitha opened her eyes. His blue stare looked desperate, wild, hungry . . . yet so focused on her as he hardened inside her and let go.

He groaned long and loud as he released inside her, his head falling back as he pressed their bodies ever closer and held her tight, as if he'd never let go.

"Tabby . . ."

The word was like melted caramel pouring all over her, and she sighed. He sounded torn. And what could she say? Raiden knew how she felt.

Suddenly, he stiffened and his eyes flared wide. "Bloody fucking hell!"

In a split second, he withdrew, fastened his jeans, and thrust on his sweater.

She guessed that meant he regretted showing emotion to her or whatever his latest hang-up was.

"Get dressed," he hissed, shoving her bra back into place.

"Look, if you're wishing now that you hadn't touched me or been real or—"

"That isn't it." He scowled as he handed Tabitha her shirt. "Hurry! Someone's coming."

Chapter Seven

*T*abitha struggled into her shirt as Raiden pushed her toward the door, wondering if they'd make it out alive. He understood the reasons the Council had made teleporting in and out of government facilities impossible, even nearly deserted ones like this. Security against the nosy and unexpected was important—but damned inconvenient.

Raiden cursed. This was his fault. If he hadn't been so dazzled by Tabby, and so drawn to the idea of savoring her sweetness, he would have sensed the intruder's approach much sooner.

Now, it might be too late. *Bloody stupid!*

With efficient fingers, Tabby tied her shirt around her still trim waist, only bothering with the button over her breasts. "Can you hold off whoever is coming?"

Raiden was about to ask what the hell she thought she would be doing in the meantime, but she dashed around the desk and yanked a drawer open, rifling through the contents inside.

"We don't have time for this." He grabbed her wrist to pull her to the door.

She wriggled from his grasp and continued on her quest. "If someone is coming, they know we're here. We won't get a chance to search this office again, and I can't let my family have died in vain. My father wanted this family tree protected. If I have to die for it . . ." She shrugged. "Let's not argue. Just go!"

"You're pregnant. If you die, the baby—"

"Dies with me, I know! Do whatever you can to make certain that doesn't happen." She slammed the first drawer shut and dove into the second, rifling through one file folder after another.

"Three minutes," he growled. "If I send up a red spark before then, it means get the hell out now."

She nodded, and he looked at her one last time, fear for her thrumming through his bloodstream.

Stubborn woman. He understood her need to fulfill her father's last wish. After today, this opportunity would be gone. But damn it, allowing her to put herself and the baby in danger . . . Raiden almost couldn't do it. For her, he tried.

Leaving the office, he crept into the once-bright reception area, staying in the shadows falling across the dusty walls. There were two entrances onto this floor. The one in front of him still showed a door firmly closed. The one around the corner he couldn't see.

It was a risk, but Raiden closed his eyes and filtered through all the sounds and scents in the building, searching for the ones that signified a living, breathing creature. Or more than one.

There in the stairwell. Footsteps.

A creaking door a moment later confirmed his worst fears. Whoever stalked them had just entered the floor and closed the door behind him soundlessly.

Too late to call for backup now. He had to hope that their surprise visitor couldn't sense him waiting and counter his surprise attack. Otherwise, he and Tabby were dead.

As the intruder came closer, Raiden sensed more. Male based on the scent. Sweat hung in the air. Excited but not nervous. Raiden would bet his very wand that the encroacher thought he had them cornered.

And he was probably right.

Twenty meters, fifteen, ten . . . Raiden held in a breath, his wand at the ready. He'd get one clean swipe at this bastard before the fight would be on.

Finally, a tall figure eased around the corner, light on his feet, almost elegant. Poised for battle.

Raiden zipped out a spell designed to stun a wizard unconscious.

At the last second, the intruder stepped aside with a laugh. "Really, is that the best you can do?"

Mathias.

Oh, shit.

The magical sociopath whipped his wand and an arc of green light jetted out the wall of windows behind him, bursting across the sky with an eerie glow before fading.

He was calling in the reinforcements.

Fuck. Raiden knew that he and Tabby had moments to get out of here, but he couldn't run into Lowery's office to get her. Besides alerting Mathias to Tabby's presence, he'd trap them inside with no escape route except out the window and a four-story free fall.

Suddenly, a jagged bolt of white light arced across the space between them. Raiden hit the ground, barely dodging it. He felt the lethal heat of the spell skate over his head, singe the little hairs on his arms. Mathias cursed.

Raiden charged to his feet, scurrying across the floor. He had to get smart and use the deep shadows in the room to any advantage possible.

Making his way to the far wall, he hid behind a big potted plant and hurled a fire spell at Mathias, the orange ball crackling and screaming through the air.

It hit him, setting the bastard's sleeve on fire. He shot an evil glare in Raiden's direction and lifted his other hand above his forearm, fingers dangling down.

Raiden didn't waste time watching. He crawled across the floor, rolling toward Tabby's father's office door. Shoving his wand under the crack, he sent up a quick red spark and hoped like hell she didn't just come tumbling out into Mathias's path.

When Raiden looked up again, water trickled from Mathias's fingers like a faucet, extinguishing the fire. What Raiden had hoped would be a game-changer had really been nothing more than a moment's annoyance for someone with Mathias's heavy-duty power.

Bloody hell, he'd had no occasion to fight the villainous wizard one-on-one. He'd trained for it. The Doomsday Brethren had discussed it. He'd heard war stories. But face-to-face alone with one of the most cunning wizards in magickind's history? His worst nightmare. The fact that Tabitha was caught in this deadly struggle only made everything more horrifying.

"Come out, come out, wherever you are," Mathias singsonged with a laugh. "I'll make certain your death won't hurt. Much, anyway."

Raiden rolled beneath a low bench just beside Lowery's office door. Tabitha's footsteps approached slowly. He could sense her fear and caution. Raiden was the only thing standing between Mathias and Tabby, and he'd have to do whatever was necessary to distract Mathias so she could escape.

Rolling out from under the bench, Raiden leapt to his feet and charged with a roar. Mathias whirled, wand poised, as Raiden jumped onto the round table in the middle of the reception space.

From above, he could see everything. Mathias had no place to hide. But Raiden also knew it made him a huge target.

With a grunt, he kicked the flower arrangement on the table toward Mathias's head. The wizard ducked to avoid it, then flicked his wand. Raiden didn't want to know what spell that evil blue streak held as it headed his way. Instead, he jumped over the bolt, then whipped his wand at the bench that had once been his hiding place. It hurtled across the room toward Mathias, who ran, taking cover behind the reception desk. The bench crashed against the desk with a clatter.

In that same moment, Tabby opened the door to her father's office and peeked out. With one hand, Raiden gestured her to the stairwell. With another, he sent a fireball at the reception desk. It burst into flame and exploded.

Mathias dove away from the fire and glared as he whipped up a wall of water, dousing the flames. Raiden could feel his anger seethe.

"This game grows tiresome, neophyte."

Raiden felt every one of Mathias's centuries of warfare and his own decided lack of experience. He'd only attained his magic in the last sixty years, and he'd spent most of those being a lover, not a fighter. Today it showed, and he cursed every night he'd spent carousing instead of learning how to defend himself and the ones he cherished.

On the far side of the area, he sensed Tabitha approaching the other stairwell. They were well lit, and the second she opened the door, the light would spill into the darkened reception area—unless he masked it.

Clenching his teeth and focusing his energy, Raiden whipped his wand and thrust his arms wide. Blinding light filled the entire space. He screamed with all his frustration and fear, praying the sound would cover Tabitha's exit. If he died protecting her, the sacrifice would be well worth it. He just had to get her out alive.

Mathias rushed across the room, shielding his eyes with a nasty curse. Raiden knew he wasn't going to beat the wizard magically, but thanks to Marrok, the Doomsday Brethren's only human warrior, he was a well-trained machine in conventional fighting methods.

With a shout, he leapt off the table, onto Mathias. The evil wizard tried to scramble away, but Raiden tackled him, pinning him to the floor with his larger body. Mathias's wand clattered out of his hand. With grim satisfaction, Raiden reached for the knife in his boot with every intention of slitting Mathias's throat. The other wizard roared and managed to brace one foot against the floor, pushing off and rolling them over. Suddenly, Raiden struggled beneath Mathias, who smiled down with malice.

"Enjoy your death. Send me a postcard from hell." He conjured a knife and held it over Raiden's throat.

A moment later, Raiden felt the sensation of sharp, cold steel pressing at his neck. Blood broke out across Raiden's throat and ran down into his ears. He was going to die. He could deal with that—as long as Tabitha had escaped.

Mathias lifted his hand and the press of the blade abated, but then he clenched his fist, blade gleaming, and stared with wicked glee. Then his hand plunged down.

Before the blade struck deep, Mathias went limp.

Raiden scrambled out from under him and looked around. Tabitha stood by the stairwell, wand outstretched, shaking. "I don't know much self-defense, but Father taught me to immobilize people once."

Heart beating wildly in his chest, he ran across the room to capture her in his arms. "You should have gone."

Her head twitched back and forth. "He would have killed you."

"The point was for you to escape." And arguing this here and now was dangerous.

Raiden looked back at Mathias, then hurled a blood red spell at him, designed to evaporate all his blood and kill him. The other wizard merely jolted and began to rouse.

Damn it! According to legend, Mathias had already died once. Could he ever be killed again?

Raiden couldn't wait around to find out. Despite exchanging energy with Tabby minutes ago, those spells had exhausted him. He must rest—or recharge—and soon.

He grabbed her hand. "Let's go."

Tugging her into the stairwell, Raiden kept her as close as possible. His mind raced. After the way he'd abandoned her, she had come back to save him. She had risked herself with the most dangerous wizard in magickind's history, and if not for her, Ronan would have been mourning his twin. Raiden didn't have to ask why; he knew she loved him. And it humbled him like nothing else. She was an amazing woman.

"Do you face danger all the time?" she panted as they flew down the stairs, racing for the entrance.

"Yes."

"You . . . you've met him in battle before?"

"Not alone. The Doomsday Brethren fight his army together."

Her hand tightened on his. "But there are only seven of you."

"Yes."

He saw the glass doors in front of them at the same time he sensed other beings making their way into the building's main lobby, closer. Shoving Tabby behind him, he summoned the last of his energy and flung a fireball at the nearest one, felling him instantly. Another ran for them, sending streams of something that looked like red water headed their way. Tabitha gasped, and he tried to think of a defensive spell, but his overtaxed body was diverting energy from his brain.

The next thing he knew, Tabby reached him and flicked her wand. "Damn it, I put you behind me."

She just pushed him forward, then grabbed his shirt to hold him behind the thick clear protective wall she'd erected.

"It won't block much or hold for long. Maybe two minutes." Her voice shook with exhaustion.

He needed to get her out of there now.

The rage and frustration he felt at Tabby and

the baby's being in danger he funneled into a wall of wind he hurled toward the remaining dozen Anarki. It swept the lobby furniture, then began whipping bodies into its frenzy, at least for the precious seconds he and Tabby needed to escape.

They rushed outside, into the winter dusk. Raiden clamped an arm around her and thought of Ice's caves in Wales. After a few disorienting moments, they hovered outside the dwelling on the windswept rocks, looking into the sea.

Tabby staggered, and he held her steady in his grip, panting with exhaustion.

"It's safe here," he murmured. "Let's get inside."

She nodded and followed him through the arched entrance. "That was the most frightening thing I've ever done in my life."

Raiden couldn't disagree.

"How will you and the other wizards ever be able to fight him off?"

The million-dollar question. He sighed. "Honestly, I don't think we can. But Ronan is devoted to this cause. I'm with him, and now devoted to whatever it takes to keep you safe. But it's another reason you're better off without me. I don't know how to be the mate you want, and I won't be alive long enough to figure it out."

That reality ate at his insides. The last thing he wanted to do was give her to Sean Blackbourne, but it was for the best, especially now that he'd failed her at Lowery's office.

"Raiden—"

"No. It's true. And I'm doubly sorry that you risked your life to go to your father's office, only to come away empty-handed."

"But I didn't." She peeled her hand away from her chest and revealed the family photo that had been on her father's desk.

His spirits sank. He'd been hoping for something useful, rather than sentimental. "I'm glad you've come away with something meaningful."

She shook her head, all that gorgeous red hair that had tumbled from her proper clips tousling on her shoulders, reminding him yet again of one of the million reasons he always wanted her.

Tabby grabbed his arm. "I know what Mathias wants. I found the tree."

Chapter Eight

From the back of the picture frame, Tabitha extracted a long piece of paper. Raiden sidled closer as she unfolded it. Names, dates, multiple branches on one long tree stretching back thousands of years. Throughout, a handful of names had been highlighted.

"What does it mean?" He had no damn clue.

"I don't know." She shrugged.

Raiden looked it over again, but he might as well have been reading gibberish. However, the bottom of the page had been altered. On the last entry in the family tree, the child's date of birth remained, but the name, once highlighted, had been deleted.

"I think I know someone who might be able to help us," Raiden mused. "Come with me."

"Someone trustworthy?"

"There's no one I'd trust more."

He took Tabby's hand and prowled the caves until he found Bram's sister, Sabelle, who sat in the kitchen, drinking tea. After introductions, the beautiful witch looked between him and Tabitha and smiled.

"Did you finally pull your head out of your arse? I'm hoping so, and that the fact you haven't mated with her is merely temporary. Ronan says you love her."

Raiden resisted the urge to throttle Sabelle. "Stifle the matchmaking. We were chased minutes ago by Mathias and some of his goons while retrieving this. What is it?"

He thrust the paper under her nose and Sabelle took it, studying it intently, her blue eyes growing wider and wider. Then she peered up at him, looking suddenly pale. "Where did you get this?"

Tabitha grabbed the scroll back, defending their find. "It was my father's, Nigel Lowery."

"The record keeper?"

"Yes. Mathias killed my family for this, I think. My father's last words were to protect the secret tree and—"

"This is, indeed, a great secret." Sabelle hesitated, as if she was searching for the right words to impart bad news. "It's the family tree of the Untouchables."

Raiden felt his stomach drop to his knees.

Beside him, Tabby gasped. "Oh, dear God."

A sacred race, the Untouchables had blended in with humans long ago. In fact, most *were* ordinary humans. But every thousand years, some recessive trait rose to the fore and the lineage produced a child far more than human—but one completely unaffected by magic. According to this document, one had been born in London a mere twenty-five years ago. Tabby's father had erased that child's name.

"The hospital we visited when I was just a girl!" Tabby covered her gaping mouth.

Raiden nodded. "The Untouchable's sire persuaded your father to keep her name secret."

"Yes, and they gave the baby, a little girl, up for adoption that very night."

"To protect her, I imagine." Sabelle's face softened with compassion.

Any business involving Untouchables was always dangerous. They were often killed not only for their seeming immunity to magic but also for their ability to suppress magic near them. Likely,

Matthias saw her as a threat. Whoever this girl was, she was in terrible danger if Mathias learned her name.

"Look here." Raiden pointed to the mother's name on the parchment. "The Untouchable's mother died shortly after giving birth."

"I wonder if it was for refusing to divulge her daughter's name." Tabby looked discomfited by that possibility. "And her father passed just a few weeks ago."

And he'd been far too young to die of natural causes. Raiden's gut clenched with worry. Clearly, Mathias hadn't yet learned the woman's identity if he still sought this page. And all of the deaths in the evil wizard's wake showed that he'd have no problem killing Tabitha to get what he wanted.

"Do you think Mathias plans to kill the Untouchable?" Raiden asked.

"If he learns the woman's identity, likely so." Sabelle frowned suddenly. "Except . . . why find her now? If she could derail his plans, why didn't Mathias hunt for her immediately after he'd risen from exile? What's changed?"

A terrible possibility hit Raiden. "Or perhaps the Untouchable is to be a weapon used against the Doomsday Brethren, meant to disable our magic long enough for Mathias to wage some terrible attack on magickind and gain control."

"A very real possibility." Sabelle shook her head. "Let me think on it. And I'll take it up with Bram when he returns. But regardless, in case Mathias could somehow use this record, it must be protected."

"Agreed. Where is Bram?"

She shrugged. "He left with Duke, Ice, and Marrok about an hour ago. Said something about solving a mystery. Hopefully, we'll hear from him soon."

Raiden rubbed a hand across his throbbing forehead. "When he returns, have him find me."

Sabelle agreed. Raiden thanked her and took Tabby's hand again, leading her through the shadowed, narrow caves to his own.

By all rights, he should send a message to Shock right now advising him that the Untouchable family tree was now in the Doomsday Brethren's possession. That missive should reach Mathias quickly and lift the threat from Tabby. Then, Raiden knew, he should deliver her to Sean Blackbourne, the man who would be responsible for her safety and happiness for the rest of her life. Then she would be safe. Mathias should have no cause to hunt her.

But he couldn't—not yet. First, he must talk to Bram, ensure this was, in fact, the secret family tree. In all likelihood, yes, but . . . better safe than sorry. And really, that was an excuse. Truth was, he yearned to keep Tabitha for another night. A whole night. Not merely long enough to make love to her. Not simply to comfort her after a staggering loss or to shield her from more danger. But because he needed her with him, from sunset to sunrise, in his arms, in his bed. *His*.

Swallowing, Raiden finally reached the door of the cave in which he'd been staying. He ushered her inside. "I know you're used to better. Your father provided for your family admirably, and this cave is temporary—"

"A bed! I'm exhausted." And she sounded thus. "Do you have a shower as well?"

He pointed the way, and Tabby closed the door between them. He spent the next twenty minutes listening to the sound of water sluicing over her naked skin and fighting the urge to break down the door and ravish her.

Just as his patience gave out, she emerged in a cloud of steam. And he caught his breath.

She wore his black terrycloth robe. The sleeves fell past her hands, and the hem dragged on the ground, but something about seeing all that fiery hair of hers streaming over his robe made him hard as hell. He needed her madly. Now.

"Raiden?" She looked at him with wary eyes.

He should let her sleep alone and in peace. It was the honorable thing to do, since she didn't belong to him and never would. But he'd never been accused of being honorable before.

Rising from the bed, he crossed the room and took her shoulders in his grip. "Tabby. I . . ."

Where to start?

She looked down. "I know. Now that the secret tree is safe, you're going to take me to Sean."

He refused to lie to her. God knew he wasn't mate material or even a wizard of high morals, but he wouldn't intentionally hurt her again. "I must. For you." He dropped a hand to the gentle swell of her abdomen. "For the baby."

Tabitha shook her head, her red hair tousling everywhere. "If you're worried about the danger to us, then leave here! Don't fight this war. Don't put yourself in danger."

In other words, stay with her. Bloody hell, it was so tempting. He'd love nothing better than to wrap Tabitha in his arms, and maybe, if magic-kind had been peaceful, he'd have put their futures and their hearts on the line and tried to mate as any normal wizard would. But everyone knew he wasn't normal. He laughed. There were still bets out there among a skeptical few on the duration of Ronan's mating to Kari. And of the twins, Ronan had always been the more steadfast. Raiden feared he had zero chance of making Tabby happy for more than a night.

And magickind wasn't peaceful.

"I can't leave Ronan, Bram, and the others to fight alone. But I won't have you in the middle of the danger. Blackbourne will care for you. His mate passed to her afterlife without birthing a youngling, so he will cherish yours. He's connected and powerful and—"

"Not you." Her face crumpled as tears welled in her eyes.

Raiden's heart turned over. Why did she love him? He shook his head, still trying to understand.

"He won't mean to me what you do." Her hazel eyes sparkled with unshed tears. "He won't make me feel desired. He won't challenge me. He won't make every day an adventure. He isn't the other half of my heart."

Oh God. Raiden closed his eyes. Her plea was persuasive, and the urge to throw caution to the wind strong. He steeled himself. This was their last night together. It had to be. And he would make every second count.

"I'm sorry, Tabby. I can't." Raiden held out a hand to her. "Be with me?"

Tears fell down her cheeks and she shrugged. "You know it's impossible for me to say no to you."

And saying no to her sweet pleas had been the hardest thing he'd ever done.

Raiden didn't say a word, just pushed his robe off her delicate, pale shoulders, unbelted it, and let it drop to the floor, baring her sweet curves to his gaze.

Breath left his body in a rush. Dear God, she was beautiful. He knew that, but every time he saw her, Tabby reminded him all over again. And not just physically beautiful. She oozed warmth, intelligence, sass . . . along with an alluring vulnerability and a pure heart. She opened herself totally every time he touched her, and there was something so compelling about falling deep into her. It felt like finding home.

Laying her on his bed, he quickly disrobed and

covered her body with his. He captured her lips, knowing this would be the last time. And that hurt like a bitch. In a perfect world, he would do this every night: kiss her, caress her, show her how much he wanted her.

But in this flawed world, he had only tonight.

From the first touch, Tabby arched up to him, and Raiden closed his eyes, slipping into fantasy, a place where she was his—and always would be. Every night would be filled with her love. And after he'd swallowed her sated cries with his kiss, he'd roll over into blissful, untroubled sleep with her by his side and their youngling growing strong in her belly.

The thought was a powerful aphrodisiac. He deepened his kiss, claiming every inch of her mouth as if he'd been able to make his wish reality.

He drowned in her sweet taste, sinking into a pool of want so deep, he knew he'd never emerge. And he didn't want to. He let the undertow of desire drag him under as he caressed her so-soft skin, down her neck, to the swells of her breasts. Her sighs tugged on his heart. This last time, he wanted her experience to be so special. She might mate with Sean Blackbourne and give her body to him for the rest of their days, but Raiden wanted to believe that she would never forget him.

He swept tender kisses across her skin, lingering at the sensitive peaks of her breasts, reveling in her slender fingers filtering through his hair, holding him close. He worshipped both nipples, laving them with attention for long minutes until she writhed, until the scent of her arousal grew unbearably, drawing him lower.

Raiden caressed the swell of her belly again, regretting like hell that he wouldn't see his youngling born or know what it was like to hold him or her. After tomorrow, he'd lose most rights to the child. Yes, everyone knew he'd fathered Tabby's baby. But as her mate, Blackbourne would be seen as its father.

Shoving the thought aside, he lowered his forehead to her stomach and cupped the swell in his hands. Tears pricked his eyes, and his mouth drifted across the little mound.

"Raiden . . . I'll stay. The danger, it's—"

"No. Please. Just let me . . . say good-bye."

Tabby tried to wriggle up, no doubt to argue, but he eased her back down and found his way between her legs, kissing the sweet, silky-wet flesh there. He'd never forget her taste, no matter how many women he took to maintain the energy to fight. There would be no one like Tabitha.

Beneath his caress, she mewled and bucked, selflessly giving all of her pleasure to him so easily. God, even after everything, she trusted him with her body in a way that both humbled him and blew his mind.

As she convulsed and her cries of pleasure echoed off the cave walls, he rose over her and slid inside her. Deep, deep, so damn deep, Raiden didn't know how he'd ever find his way out. She welcomed him, her slick heat a haven, the place he'd always crave. The place he'd want to stay in forever.

Ronan believed that Raiden loved Tabitha. Ronan was right.

Fucking impossible time to realize it.

He cupped her face in his hands, refusing to look away from her for a single second. Instead, he made love to her with a soft, reverent stroke, guiding her body up until she moaned, tensed, gasped, then surrendered her pleasure to him completely. Lost to her, Raiden followed Tabby into the abyss. And when she fell asleep in his arms, curling up like a trusting little kitten, he burrowed deep under the covers with her, hand over her belly, and drifted off, pretending that when he woke tomorrow, Tabitha would still be his.

Chapter Nine

The following morning, Raiden woke with Tabitha in his arms, her legs tangled in his. He buried his face in her neck and inhaled. Her natural perfume, like cinnamon and fresh spring rain, made him ache instantly. He'd know it anywhere. And he'd miss that scent forever.

The sun hadn't yet risen, but his fantasy night was over. Though he'd awakened her several times to make love, it hadn't been enough. It never would be. But the time had come to face reality. Keeping Tabby and the baby safe was his first responsibility, even if that meant cutting out his own heart.

After pressing a kiss to her forehead, he untangled himself from her and rose. Stomping down his regret, Raiden showered and dressed. He found Bram in the kitchen, drinking coffee.

He poured himself a mug and sipped, wincing. When Bram made it, the brew could take the paint off walls. Today, Raiden feared he'd need it.

The Doomsday Brethren leader wore an edgy, watchful expression that didn't bode well.

"Do you have a minute?" Raiden asked him. "I have a problem."

Bram sipped coffee. "A minute, literally. I must meet Duke this morning. Long story."

Not one with a happy ending, clearly.

Quickly, Raiden told him about nearly everything that had transpired over the past two days, including the parchment outlining the Untouchable family tree he and Tabitha had retrieved.

"Bloody hell." Bram shook his head. "Well, the good news is, there's no need for you to worry about Tabitha's safety now. Mathias knows the identity of the Untouchable. Duke found her last night and is bringing her here. I'll fill you in later. I'm expected to meet them now."

Before Bram could leave, Raiden grabbed him by the shirt. "You're saying that Mathias no longer needs the information Tabby's father begged her to protect?"

"Precisely. We found the Untouchable last

night, and Mathias is on Duke's arse now. He shouldn't bother Tabitha again."

With a grim nod, Bram disappeared out of the room and left the caves. Raiden melted against the wall and loosed a staggering sigh of relief. Mathias had no cause to hurt Tabby now. She was safe. And as soon as Raiden could get her away from him and settled with Blackbourne, he could rest easy, knowing she wouldn't be caught in the crossfire of this bloody ugly war.

Thank God.

Except now this really meant good-bye.

That reality settled in as Raiden ambled back to his cave in a sightless daze. His legs moved as if they'd become leaden. Tightness banded his chest, and sharp pains tore through him. Breathing fucking hurt. Tears stabbed his eyes like needles.

Today, he'd lose Tabitha forever. He'd never know her kiss or her love again. He'd never hold their youngling. He'd never imagined this moment would bring him to his knees, like an army of dull knives gouging his soul.

Better that than Tabby widowed or dead. Knowing she was safe had to satisfy him for the rest of his life.

❈   ❈   ❈

Tabitha paced the little bedroom, her hair tucked up at her nape, her skirts swishing around her. Worry jabbed her stomach.

When she'd awakened, Raiden had been gone. Wasn't that a metaphor for their relationship? Only now, she wasn't worrying that he simply didn't love her. The way he'd made love to her last night, she knew better. No, what concerned her now was his safety. Had he left her to fight? Would today be the day Mathias bested Raiden, killed him?

Seven against an army. Staggering odds, to be sure. For the youngling's sake, she should be happy that Raiden would soon deliver her to another man who would make her and the baby his responsibility.

True, she didn't have to be Sean's mate. Her father had left her with much. She could rebuild the house and live comfortably for the rest of her years. But he'd wanted this match for her, wanted a father for her youngling. Raiden couldn't—or wouldn't—fill the role. She understood, really. If Mathias attacked them here and she had to escape, smuggling a youngling to safety . . . odds were, Mathias would kill them.

Sean was a kind man, and he made her laugh, feel secure. As matches went, it was a good one. He would never demand her heart and soul, yet would always put her first. It was more than many of magickind's arranged matings. But now that she'd known joy in Raiden's arms, Tabitha feared that mere comfort would never be enough.

Still, how could she naysay her parents' wishes? And Raiden's as well? He fought for such a noble cause and tried so hard to keep her safe.

She couldn't. And arguing would only make them both hurt more.

A moment later, Raiden entered the little bedroom, resignation all over his face. Dread crashed into the endless pit of her stomach.

Tabitha tried not to think about the fact that he would never make love to her again. From today on, that would be a virtual stranger's right.

"Bram says the identity of the Untouchable is no longer secret. Mathias knows who she is. The danger to you is gone."

And so was her reason to stay. Raiden was, no doubt, eager to send her on her way.

"I'm sorry for her, then."

"Indeed. Would you like coffee? Breakfast?"

Before he dropped her off and left her forever? "No, thank you."

He nodded. "I've already talked to Blackbourne's household staff about taking over the rest of the details for your family's burial. They will work with you. The bodies are being transferred now, so you needn't trouble yourself."

She swallowed down her rage and guilt and endless sadness. They swirled together, making her stomach pitch and roll. She placed her hand over her belly, where the life she and Raiden had created together rested. He would never know his son or daughter. She could never share the joy of parenthood with him. Desperate tears burned her eyes.

"Thank you," she choked out, then looked around, realizing she had no reason to delay the inevitable. "I have nothing to pack or take to Sean."

Raiden shook his head, clenching his jaw as if he held back a terrible pain inside. "He'll have you. He needs nothing more."

Tabitha felt more tears sting her eyes, and she stared at the ceiling, willing them away. But nothing could stop them.

"Can't we . . ." *What? Find some way to be together, yes. But how?* She had no idea.

"No," he bit out. Then he kicked the bed with a frustrated roar. The mattress lurched across the floor, shuddered, stopped. "The last thing in the world I want to do is let you go. But you saw Mathias yesterday. He and his Anarki are relentless. In the past, they've attacked us at Bram's house, burned it down. We've engaged them in battle repeatedly. It's only a matter of time until the casualties mount up. The rest of these wizards have mates, and I don't understand bringing them into danger." He shook his head. "But none of them have a coming youngling. If this fight with Mathias drags on for decades, as it did during his first existence, then raising a baby constantly in danger . . . no. Besides, I don't know how to care for you the way you deserve. And you deserve everything."

She cupped his face in her hands, willing him to understand. "You care for me in every way I could want, Raiden. If not for the baby, I would do whatever it took to stay with you."

"And God help me, I would probably let you." He grabbed her shoulders. "I'm so damn weak where you're concerned."

She caressed his cheek, and he closed his eyes, a shudder racing through him.

Then he leaned down and pressed a lingering kiss to her mouth, soft, full of regret and good-bye. "I love you."

Tabitha felt those three words light up her whole body. The air left her lungs. He loved her? Really? Yes, it was there in his blue eyes. He looked straight at her, not blinking, not flinching. Finally, he let her see how much she meant to him.

"Why now?"

"Because I'm selfish. You'd recover from me more quickly if you believed I didn't care, but I can't stand you thinking that I'm too much of a bastard to love you. And because there's a part of me that hopes you never forget me."

"Never," she vowed. "I'm praying our youngling has your eyes so I can look at him or her and remember you each day."

Tabitha held back a sob. God, this was tearing her up inside. While she would be safe and protected with a man who would watch her and her youngling, Raiden would be alone, fighting the war that most of magickind was too cowardly to wage—and likely dying. And knowing all the while that once Sean Called to her and she spoke the Binding, Raiden would lose her forever.

To keep her and the youngling safe, he was causing himself immense pain. As much as she hated the situation, she loved him even more for his sacrifice.

"Don't do this. I'm willing to risk the danger to stay here with you."

He closed his eyes and shook his head. "I'm not. Your safety means more to me than . . . anything."

Damn it, under that playboy surface, he was a good man. "But *you* won't be safe."

Raiden shrugged. "All I ask is that you remember me. Tell the youngling about his or her father, please."

She nodded, but everything inside her was falling apart. "I don't want this."

"It's for the best." He held out a hand to her. "Let's go. Blackbourne is expecting you."

As she linked her hand in his, her insides crumbled. Tabitha fought to stay on two legs and not throw herself against his chest and beg. Her heart hated this. Her head knew he was right.

Together, they ventured through the cavernous structure, then exited to the rocky outcrop overlooking the sea. The winds were calm today. The sun rising over the water looked magnificent with the promise of a new day, a new beginning.

"I can make my way from here," she whispered.

Raiden squeezed her hand. "I'll see you there safely." He hesitated. "Don't make me let you go before I must."

Tabitha held back tears and nodded. A moment later, the vacuum swept around her head, and she staggered, her balance off as Raiden transported her to Blackbourne's estate.

When they arrived, he gave her hand one last squeeze . . . then released it.

She wanted too badly to grab him again, hold him one last time, but in front of them were the imposing black wrought-iron gates protecting Blackbourne's rambling house from intruders. On the other side of the gates, Sean walked toward them with a purposeful step.

He was still in his prime and a handsome man in his own right, and Tabitha knew she should feel fortunate. She didn't.

Sean raised a hand. Moments later, the gate opened. Raiden guided her through until they stood before her mate-to-be.

"Thank goodness you're safe," he murmured, taking her hand. "After I heard of your family, I worried for you and the youngling."

"I'm fine." Physically, yes. On the inside? Dying. How could she mate with this man? Or any man other than Raiden?

Sean directed a firm stare at Raiden. "You're giving her to me, correct? You understand that once you leave this estate, she will be mine and you will no longer be welcome to see her?"

Raiden didn't look at her, didn't hesitate. "I understand. It's as her parents wished. You will keep her and the child well."

Sean curled an arm around her and brought her close. Nothing about him repulsed her. She simply didn't love him and knew that she never would.

"Well, then." Sean sent Raiden a tight, polite smile. "There's nothing more to say."

Raiden shook his head. "One more request: when the youngling comes, if I'm still . . ." He hesitated.

Alive. That was the word he sought.

He cleared his throat. "If I'm still . . . fighting, will you send word of the youngling's birth? I'd simply like to know that he or she is delivered safely."

Blackbourne hesitated. "I will. But don't ask for anything more."

Chapter Ten

*R*aiden paced the barren turf around the perimeter of Blackbourne's estate like a damn stalker, sinking into the newly-rain-soaked soil as he eyed the towering gates and the imposing house beyond. He should leave: Tabby—Tabitha—was no longer his. But he remained. Wind whipped his hair, tugged at the bare branches of the trees above, and echoed hollowly around him.

Two damn days since he'd dropped her off with Blackbourne and the wizard had taken her into his home. Had he Called to her already? Claimed her?

Raiden clenched his fists. Likely so, and it was best for Tabitha. But damn if it didn't hurt like hell.

Gnashing his teeth at the futility of his pain, Raiden heard a whooshing sound behind him.

Then another. Followed by several more. Heart pounding, he tucked himself deeper into the shadows, crouching behind a massive tree. He peered around the gnarled trunk.

Mathias and a dozen Anarki emerged into the spill of light at the perimeter of Blackbourne's gate. This wasn't a social call. Everything about their manner screamed violence.

Fuck! Why were they here? Between the Blackbourne family connection to Mathias and the fact that he already knew the Untouchable's identity, Tabitha should have been safe now. This show of force made no sense.

Except Mathias's expression said he had revenge on his mind.

Raiden didn't dare teleport away. This close, Mathias would hear. And he couldn't leave Tabitha alone. But he also couldn't fight a half-dozen Anarki by himself.

Sending up a prayer that his unconventional idea would work, he whipped out his mobile phone and snapped a picture of Mathias and his goons, then sent it to Bram. He added a text: *Get ur arses 2 Sean Blackbourne's & b quiet.*

Unless and until reinforcements arrived, Raiden had to slow the Anarki's entry into the house. Because if Mathias reached Tabitha, the fighting would likely be brutal, swift, and one-sided.

As the wind turned particularly brisk, he aimed his wand at the nearest tree and lopped off a heavy, dangling branch. He sent it hurtling into two of the formerly human soldiers. Their undead corpses toppled over, one decapitated. The other grunted, losing his arm and bleeding an oily black.

Mathias tensed and glared at the tree. Raiden knew he was sizing the situation up and wondering, *Natural causes or magical?*

Raiden plastered himself behind, low to the ground, trying to figure out how the hell to stall Mathias now.

A moment later, he heard a gentle whoosh to his right. Raiden tensed, but Bram, Ice, Caden, and Ronan appeared in the shadows beside him, against the wall. Raiden whipped his gaze around to see if Mathias had heard or sensed their arrival. But the Anarki had already vanished, ripping the wrought-iron gates wide and stomping onto the grounds behind the brick walls.

Raiden stood, thoughts burning through his

head. He motioned the others over. "We have to go in now. Tabitha is inside—"

"We don't know what we're walking into," Caden argued.

"I don't fucking care. He can't . . ." God, Raiden was so terrified of the possibilities, he couldn't get the words out. "I will not let him touch her."

Ice and Bram exchanged glances, then nodded.

"We'll split up. Caden, you and Ice head to the east side of the house. See if you can determine where Mathias has gone and what he's done. The rest of us will take the west side and do the same."

No one was in sight as Raiden and the others sprinted across the expansive grass and approached the rambling house.

As they crept around the west side, one look into the windows proved to be Raiden's worst nightmare. Blackbourne lay facedown on the ground, unmoving. Unconscious? Dead? And Mathias clamped a cruel hand around Tabitha's arm, smiling with malice as he said something that made her flinch.

Terror pumped through Raiden. He prepared to launch himself through the window. Mathias could not touch her for another second without Raiden losing his fucking mind.

Bram grabbed his shoulder and forced him down. "Do you want to ensure her death? We need a plan."

Mathias used his free hand to rip the top button of her dress. She shrank away with a scream. He laughed and reached for the second.

"We don't have time for a plan." Raiden shook off Bram's grip. "If you want to help me save her, come with me. Otherwise, leave me the bloody hell alone."

This time, he leapt through the window. Glass shattered everywhere, and Tabby turned away to avoid the spray. Shards peppered deep into Mathias's face and chest. With a nasty scowl, he cursed.

Raiden reached for Tabitha to teleport her away—but Mathias stepped between them. Glaring, he magically wriggled the glass free from his skin. The bleeding cuts healed an instant later.

"Coming to your *encinta's* rescue? How touching." He grabbed Tabby tighter.

She fought and kicked, but Mathias slapped her soundly—a sharp crack of palm to cheek. Her head snapped back. Then she went completely limp.

Dear God, was she dead?

Seething bloody murder, Raiden charged, only to see Mathias raise a hand—and an invisible shield.

He bounced off the force field and snarled. "What the hell have you done to her?"

"She's merely unconscious," Mathias drawled. "Until I deem otherwise."

"Tabitha doesn't have the information you want. I do. Leave her be."

"Oh, it's not the information I require. And you're in no position to give orders." With a menacing grin, Mathias hovered one hand above Tabitha's throat, mimicking a strangling grip. Even in her unconscious state she choked, turned red, thrashed.

Raiden tried desperately to push past Mathias's invisible barrier. But damn it, the wizard had five hundred years' experience on him.

Still, Raiden refused to give up. "Don't hurt her. She can't help you."

"But you can. I'll release your encinta unharmed if you give me the Untouchable within an hour. I know you, Bram, and that ridiculous Duke are sheltering her. Give her to me, and I'll leave your sweet Tabitha alone."

Duke would never allow that. He'd given

up virtually everything to keep the Untouchable woman safe. Besides, surrendering such a weapon to Mathias . . . they could all die an unpleasant death.

Raiden shook his head. "You'd never turn Tabitha loose unharmed. I think you'd kill her for the sport alone."

Mathias raised a brow. "It pays to know your opponent. Clearly, you do. Bravo!"

While Mathias verbally jousted, Raiden caught site of Caden and Ice quietly creeping up behind the wizard, slowly drawing their wands. Both were covered in black blood, indicating they'd killed more than a few Anarki.

Out of the corner of his eye, Raiden saw Bram and Ronan approach Mathias's blind flank, wands in hand. God, would they finally catch the bastard and vanquish him once and for all? Could it be that simple?

Caden pointed his wand at Mathias's head, fury and hate all over his face, then took a step closer.

He bounced against Mathias's invisible wall. And their surprise was blown.

Suddenly, the chilling bastard whirled to growl at them all and, arms raised, sent a massive wall of water crashing in every direction. Water gushed with ear-splitting power, dousing everything in sight. They staggered back. The strong current swept Raiden's feet out from under him and rolled above his head. Ahead, he could see Tabitha wriggling, a tangle of legs and skirts in the thick water as she fought Mathias.

Then another wave sucked him under.

Gasping for air, he fought his way to the surface, following the trail of bubbles. When he emerged, he sucked in a deep breath—and saw Tabby swimming across the surface toward him. Surprise jolted him like a live wire. She was alive! Free!

Greedily, he clutched her against his chest with one hand, wand in the other, while he scoured the room for Mathias. She grabbed Raiden tightly, buried her face in his neck, and sobbed.

As the water flooded out the open window and dissipated, Raiden realized Mathias was nowhere in sight.

"Damn it!" Caden shoved his wand back into his jacket.

Bram pocketed his wand and glared at Raiden. "We could have cornered the bastard, but we didn't have a bloody plan. You jumped in without thought."

With a glance, Raiden told the group's leader that he could fuck himself. Yes, he wanted Mathias dead . . . but he needed Tabby alive more.

Ronan clapped him on the shoulder. "I'm glad she's safe."

"Besides," Ice added, "we don't actually know how to kill a wizard who's already risen from the dead. There's nothing to say that even with a plan, we would have succeeded tonight."

In fact, they'd all wondered before if killing Mathias was a mere fantasy. Incarcerating him was nearly impossible, which left them wondering how the devil they could vanquish him once and for all. Raiden only knew they wouldn't stop trying.

In his arms, Tabby pulled back and sent a terrified hazel gaze his way. "He's gone, Raiden?"

"Yes. I'm here, love. How do you feel? How did you get free?"

"I'm fine. When he slapped me, I pretended to pass out, hoping he'd drop me or think me useless as a hostage."

Wishful thinking.

"When Mathias blasted the water through the room," she continued, "I-I felt him dissolving himself into the water. The way he grabbed me, I knew he meant to take me with him. And if he did, he'd kill me. So I surprised him by kneeing him in the groin and shoving away just as he dissipated."

If Mathias hadn't already been in the midst of breaking down his form to float away with Tabitha, he would likely have remained behind and killed her just for spite.

Raiden clutched her tighter. He hadn't saved her, damn it. She'd saved herself. Her cunning and bravery made him love her that much more.

"You amaze me, Tabby."

"Please don't leave me again."

He didn't know what to do. But he couldn't give her back to Blackbourne if the other wizard still lived. That, he *knew*.

"You haven't mated yet," he observed by studying her signature.

"I-I told Sean I needed time to mourn, that I couldn't pile what should be the happiest time of my life on top of the saddest."

Raiden closed his eyes. He'd wanted Tabby safe . . . but the thought of her being Blackbourne's had ripped his heart out and poured acid in the empty hole.

"But Sean suspected," she went on, "that I was stalling. He knew I mourned you as well."

Raiden hesitated. He'd brought her here for safety, but if he hadn't returned tonight, Blackbourne would have failed her. She might, even now, have been dead. Or worse.

At his feet, Sean Blackbourne staggered upright and saw Tabitha in Raiden's arms. Blackbourne froze, resignation settling across his features.

"You've come back for her, then?"

Raiden looked between him and Tabby—and realized that even with the risk of war, she'd be safer with him and the rest of the Doomsday Brethren. As long as Mathias roamed free, trying to overtake magickind, there would be danger everywhere. Raiden had seen plenty of casualties among magickind's innocents, who had no defense against a maniac like Mathias. "Civilians" like Blackbourne were ill-equipped to fight this terrible threat. Mathias could come for Tabitha again and again. Raiden shuddered to think what would happen if he wasn't by her side.

Meeting Blackbourne's stare, he simply said, "Yes."

Blackbourne sighed with regret, then looked at Tabitha. "I don't have to ask what you want. It's clear that you love him."

Tabitha's lips pressed together as she slowly

made her way to Blackbourne and kissed his cheek. "I'm sorry, but . . . I do."

A sad half smile crept across the older wizard's face. "Your haunted eyes made that hard to miss. At first I thought that mourning was strictly for your family, but when you said his name, I knew." Then he glared up at Raiden. "You're mating with her, correct? No more crap about lacking instinct?"

Raiden stiffened. "That's something Tabitha and I will discuss."

"See that you do. Quickly."

Biting back anger, Raiden resisted telling Blackbourne what he could do with his edicts. But the wizard was letting them go with no malice, and getting Tabby to safety was more important.

With Blackbourne's permission, they all teleported away from his estate and back to Ice's caves. The other wizards quickly made themselves scarce. Raiden took Tabby's hand and dragged her to his cave, then set her on the edge of his bed.

He knelt beside her, resisting the urge to fidget. "You deserve much better than me."

"You've done your very best to keep me safe," she argued quietly.

"It hasn't been enough."

"You don't have to do it alone. Together, we survived these past few days. We will in the future, as well."

"You don't know that!" He jumped to his feet.

"I know without a doubt that you'll do everything in your power to keep me and our youngling safe."

True. And he'd never stop.

"This war is dangerous. I may not live to see old age."

"I'll cherish every moment we have, but I have faith you'll do everything to return to me safely."

Another truth.

Tabby grabbed his hand and urged him back down with a gentle tug. "Life doesn't come with guarantees. These are dangerous times. Is anyone safe?"

No. And he knew it, had thought it himself mere minutes ago. "You're right, but I'm . . ." Raiden shook his head, trying to force the words out of his mouth. He wanted Tabby so badly. But he wanted her happiness more. "I'm terrible mate material."

"How do you know that for certain? You've never tried mating."

Closing his eyes, Raiden hung his head. Shame clawed through him. He'd wasted years, focused on nothing more than conquering one female after another. It was all he knew. "You know my reputation."

"Indeed." She sighed. "If I released you now and gave you leave to bed any woman you wished, are you certain you wouldn't choose me?"

Not choose Tabitha? No woman had ever affected him so much. He'd choose her every time. "You know I want you. God, so much . . ."

"Have you ever felt about another woman as you do about me?"

Until her, he'd never fathomed feeling about any witch as he felt about her. "No."

"Have you ever told another woman you loved her and meant it?"

Say the three scariest words to some meaningless lay? "No. But your parents wanted—"

"My parents believed that you would never love me. If they were here now, what would you tell them?"

A wave of emotion broke over him. A realization. Sadness, joy. Raiden's love for Tabitha flowed through his veins, as natural as breathing.

Suddenly, he knew exactly what he wanted.

Always before, he'd been afraid to believe in it, fight for it.

Not anymore.

Raiden took her face in his hands, feeling tears well in his eyes. "I'd tell them that I'll defend you to my dying breath, that I will want you always, and that I love you more than my own life."

She smiled softly, tears running from those thick-fringed hazel eyes. "That's what I hoped you would say."

His thoughts raced. Only one thing stood between him and Tabby now. He'd faced down Mathias tonight with less terror than asking his encinta the question on the tip of his tongue. "Do you have any reservations about mating with me?"

She caressed the side of his face and sent him a huge, bright-eyed smile that lit up his heart. "Call to me and find out."

Issue the formal vow of a wizard to his mate. Right. Hell, did he even know the words?

Raiden closed his eyes and pictured the rest of his days with Tabby. In contentment, shrouded in love.

The sacred words filled his head.

"Become a part of me, as I become a part of you. And ever after, I promise myself to thee.

Each day we share, I'll be honest, good, and true. If this you seek, heed my Call. From this moment on, there is no other for me but you."

Tears flooded her beautiful eyes, and Raiden swore that even with her hair half-tumbling out of its knot and her clothes soaked, she'd never looked more radiant.

"Was that so difficult?" she whispered.

No. In fact, he'd never felt more certain about anything in his life. Except . . . "Are you going to answer?"

"I can't wait." Tabitha pressed a kiss to his lips, and nothing had ever tasted sweeter. "As I become a part of you, you will become a part of me. I will be honest, good, and true. I heed your Call. 'Tis you I seek. From this moment on, there is no other for me but you." She smiled again. "We're officially mated."

"We are, indeed." He tore off his shirt and hovered above her to remove the last of the pins from her hair. Then he sent her a lopsided grin. "I need to make you mine. Now."

She sighed as she unbuttoned her dress. "I already am."

Darkest
Temptation

Sharie Kohler

Chapter One

The car rolled to a hard stop beside the house's perimeter wall. Lily's head bounced against the headrest, her seat belt biting into her chest. The moon-soaked night throbbed around her. *Alive.* As palpable as heavy fog.

This was it. Where *he* lived. She knew it. Felt it in the tightening of her scalp. The tingling of her flesh. The dull, nagging throb at the core of her. Already, she felt the change. The difference, *her humanity fading.*

Fighting back a swell of nausea, she rotated her still tender arm, gently fingering the deep wound there, cringing at the sticky warmth of her blood.

The man beside her spoke, his voice as rough and gritty as the asphalt burns on her hands and knees. "Remember what I said. If you lose the gun, use the knife. Lose both, and you're dead. Nothing else will work on him. Got it?"

She turned to stare at the hunter. *Curtis.* Moonlight streamed through the dirty windshield, limning his narrow features a pearly gray. He reminded her of a rat with his straggly hair and hooked nose. His small, dark eyes darted anxiously around them, as if he expected an attack. "I've been hunting this bastard a long time. Fail me and you die."

She nodded once, wishing he would stop talking and let her get it over with so she could put this nightmare behind her. She recalled his brutality. He had cut down those . . . *things* without a blink. She was nothing to him. A means to an end. Expendable. She knew what needed to be done.

"Fuck him if you have to, just kill the bastard."

She flinched at his harsh words despite all she'd been through. All she had seen tonight. All she still felt . . .

Bile rose in her throat and she shivered. She'd only ever been with one guy—her high school boyfriend. Before he'd graduated and left for Berkeley. Before Mom had gotten sick and Lily's life had become about working two jobs, paying bills, playing nurse. About making it through the day, the week, the year. About giving up on her dreams in order to survive.

He chuckled and closed a hand over her bare thigh, sliding moist fingertips beneath the edge of her skirt. "You're a nice enough piece. You got that going for you. Use it."

She pried his hand from her thigh, gritting the words, "I'll do whatever it takes." And she would. She always had. For her life. For Mom.

He grunted and motioned for her to get out of the car. "I'll be around. Don't screw up."

She stepped from the vehicle, eyeing the stretch of white stucco wall that guarded what lay within from the outside world. A shiver chased down her spine. *You know what lies within. You came face-to-face with it over an hour ago. Watched as it made a meal out of Maureen.*

Gleaming silver eyes, swiping claws, and gore-stained teeth flashed in her mind. She shoved the images back with a ragged breath. Maureen's short-lived scream echoed in her head. Lily closed her eyes against the stinging memory and sucked in a deep breath.

Clasping a hand over the nasty bite on her arm, she assessed the wall, the headlights of Curtis's car warm on her back. Gnats and mosquitoes danced around her, attracted to the light and the aroma of spilled blood—hers and Maureen's.

Craning her neck, Lily tried to imagine a way over the ten-foot wall and not think about what waited on the other side. The gun tucked in her jacket bumped her hip, offering solace as she walked. Curtis's eyes burned into her from where he sat in his car.

She could do this. She had to. She couldn't fail. Couldn't vanish and leave Mom alone. Not now, so near the end.

Fueled with determination, she climbed up a large oak tree beside the wall, biting her lip against the pain in her arm. Blood ran over her teeth, warm and sweet, but still she climbed. She worked her arms and legs, fingers digging fiercely into rough bark. Fresh blood rose on her scraped palms, making her grip slippery as she dragged herself onto a branch. Inch by slow inch, she progressed further, holding her breath, praying the branch did not snap beneath her weight. Finally, as far out on the bowing limb as she dared, joints stretched and screaming in protest, she jumped.

With a muffled shout, she caught the wall. Grunting, she clung, slippery hands curling around the edge. She hauled herself up, dragging her body. Chest heaving, shoulder screaming in protest, she collapsed atop the wall. She had done it.

Curtis reversed and turned his car around, the lights swinging wide. She watched the taillights disappear down the hill, the purr of the engine fading as he vanished into the night.

She had made it over the wall. Now she was on her own.

For several moments, she fought for breath, the coolness of the stucco seeping through her, chilling her legs, penetrating through her jacket and silk halter top. The halter top Maureen had loaned Lily when she'd shown up at Maureen's house wearing a *"boring blouse"*—Maureen's words. Fresh-hot pain rolled over her. *Maureen.* Dead. Mauled and rotting behind that nightclub. The image flared, a burning imprint in her mind. She jammed her eyes in a tight blink, but the horrible image clung, scraping behind her eyelids.

Opening her eyes, she stared at the moon burning brightly through the night's clouds, seeing it with fresh eyes. The eyes of someone who knew its curse, understood its power. It would be the end of her if she let it. Its intense force seemed to flow to her even now, reaching for her, *into* her. The wound on her arm tingled in response.

"The hell with you," she growled. "You're not going to get me." Sucking in a breath, she surveyed the drop down from the wall.

Turning on her stomach, she slid her legs over the edge. Feet dangling, she lowered herself until she hung by her fingers. Arms burning, muscles stinging from the strain, she dropped . . .

And landed hard, toppling and rolling to her back in a winded pile.

She rose slowly, assessing the grounds around her. Well-tended lawn cushioned her feet. The perimeter lights of a large house with a surfeit of windows winked at her through the wind-brushed trees. The windows gleamed like dark sheets of ice in the night. It was beautiful, a showpiece. But oddly soulless.

She stepped forward, every muscle tense, ready. Do-or-die time. She couldn't leave Mom. Not now. Not after sticking with her through all these years.

Body taut as a bowstring, she advanced through the trees, hoping they would shield her, offer some cover until the last possible moment.

"Fuck him if you have to, just kill the bastard." She ground her teeth to block the thick rise of bile in her mouth. She would do whatever it took to win back her life . . . *to keep her soul and not turn into a monster with a taste for human flesh.*

To be there with Mom at the end.

She thought of tonight again, of Maureen's screams, of the white-hot pain as teeth ripped into her. That wasn't going to happen again. Now that she knew monsters were more than make-believe, *more* than the stuff of nightmares, she was ready. Her hand slid inside her jacket's pocket.

I'm the hunter now.

Luc crouched high in a tree, more shadow than man, watching the interloper through narrowed eyes. He had felt her the moment she'd stood outside his gates. *Smelled* her. The female heat of her. The freshly spilled blood she wore like perfume. The fear.

Inhaling her scent, faint and earthy beneath the taint of blood, his throat thickened. The old dark hunger rose in him as he observed her weave through the trees.

Silent as the wind, he jumped to another tree, loosely climbing the trunk and perching on another branch with the agility of a jungle cat. He flicked an angry glance at the moon. Bad timing for her. Its lure thrummed through him. The heavy pull alive and strong in his muscles and bones. He would be hard-pressed to control himself tonight. She was a fool to come during moonrise. When he felt so little restraint. When hunger rushed him. His heart raced with predatory speed in his chest.

She was not the first. Others had come. Mortals and lycans alike. Although never alone. Hunters came in groups. Lycans in packs. They hunted him for one reason only. To kill him.

As he watched her, he knew the same purpose filled her, saw it in her deft, determined strides. Felt it in the vibrating tread of her feet over the ground. And he knew he would do what he had done to the others. Destroy her. Leave no trace behind. Those who intruded on his life never lived to carry tales or spread word of his existence. They thought him something else. Another lycan. Only too late did they learn he was more. *More* dangerous. *More* of a threat.

He would destroy her and then move on. Continue. Cursed and alone. Existing. But not living. Never living.

He had carved for himself the closest thing to peace he had ever known here. Far from his cousin and the army of evil he'd built. Brethren whose taste for blood was not limited to moonrise. Nothing save total dominion over the world would satisfy Ivo. Luc wanted no part of the mad schemes, wanted only to escape from the corruption.

He glanced a final time through the branches at the moon that called, beckoned, tugging him down dark paths. The same moon that had conquered Ivo. *And Danae.*

Luc looked down, cocking his head and watching the female as she moved. He inhaled through flaring nostrils. Hunters always carried a certain stink to them, righteous zeal combined with the odor of stale blood from countless kills. He had never come across a female hunter. Not in Europe. Not in the States. He did not think they existed. He frowned, shaking his head.

Moonlight sifted through the latticework of branches. Her hair, glossy dark under the kiss of pearl beams, fluttered through the wind as she moved. His body leaned forward, eyes following the path she cut. He inhaled her scent again, her woman's heat filling him. Earthy, musky dark and ready to mate. His cock grew heavy. Need pulled at the back of his skull.

He growled low in his throat. Time to finish this. *Her.* Before he surrendered to those urgent needs and fell victim to the curse he had spent lifetime after lifetime avoiding. Somehow, he'd clung to his soul through all these years. One tasty female would not break him now.

With an epithet burning the back of his throat, he dropped twenty feet, his large frame landing lightly before his prey.

Chapter Two

*H*e dropped from the sky like a hawk, landing on the balls of his feet in a crouch, an animal ready to spring.

Swallowing down a scream, she spit out with forced bravado, "Nice trick."

He would expect her to cower. To scream. To beg for her life. She would disappoint him.

He answered her with a low growl.

She could make out little beyond his enormous size and the flash of eyes homing in on her, a predator intent on the kill. Doubt clawed hot fingers through her. Something was . . . different. He was different. His eyes glowed down at her a yellowy-brown. Nothing at all like the pewter-colored gazes of the beasts that had attacked her outside the club. Baltic amber with white fire flaming in the center.

He flew forward then, slamming her down on

the ground. Her teeth clacked together at the sudden collision with hard earth. He loomed over her, around her. Like the night, he was everywhere all at once. A massive wall of flesh, bone, and muscle . . . indestructible, yet she had to destroy him. *She had to.*

Her hand flew inside her jacket, the once stylish black suede her mother had bought her two Christmases ago now a shredded mess. The thought of her mother made her chest burn. She had to strike. *Now.*

Her fingers closed around the cold grip. She slid it from her jacket. Before she even had time to aim, he grasped the weapon and twisted it from her hand, turning it so that the cold barrel aligned with her throat, the mouth pressing directly beneath her chin, the gun's cold lips a deadly kiss on her shivering flesh.

Shit. He'd disarmed her with pathetic ease.

The wall of man —*beast*— around her pressed closer.

"C'mon. A bullet isn't really your style," she choked, her skin simmering too hotly for her to care about the wisdom of provoking him. "Shouldn't you be mauling me like a dog right about now?"

"You're either very stupid or incredibly brave."

How about desperate? And pissed? His kind had killed Maureen and infected her. If he was going to finish her off, she was going down spitting in his face.

The gun dug deeper beneath her chin, punishing.

Sucking in a breath, she waited for the pain. Waited for death. A moment passed and nothing happened.

Slowly, she focused on his face, all shadowed angles but undeniably human. Baltic-gold, deep-set eyes drilled into her beneath dark brows. Mesmerizing. But not a beast like from the club. He was nothing like the monsters that had attacked her and killed Maureen. The realization gave her a start.

Why had Curtis recruited her to kill him, then?

"Silver bullets, I take it?" He leaned in to sniff the gun before nodding. "You came prepared. Except you can never be prepared enough for me." His face descended in a blurring rush of speed. She gasped. The warm tip of his nose brushed her cheek, moving over her skin until his lips grazed her ear. And damn her traitor body if she did not respond, did not arch against his chest—against the hard body of a faceless stranger holding a gun beneath her chin.

He inhaled deeply. "What are you?" His voice rippled heat through her body. Warm and guttural, like smoke curling in her veins. And foreign. The exact origin indecipherable.

As he leaned over her, she felt the thick bulge of him, hot and heavy against her belly. Dread filled her at her rising hunger. She throbbed at her core, and moistness rushed between her legs. She groaned, hating herself—the terrible thing she had become—and hating him but ready to have him. All of him, hard and thrusting inside her right here. Right now. Like two animals in the dirt. And she still couldn't clearly see his face. She couldn't live this way.

God. She shook her head and stopped, the slide of the gun's mouth beneath her chin too real, too terrible.

"You're trespassing." He sniffed again, then exhaled, his breath a hot gust on her flesh. A dragon breathing against her cheek. Her heart clenched. His will alone stopped the killing fire from spewing forward. This she knew. Somehow. Intuitively. She knew a beast surrounded her despite his human appearance. Curtis must have been wrong when he'd explained the rules that governed lycans. Hope unfurled in her chest. Maybe that meant she wouldn't be a slave to the moon and primitive urges, a slave to the insatiable need to kill, to feed on human flesh . . . to screw anything with a Y chromosome.

"But you know that." A thread of laughter laced his voice. "Come to kill me, have you?" The hair near her temple feathered, and she realized his fingers touched there, rubbing her hair as if it were something to test between the pads of his fingers. The instinct to turn into his touch and purr like a cat seized her.

"You're no hunter," he announced. His nose buried in her hair then, breathing deeply. She shivered. She heard the frown in his voice as he demanded, "What are you? Why do you wear your own blood?"

"I—" She stopped, swallowing at the horrible croak of her voice. "I was attacked. Bitten." She stopped again and bit her lip to keep from saying more. Saying the rest.

He pulled back, a tension that hadn't been there before seizing him, washing over him— pouring into her. "When did this happen?"

"A few hours ago."

"How did you get here?"

She opened her mouth, hesitating.

"How?" he barked.

"A hunter dropped me off. He said he was an agent from . . . some group."

"NODEAL," he muttered. "National Organization of Defense Against Ancient and Evolving Lycanthropes."

"Yeah, that's it." She swallowed before adding, "He said this was your fault. That you're some big pack leader. An alpha. That if I killed you . . ." Her voice faded.

"Ah. Did he now?" He smiled then, although no humor lurked in the shadowed bend of his mouth. "So you think I'm your alpha?"

She nodded her head against the ground.

"And," he drew out the word, "he told you killing *me* would save you. Would break your curse."

"Yes." She surged forward with renewed strength, struggling, stopping at the cold press of the gun.

"Wrong."

She blinked. Wrong? What did he mean, *wrong*? This was her life . . . and her mother's. Killing this monster was her only chance.

"If I die, you'll still be a lycan."

"But you're a—"

"I'm not a lycan. I'm something else."

The announcement twisted like a knife in her chest. "You're lying!"

"Sorry—either your hunter friend lied to you or he was mistaken. Your alpha is out there somewhere, but it's not me. You're one of them—" He rose higher above her, a lengthening shadow, removing himself from her even as the gun deepened its kiss beneath her chin. *He meant to kill her.*

"No." He was lying. She didn't know why, but he was. He had to be.

"You're infected."

"No—"

"You're ruined."

Her voice fell harder, her denial hotter. "No! I'm not. I'm a person! Not a monster."

"Not anymore." He pulled back the hammer, the grinding click twisting her stomach, and she realized all the shouting, all the no's in the world, would not stop him. He meant to kill her. To end her life here on the cold ground of autumn, miles from Los Angeles, miles from her mother. She closed her eyes in a long, agonized blink.

"Please. My name is Lily." The words rose from

deep within her. She was a person. With a name. Not some monster in need of killing. Not like the thing that had bitten her. He had to see that.

Gradually the pressure beneath her chin eased. The gun moved away. His weight lifted as well. Before she had time to orient herself, she was pulled to her feet.

"Come," he commanded, moving ahead of her. *Leaving* her.

For a moment, she stood alone, surrounded by trees and quiet night. Moonlight infiltrated the thick canopy of branches as she watched his lithe movements carry him forward, confident and fully expecting her to follow.

And for whatever reason, she did. Nothing had changed. Her mission was the same. She didn't believe his vague *I'm something else*. Right. He was the key to her survival. Killing him meant life. That had to be true. She wasn't giving up.

Lily.

A flower. Sweet and pure. He dragged a hand over his head to the back of his neck. Even better. Now she had a name. Now he would think of her as Lily. Lily with the great hair. With breasts that wouldn't quit. With the fascinating scent that affected him on a primal level. Oh . . . and a fresh lycan bite on her arm that marked her as property of some pack out there. Lily, who would turn in the next month and no longer be so sweet, so innocent, so pure. *So just take her. What does it matter? Satisfy your lusts and then destroy her.*

Lily. The name cracked his resolve. She was too vulnerable, too . . . *human.* A girl. A woman.

Even if she wasn't anymore.

Except for the bite on her arm, everything about her still screamed "human." Vulnerable mortality. All that he had ever wished to be.

He couldn't recall the last time he'd shared an honest moment with a mortal. His mother's family had raised him, reviling him as a child, then, later, as he grew into a man, fearing him.

He had never justified their fears. Never harmed a human who hadn't tried to kill him first. He'd never wished to dominate and enslave man—as Ivo did. Luc believed humans to be generally good. Even the hard-core agents for NODEAL and its European counterpart, EFLA.

He'd witnessed war and atrocities in his lifetimes, but he'd also seen goodness and honesty and dignity within mankind. And that was what he saw in her. *Goodness. Honesty. Dignity.* He couldn't destroy that. Lily—his first brush with humanity in countless years. And he couldn't make himself destroy that—*her*. At least not yet. On the next moonrise, he would. When there would be no mistaking what she was. When all the humanity had faded from her DNA.

He could feel her stare drilling into his back as she followed him, could *feel* her uncertainty, her confusion. Because he'd denied being her alpha. Because he hadn't killed her. A delay only, he assured himself. A way for him to do what needed to be done and not suffer guilt for the rest of his too-long life.

He strode inside his house, waiting for her in the mosaic tiled foyer, pausing near the stairs, one hand clutching the iron railing until he felt her arrival. Once her soft steps cleared the threshold, he pushed on, not daring to look over his shoulder and see the temptation he heard with every step . . . or smelled with every breath. He didn't need to. He had seen her perfectly in the dark, his vision homing in on a face alluring in its sweetness. Round and apple-cheeked. Fresh. She would look young at forty. Not that she would ever see forty. She was lost. He would do well to remember that unless he wished to join her in the afterlife.

Blinking hard, he shoved back the stinging thought. He might struggle now with what needed to be done. But not later. Later he would perform his duty and not blink an eye.

Maybe he needed to venture into the city and find a woman for the night. Occasionally he succumbed and did such a thing, although he hated the risk, never fully trusting himself.

He walked down a corridor of bare walls, the soles of his boots sinking into the plush runner. He'd bought the house fifteen years ago, already furnished and decorated for some Hollywood big shot who had run out of funds before closing.

She trailed him silently, the sweet fragrance of her blood wrapping seductive tendrils around him. He passed through the kitchen, striding past top-grade utilitarian appliances, the gleaming steel of the oversized refrigerator revealing a blurred reflection of himself. The sharp blade of a nose. The harsh set of his dark brows over primal eyes. The black, close-cropped hair. Once, before his fourteenth winter, his eyes had been a light hazel, dark moss when he'd laughed. Or so he'd been told. Scarce laughter had filled his childhood. He and Ivo had had only each other. Born two days apart, they'd been more brothers than cousins. Cursed before they'd even left the womb.

Shoving thoughts of Ivo away, he descended to the cellar. Her steps echoed behind him. Standing in the center of the icy-cool room, he pulled the chain of the single bulb dangling near his head and faced her. The bulb danced wildly, sending light around the room like some kind of dizzying strobe.

She was tall. Her body full, like women used to be, when a little meat on your bones had meant wealth, prestige, status. A time he remembered. Ripe breasts pressed against the silky fabric of her top, the nipples prodded to attention. He could make out the tiny bumps dotting her areolas. His cock grew hard as he stared. Her eyes stared back at him. She had yet to survey the room . . . her prison for the next month.

Her dark eyes feasted on him in the sudden light, pupils dilating as they crawled over his face, seeing him for the first time, missing nothing. He felt the rise in her body temperature, noted the slight increase of blood flow in the heart that already thundered in her chest. He saw. He felt. He heard. He *knew*. One lift of his finger and he could have her. Could spend himself inside her until his animal passions subsided. The thought of sinking between those ripe thighs tormented him.

Quickly, desperate to flee, he lifted his arm and pointed to the wall, where chains hung, dark as slate, against the gray concrete. A mattress sat on the floor below the chains. They were there for him, although he'd never used them before. Never had the beast risen inside him to the point that he'd needed to restrain himself. He simply needed to be prepared. Needed precautions in place. If that day ever came.

"There," he growled.

Her eyes widened and she shook her head, the brown waves tossing. "You cannot mean —" Her mouth trembled, those plump lips so appealing, so tempting . . .

"Get on the mattress." Urgency sped through his veins, mingling with the pump of hot sexual need. He had to get out of here. Away from her. *It had been too long.* "Get on the mattress. Now."

Chapter Three

Heart beating like a drum against her too-tight chest, Lily bolted past him. Only he was too strong. Too fast. *Not a lycan, my ass!*

He lifted her off her feet, one steel-muscled arm wrapped around her waist. She kicked, landing several solid blows, but it did no good. He didn't slow, didn't even grunt from the sharp dig of her boot heels. He was too tall, too big . . . too male. She was not a small woman, but his body swallowed hers.

He was something all right. *Something* inhuman. Something Curtis hadn't gotten around to explaining, but she would bet this guy was still the key. The key to her survival. If she could just manage to kill him. To get the knife from her boot . . .

He stopped beside the mattress, the soles of his shoes making a rough slide on the concrete.

She twisted in his arms, her hand snatching a fistful of his short hair and pulling with enough force to rip out the roots. Still, he did not react, did not even appear to *feel* pain.

A sob scalded at the back of her throat. Struggling was useless. *Lily girl, you're in trouble.*

She fell limp, breathing heavily within the hard clasp of his arms, her mind working feverishly, trying to figure a way out of this nightmare.

"Are you done?" he growled against her ear, his lips soft. Soft, as they shouldn't have felt. For a man. For him. For whatever he was.

Then she remembered. Curtis's ugly voice floated inside her head. *"Fuck him if you have to, just kill the bastard."*

Could she do it? Her gaze scanned his face, the glowing eyes, the square jaw, the wide mouth with its top lip sharply defined over a fuller bottom one. "Attractive" didn't accurately describe him. He was beautiful.

Closing her eyes to the dark temptation, she thought of her mother . . . of the last seven years they had endured together. According to Dr. Grazier, the end loomed close. Lily hadn't given up on her dreams in order to care for her mother just so she could end up chained to some monster's wall. She'd be there with her at the end. One way or another. She would do whatever it took to survive.

"Are you done?" he repeated.

"Yes." She hardly recognized the breathy gasp of her voice. "I'm done."

She hadn't even started.

Slowly, he released her, relishing the slide of her body against his. Satisfied she wouldn't run again, he pointed fiercely at the mattress and chains.

Defiance still gleamed in her eyes. And then there were those ripe, trembling lips . . . hell, there was a reason he avoided the world. He didn't need this. Didn't need some newly turned lycan showing up on his doorstep to torment him.

His eyes fixed on her mouth again and he cursed, dragging a hand through his short-cropped hair. He needed her out of his sight. And quickly. Before he surrendered and acted out his every primal instinct on her.

Gritting his teeth, he ground out, "Get on the mattress and put the manacles on."

Her chin came up. "Make me."

Dark fire sparked inside him at her words. "You don't know what you're dealing with, little girl." He stepped forward, schooling his face into an unforgiving mask. Hard. Inflexible. No way would he let her know how much she tempted him or how difficult it would be to destroy her. But he would. He wasn't a killer by choice. Not like Ivo. But when necessary, he got the job done.

His hands closed around her arms, and he felt the heat of her flesh, the rush of her blood beneath the fabric of her jacket, beneath her soft skin.

Something flickered in her gaze. Something dark. Unreadable.

She glanced down at the mattress beside them. Moistening her lips, she faced him again, those liquid brown eyes with their fast-fading humanity twisting his insides into knots. "It looks soft enough," she purred.

Even as he held her, she leaned forward, straining, pressing herself against him like a cat in heat, itching to crawl into him. And, God, he wanted her to. It took every ounce of will he possessed to hold her away.

"What are you doing?" he growled, fingers flexing on her.

"Trying to get to know you."

Yeah. Right. It might be a full moon. And he might be a slave to his impulses. But he wasn't stupid. He didn't buy for a second that she wanted to go at it with him. She'd come here for one reason and that was to kill him. "So you can get close enough to kill me?"

"You took my gun," she reminded with a coy arch of her brow.

"And that should make me trust you?"

Her lips curled in the barest hint of a smile. "Don't you want to be friends?" She strained harder against his hands, and his gaze dipped. Her jacket parted wide. His focus fell on the breasts being hugged by her silk blouse. His mouth alternately dried and watered at the hard nipples pushing against the sheer fabric, prodding points he ached to palm.

Fire scored him. His gaze shot to her face. "You're playing a dangerous game."

Her smile deepened, a single dimple appearing in her right cheek. "I like games." Her voice teased, brushed him like the stroke of a feather.

"You want to fuck me?" he drawled, desperately needing the harshness of the question . . . hoping it would scare some sense into her. And jog reality back into him. The reality of what she was. What he was. And why they couldn't do this.

Her wantonness was the beast asserting itself. It had to be. Either that or she was into one-night stands with supernatural creatures she had determined to kill. "Is that it?"

She shrugged and glanced down at the mattress. "Doesn't seem like such a bad idea."

And it *didn't*. At least not with his blood a burning rush in his veins and his logic fading fast. *Shit*.

"You want to go at it? Right here? With me?" he bit out, his voice thickening to an animal growl that sent a bolt of alarm through him. *Careful. Steady.* "Some guy you came here to kill?"

"I don't want to kill you. Not anymore." Her voice purred on the air, stroking a fiery trail through him. He let it burn its path, weave a spell of seduction.

She had a great mouth. Wide with the corners permanently angled upward, the top lip nearly as full as the bottom. Those lips moved slowly now, hugging every word as she spoke, her words a slow, sexual drip. "Just . . . a . . . kiss?" she coaxed.

Cursing, he hauled her fully into his arms, claiming her lips as she had taunted him to do.

It had been too long. Too long since a woman

had melted against him, too long since he'd risked intimacy. Too long since Danae. Otherwise he wouldn't have been kissing a lycan. Newly turned or not. Damned or not. Either way, she was as good as dead.

She touched her tongue to his, and the kiss turned raw, blistering. Their teeth clanked and he tasted a hint of blood, Still, he kissed her. And still, she kissed back just as hungrily. Giving. Taking. Her fingers curled, digging into his shoulders, pulling him down on the mattress. Over her.

He fell between her thighs. Her skirt pooled around her hips. He pulled back and ripped her scrap of small black panties in one feral swipe.

His mouth devoured her lips again. She gasped into his mouth as he rubbed between her legs, playing with her satiny flesh, spreading her moistness. She lifted one boot-clad leg and hooked it around his waist. He slid a hand along the warm flesh of her thigh, squeezing, kneading, caressing his way to the smoothness of her ass.

He wedged himself deeper between her legs, regretting the barrier of his clothing as he pushed himself against her sex, the moist heat there too much. He moved to free himself—only to freeze at the sudden sharp tip of a blade to his back.

He blinked down at the woman beneath him, all hint of seduction gone from her eyes. Hard resolve glittered in its place.

"This is your game, then."

She smiled those full lips, bruised from his kisses, a brutal curve. "I told you I like games."

"A knife won't kill me," he announced in a voice surprisingly calm given the aching burn to possess her singeing his veins.

The point of the blade dug hard into his back, grinding into his spine. Her face inched closer as she hissed, "No? How about a blade dipped in silver chloride?"

He tensed, wary. "That might slow me down a bit." Silver wasn't the deadly allergen to him that it was to lycans. But it definitely took him some time to recover from it.

"Liar!" Desperation tightened her voice. "It *will* kill you."

"I already told you I'm not what you think."

A flicker of apprehension crossed her face before the cold resolve returned, slipping back into place. "No? If you're not a lycan, then what the hell are you? You're not human."

"I'm a hybrid. A dovenatu."

"Dovenatu?"

"Loosely translated to mean 'double birth.' The easiest way to explain it—I'm a half-breed lycan. I can shift at will, not just at moonrise. And silver can't kill me."

While she digested this, he twisted around to grab the knife. The move sent the blade into his back. Not too deep, but just the same, he hissed. Her eyes flared in horror. Clearly a woman unaccustomed to administering pain.

He slammed her arms down on either side of her, flattening his body over hers. Her blade fell softly to the mattress.

"You cut me," he growled, relishing the mash of her breasts against his chest.

She glanced left and right to where he pinned her wrists.

"What's wrong?" he mocked.

She snapped her gaze back to him, and the raw fury there flayed him. Moisture shone in the brown depths.

"Don't you dare cry on me."

"I don't cry," she denied hotly.

Before he caved and lost all his good sense, he tightened his grip on one of her wrists. Doing his damnedest to ignore the delicate sensation of her bones, he clamped one manacle around her. She didn't protest. Simply stared at him with her wide doe-brown eyes, something else creeping in, edging out the fury. Understanding. Acceptance. *Defeat.*

"I'm really going to turn into one of those monsters," she whispered.

He sighed and dropped her bound wrist. The manacle scraped the wall, echoing somewhere deep inside him, where he'd thought feelings, emotions, forever buried. "Yes."

"Killing you won't change that. Won't save me."

"No. It won't."

Lily nodded, dark shiny waves of hair rolling against her shoulders. "I just wanted a night out. Some fun for a change—" She shook her head, stopping hard, whatever else she would have said lost.

She met his gaze, no self-pity visible. Most women in her position would have been full of tears and self-pity at this moment. Hell, most *men.* That she didn't succumb to weakness only made her more attractive—harder to resist. Easy to admire. To want.

"Do whatever you have to. Just don't let me become one of them." She offered up her other hand.

He circled the slight wrist with iron, feeling like a bastard. Whoever she was, whatever had happened to her tonight, she didn't deserve this. She'd simply been in the wrong place at the wrong time.

He'd been born what he was, felt its stigma since childhood. But her? She had run full force into it tonight. It was enough to drive anyone over the edge. Yet here she was . . . so strong, so alluring to his long-dead heart.

She spoke, her voice as tremulous as a feather drifting on air. "What's your name?"

He rose quickly to his feet, as if distance would cure him of his hunger for her. "Luc."

"Luc," she repeated. "What's going to happen to me?" With her eyes she really asked, *What are you going to do with me?*

The sudden image of spreading her thighs and pumping himself inside her slammed into him as hard as a rock. He gave his head a fierce shake. *Moonrise.* He was a victim of the moon's curse. Nothing more. He'd be better in the morning. Better three days from now, no longer such a slave to the hunger. To thoughts of possessing her.

He craved relief. A quick lay. Only not with her.

Even in this darkened cell of a room, he could feel the moon's full power, its strength urging him to release the base impulses he had managed to control these many years.

A quick drive into the city and he would return home sated. *Safe.* At least from her. Then, in a month's time, he would finish it. Finish her. When she was fully turned, her humanity nowhere in evidence, he would not hesitate to destroy her.

Pocketing the key, he stood over her for some moments without answering. Turning on his heel, he left her alone. Safe in her prison. For now.

Chapter Four

*T*he stink assailed him as soon as he drove outside the gate. Lycan blood. Nearby. Luc inhaled deeper, identifying the origin. Days-old blood. A mortal wore it. A man. A hunter. The odor lingered beneath the moon's glow, the scent weaving through the air in tendrils of death. *Ancient evil.*

Parking his Aston Martin down the hill, he moved stealthily through the night, more shadow than man. *Man.* Hell, he had never been that.

His first impulse was to kill this hunter, as he was clearly stalking Luc. This hunter wasn't some misguided soul with noble intentions. Luc could feel the rot of his soul as he cut through the breezeless night. This one was zealous, relentless.

Then an idea formed, teasing at the edge of Luc's dark thoughts. Moving with the speed of hurricane winds, he appeared at the driver's door before the hunter could react.

Luc crashed his fist through the glass and snatched the man by the throat. Fingers tight around his narrow neck, he pulled him through the window, flinging him on his back to the asphalt.

"Please!" The hunter waved his hands wildly. "I mean no harm."

"No harm?" Luc leaned low, hovering over the hunter's face. "Is that why you sent that girl after me?"

"She's a gift, a present," he babbled. "You don't like her? I can find another one—"

"Enough!" Luc roared, knowing just what kind of man he dealt with. He didn't doubt some hunters were driven by a higher purpose—to see lycans eradicated from the world. But something far from altruism drove this guy. "I'll have the truth or rip out your heart. It makes no difference to me. Why are you after me?"

"I . . ." He paused, wetting his lips. "Rumor has it you're running all the packs in L.A."

"Well, your information is wrong." Luc tightened his grip and hauled the hunter to his feet, slamming him against the side of the car. Shattered glass crunched beneath his feet as he stepped closer. The hunter's small weasel eyes bulged.

Luc flicked a glance skyward to the gleaming moon. If he were a lycan, he'd be in full shift now instead of battling the moon's call, the beast in him simmering just beneath the surface. "Do I look like a lycan to you?"

The hunter scanned his face with rapid ferocity. "N-no." His brow creased. "But you're not human. You're too strong. What in hell are you?"

"Someone you've vastly underestimated."

Comprehension washed over his face. "Jesus. You can't be." He shook his head, straggly hair falling in his face. "Dovenatus don't exist. It's just a myth . . ."

Luc twisted his lips savagely. "Wrong again. And that's going to cost you."

He reached around and pulled the guy's wallet from his pocket, scanning the name and address. "Listen well, Curtis. You've got one chance to live." Luc jerked his head toward his house. "It's simple. Find that girl's alpha and you live. Got it?"

Curtis's eyes drifted toward the gated house. "But I thought it was *you*. How am I supposed to find—"

"Now that you know you're wrong, do what you do. You're a hunter with NODEAL, right? You hunt lycans. So *hunt*."

Curtis gave a single nod of his head.

Luc continued, anger churning in him as he thought of the woman chained to his basement wall. "Use your fucking resources. Put together a team. I don't care how you do it, just find the bastard or I'm coming after you and your whole damn branch. Understand?"

Curtis nodded fiercely.

"One month." Luc flung him away. "Go."

Luc watched as the hunter scrambled into his car and sped away. Turning, Luc made his way back to his own car, knowing he needed to take care of one more thing before returning to his house.

The full moon followed him as he drove toward the lights of the city, to the beckoning throng of humanity, where he could find release from the urgent needs that moonrise had ignited in him. He was no fool. If he didn't find relief, he would return and follow her scent to the room below. He would take her. The beast would demand it.

A month with her in his house would be bad enough. But tonight, with the moon at its zenith, the pull a deep burn in his blood . . . she was not safe from his appetites.

He would find some dissolute soul hungry for the coarseness of a sordid tryst and leave Lily alone until he found the courage to destroy her.

Lily struggled against the manacles, fighting the steel that cut her tender flesh. Her mind raced. She thought of Mom. Maureen. The rat-faced hunter who expected her to kill Luc. *Luc. A hybrid*.

"What the hell is that, anyway?" She was still trying to wrap her head around lycans . . . around what they were . . . and the fact that she was now one of them.

Lily fell back on the mattress with a curse. Until a few hours ago, she had never known werewolves existed. Now she did. Now she was turning into one of them. She might not know all of what that entailed, but clearly an out-of-control libido was part of the deal. Great. Probably why her play at seduction had not gone as planned. She wasn't supposed to enjoy it. That enjoyment had distracted her.

Maureen had teased her about hooking up with a guy tonight. *A one-night stand will be good for you. A little pick-me-up*. Somehow making out with some hot half-breed werewolf had escaped Lily as a possibility. Maureen would laugh if—

The thought ended abruptly, before completion. Maureen would never do anything again.

Hot tears burned at the backs of her eyes. She slid to her back, the chains rattling as her arms fell limply to her sides, dead weights. Her skin tingled, crawled. Her gaze drifted. A thin ribbon of moonlight floated from a single narrow window set high on the wall, finding her, stroking her with a tender hand.

A great tiredness swept over her. A sudden lethargy she couldn't fight. Her achy eyes closed, the lids too heavy. She tried to stay awake, to think, to plan a way out of this mess. *What is happening to me?* She managed one weak blink. No use. Her body could no longer move, her eyes no longer stay open. Darkness rolled in.

Luc cut through the crowd, his arm hard around the woman's waist. She tripped on a step and he pulled her up.

"Hey, you're in a hurry," she gasped, her breath a giggly rasp over the club's heavy pounding thrum.

He stepped outside, senses alive, alert on the night. Striding across the street, he kept a firm hand on her as the beast in him coiled tighter and tighter, ready to spring unleashed.

She gasped in approval at the sight of his car. "This is yours?"

Unlocking the door, he pulled the front seat forward. A coy smile on her painted lips, she slid into the back. He followed, pressing her down onto the black leather upholstery, his body wedging between her ready thighs, his need hard and consuming, tightening his balls. He felt the dangerous pull at the back of his skull and swallowed down a growl. If he wasn't careful, he'd turn right here. Something he hadn't done in years.

He bunched fistfuls of skirt and yanked the fabric up the woman's waist.

She laughed. "Hey, aren't you eager?"

Moonlight bathed her through the back window, giving her tanned skin a pearl hue. Her flesh felt warm and toasty beneath his hands, the scent slightly acrid from her frequent visits to the tanning bed.

"What's your name?"

"Luc."

"Hmm, Luc. I like your accent."

She wasn't young. Bottle blond with dark roots rising in her part line. Bleary eyes revealed her night had started long ago. Nothing like the girl he'd left at his house. But that was good. He didn't want someone like Lily. Someone whose freshness reminded him of everything he'd never known. Everything he could never have.

He needed a woman like this. Hard and jaded with tired lines edging her face, accustomed to trysts in backseats with strange men.

A smile pulled at her lips, practiced and full of artifice, accustomed to smoky bars, late nights, and hard men. Precisely the kind of woman he wanted. One who wouldn't mind a quick tumble, minus the sweet words. One who liked it rough. With the moon bearing down on him, foreplay fell short.

She rose up to kiss him. His lip curled at her stale breath, and he dodged her mouth.

"Don't be like that," she pouted against his cheek. "Can't you kiss?" She groped her breasts through her nonexistent top. "Guys usually like these. They cost enough. Can't you say something nice about them? Maybe play with them a bit? The girls would like that."

Ignoring her, he moved a hand to his zipper.

Closing his eyes, the sight of Lily filled his head, *her* breasts, fresh, ripe . . . not readily available to every guy in L.A. Air hissed between his teeth and his cock swelled at the thought of her.

"Sorry. I'm low on foreplay tonight," he bit out, his voice thick and guttural in his mouth. He stilled at the sound, tensing, fighting the swamping sensations. His eyes flew open. Imagining Lily was a bad idea.

"Never mind. C'mere, big guy." Her hand closed around him and he shuddered. Not because of the way she worked her palm over him . . . because it just wasn't right. He saw only Lily. Tasted her. Smelled her scent swirling around him.

With the beast prowling for release, howling in need, he flung himself off the woman. "Go," he snarled. "Get out."

"Shithead," she snapped before vanishing out the door.

He dragged a deep breath inside himself and collapsed against the leather seat, the back of his hand against his brow as he stared out the window at the moon, live and pulsing in rhythm with his heart. Blood rushed in his veins, and his pulse quickened, fought against his body, urging him to turn, to shift . . . to seek his release on the female waiting back at his house.

He should remain where he was. Even if it meant spending the night in the backseat of his car.

At least he wouldn't be anywhere near the temptation that resided in the basement of his house. A woman—a *lycan*—he would have to kill in a month's time if the hunter failed to deliver her alpha to him.

She had no hope of battling her urges and resisting the shift. She would turn. A slave to her hunger. A killer. Without remorse. Without a soul.

For his sake, he should stay away. For both their sakes. Until next month.

Chapter Five

*L*uc told himself he was only checking on her to make certain she had not escaped. His steps fell silently. He ignored his reflection in the stainless steel appliances as he passed. He rarely looked at himself. Had not since his family had turned from him, rejecting him so many years ago. He resembled them, saw their faces in his own. The olive skin. Gypsy-dark looks with gold eyes. His mother. His grandparents. Aunts. Uncles. They were all there in his face. He could do without the reminder.

Ivo had been his only true family . . . and even that relationship had not lasted. Not withstood the test of time. No relationship ever could. Not the endless stretch of time that faced him, anyway.

He eased the door open, wincing at the blackness that greeted him. His eyes adjusted to the dark, instantly finding the still shape lying on the mattress. He could see his way through a subterranean cave. It was part of his gift—his *curse.*

A soft whimper scraped the air and he tensed, hearing the pain, sensing it, feeling its echo deep inside himself. *Remembering his own time.*

Initiation had begun. Long, torturous hours in which her body . . . died. And her new self was born. A new Lily.

Next moonrise, she would answer its call and shift into a beast that fed on mankind. If he did not stop her. If the hunter failed to find her alpha. Luc grimaced. He wasn't holding much hope for that idiot. The guy had thought Luc a lycan—the alpha of the pack devastating the area.

His feet slid unerringly to a stop beside the mattress. She lay on her side, her manacled hands curled in front of her. Perspiration speckled her brow. Salty-sweat drops he could smell. Waves of heat emanated from her, like the warmth emitted from a fire.

Crouching beside her, he touched her brow and winced at the fiery skin. She rolled to her back, crying out against the manacles impeding her movements. She struggled, possessed, desperate to be free.

"Don't," he commanded, even as the manacles cut into her tender wrists. The skin already glowed raw, an angry red.

The memory of his own Initiation rose up in his mind to torment him. His grandfather had locked him in the family crypt. In that dark prison, surrounded by the corpses of his ancestors, he had thrashed on the cold earth, only vermin for company as he'd suffered the bleeding-hot death of his humanity. He cast a quick glance around the dark cellar, not so different from his crypt.

A low keening moan swelled from her lips. A death cry. This girl, Lily, was dying before his eyes. Something shivered through him, and his gut tightened.

Standing, he turned, determined to walk away, determined to leave her alone to endure. There was nothing he could do to prevent it from happening. He'd endured Initiation without anyone being there for him. He'd suffered it alone. Why not her?

He froze at the base of the stairs, hands flexing at his sides, stomach clenching at her pained whimpers. He jammed his eyes tight, as if he could block them out. No use. He couldn't ignore her. Couldn't hide upstairs. Even in his room, he would still know she was down here. This strange girl who smelled of innocence dying.

Cursing, he dug the key from his pocket and whirled around. Squatting, he unlocked the manacles and freed her. He rose, holding her close to his chest, adjusting her feverish body in his arms, his jaw set in a savage clench. Her cheek pressed against his chest so trustingly, defenseless, the heat of her burning through the fabric of his shirt.

With hard strides, he carried her from the basement, taking the servants' stairs to the second floor, passing countless empty rooms until he reached the master bedroom. He hesitated before entering, knowing he could drop her in one of the guest rooms and leave her there, in a comfortable bed, satisfied he had done the best he could to alleviate her pain.

But then he remembered what regeneration had felt like. Like dying and being reborn at the same time. He simply couldn't abandon her to the agony. Couldn't let her suffer through it alone, as he had.

She moaned, and the sound cut through him,

reaching something buried deep . . . something forgotten, dark and untouched. Striding into his room, he yanked back the comforter and lowered her onto the great bed he had occupied—alone—for the last fifteen years.

Stripping her jacket from her shoulders, he tried not to caress the smooth slope of her shoulders. She arched her spine, almost as though she understood and wanted to help. Her boots followed. He concentrated on the side zipper, not the sexy, supple feel of her calves against his palms. Not the pressing need that throbbed through him, stinging his flesh, pulling at his bones until he feared he had gone too far.

Tossing each boot on the floor, he settled her in the center of the big bed. He dragged a shaking hand over his tightening scalp, watching her as he hovered above the bed. Sinuous limbs twisted, working the skirt higher, to her hips. His palms tingled, burning to feel her again. She arched her neck off the bed, dark brown strands brushing his pillow. Her body shuddered as the lycan twisted its fiendish path through her, killing the old DNA and regenerating new. A jagged moan ripped from her lips.

With a curse, he slid in beside her and folded

her in his arms. "Shhh," he said, smoothing a hand over her forehead, pushing back sweaty tendrils as he absorbed some of her scalding heat into himself.

She clung to him, hands digging into his shoulders as if she would crawl inside him. Unable to resist, eager to feel her skin against his own and knowing it would ease some of her fever, he pulled his shirt over his head. Her whimpers softened as he wrapped himself around her, gritting his teeth to keep his sigh of pleasure inside. Her hands gripped hold of him, the smooth, satiny skin of her palms sliding over his back. Her body writhed, twisted against him, desperate and hungry to both escape her death . . . and embrace her rebirth.

Her skirt puddled around her waist and he cursed himself for tearing off her panties earlier. Her rich female scent rose on the air, folding him in a fog of lust. Her movements changed. Became more deliberate, driven from blind, primitive impulse. She clenched her hands around his shoulders and thrust her moist heat against him in a simulation of sex. Air hissed from between his teeth.

He pressed a palm to her damp forehead and

made hushing sounds, willing her to still, to calm, to sleep . . .

After a while, she relaxed.

Holding her tightly, he closed his eyes and willed himself to sleep as well, to escape to where he wouldn't *feel* . . . where the beast would cease tormenting him and he could forget how much he craved the hot press of her body. Not some stranger from a bar that he sought to satisfy his body's insatiable demands, but *this* woman. One part assassin bent on his death. Another part dying innocent.

Bone-deep weariness closed its fist around her. Lily struggled through the heavy shroud of her thoughts, fleeing the heat, the flames that licked through her, intent on devouring her. Mom. Maureen. *A man with eyes of yellow amber who made her quiver inside.*

Then her thoughts slid into something else, something new and terrifying. Her senses came alive, stretched taut and sizzling with awareness. Yellow fog rose up to surround her. Yet she wasn't alone. She felt them. In the wild thrumming of her blood, in the huge moon overhead, summoning her, a pearl in the black sky. Shadows crowded her, lengthening and widening . . . taking shape, becoming *them*. She tasted their wild hunger, knew it for her own. Silvery eyes cut through the fog, homing in on her.

She ran. Fled the demon beasts, so real, so terrifying, so . . . *tempting*. They surrounded her, silver eyes glowing through a fog so thick she could not see her own hand before her. They were everywhere. They chased her. Hunting her. Tempting her. Her enemies . . . her brethren.

She winced at the heat swamping her, at the sensation of her skin tightening and pulling. Shivers shuddered through her despite the terribly wonderful burn. Moaning, she writhed, wiggled as if she could shake the fever free, as if she could lose it—them—herself, this terrible thing that was happening to her. As if somehow she could make her skin stop tingling and itching and aching all over.

Another burn began to consume her. This one a hurt she could take care of . . . if the hard body against her would press closer, deeper, ease the clenching ache . . .

She opened her eyes to a darkened room . . . but saw everything with amazing clarity. Colors everywhere. Vivid colors she never knew existed before. The golden brown of a firm chest, rising and falling with deep, even breaths. She lifted her cheek from that chest and inhaled deeply of salty masculine flesh. Her gaze drank him in. Lithe lines and sculpted muscle. Her skin tingled anew, humming with a sort of electricity. Her already pounding heart beat even harder, and she felt dangerously close to fracturing apart.

While he slept, his lashes cast crescent-shaped shadows on his cheeks. She shook her head and tried to focus on his face, to clear the grogginess from her head, her thoughts thick as syrup.

Her hand slid down the center of his chest. Down, down, down . . .

She knew him. Even in the grip of whatever seized her, she remembered. Remembered the hard hand that had torn her panties in one feral swipe. The steel thighs that had pinned her down, squeezing around her hips. The molten taste of his lips. The liquid caress of his tongue. The gold eyes that drilled into her.

The fact that she fondled the man she had come to kill did not faze her in the least. His was a body that could make her forget. A warrior's body that heightened the already throbbing pull between her legs. She shook her head, knowing such thoughts were absolutely not her . . . and still not caring. Not enough to stop, anyway.

He was too delicious. And she was too hungry, too achy in all the wrong places. *The right places.* There was that voice again, its dark little whisper whipping across her mind, directing her in all things wicked and wild. Strangely enough, that voice felt comfortable. *Right.*

The hunter, Curtis, had told her lust ruled lycans. And now she understood that. Embraced it.

With a desperate little moan, she crawled atop him and covered his sleeping lips with her own even as her hand freed that part of him she craved. *Needed.* Closing her fingers around the satisfying length of him, she stroked him, elated to find him already hard. She gasped her own excitement against his lips, directing the hard tip of him between her thighs, grateful for the lack of clothing.

A pair of hard hands closed around her arms, stopping her.

Before she could draw breath, she was flung through the air. Flat on her back, she arched against the hands imprisoning her, desperate for the pleasure she had been so close to claiming.

She growled, her gaze snapping to his. To a fierce pair of eyes, brutal enough to chill anyone's blood.

Only Lily wasn't anyone. She wasn't even herself. Not anymore.

Her blood ran scalding hot in her veins. Baring her teeth, she hissed her frustration, her desire. Desperate to tempt him, she managed to free one hand and wedge it between them. He kept her bound to the bed with his other hand, preventing her from moving an inch. As if she were some wild animal that might devour him given the chance.

Smiling, she wrapped warm fingers around him, her touch seductively gentle despite the fantastic surge of strength coursing through her. With a purr, she flexed her fingers around his increasing hardness.

"Stop," he ground out.

She pumped him in a deep, languorous stroke. Once. Twice. "That's not what you want." She didn't even recognize the sound of her voice, all thick and guttural in her mouth.

"Yes. It is."

She slid her thumb over the tip of him again, smiling in dark satisfaction at the drop of moisture rising to kiss her. "It's not what your body wants."

He snared her wrist between them, stopping her. "Fortunately, I'm a lot smarter than my cock is."

"Are you really?" She rotated her hips, locking her thighs around him tightly. He groaned at the sensation of her hot sex nudging against him. Her scent rose, heady and ripe. Every fiber of her being screamed in need. She had to have him. She would not relent until they were one. Until he was hers.

Chapter Six

Silver eyes gazed up at him, and something withered, dying inside of him at the sight. She was one of *them* now. But then he had known that would happen. Seeing her lovely brown eyes gone just drove home that she was no longer an innocent girl. No longer like the girls in his boyhood village. Girls he could not have had. The ones his family had beaten him for for even looking at.

She was something else entirely. Something even more exciting. In the throes of dark and primitive lusts, she was overwhelming to him. Something the beast in him could not resist. Every instinct demanded that he claim her, even as his conscience screamed against it—against having her, loving her body only to later destroy it. As he must.

He flexed his hands around her slender arms, his fingers tightening along smooth limbs that would tear and stretch and twist into something dangerous and terrible in a month's time. The same kind of creatures that had brutalized his mother and aunt years ago, resulting in his and Ivo's births. Creating them both—blights on the family.

Still, he craved her, and he could not keep himself from releasing her hand to continue its sensual assault on his body.

She resumed sliding slim fingers over his cock, the feverish touch of her skin deliciously hot. Dangerous and desirable. He arched into her clasp, closing his eyes tight and imagining it was her sheathing him.

He thrust several more times into her hand before opening his eyes and locking gazes with her. The silvery pewter of her eyes gleamed up at him, as wild and menacing as the animal clawing to be freed inside him. *Lycan eyes.* Beautiful in a way he'd never thought eyes like *that* could be. She rubbed the head of him against her moistness, teasing it at her opening, sucking the tip of him inside her. Exquisite torture.

Gritting his teeth, he held back, preventing

her from going any further. Any deeper. Sweat beaded his brow at the agony of it. The bliss. She was no longer human. Nor was she a dovenatu like *him* . . . like Danae, his cousin's mate. He had thought Danae loved him, had thought she'd wanted the things he had—had wanted *him*. Instead she'd chosen darkness. *She'd chosen Ivo.*

And he'd chosen this life. A life of solitude. His lip curled back over his teeth. Perhaps not the best choice if it drove him to crave the touch of a lycaness. Clearly he'd gone mad during these years of self-imposed exile.

Air hissed between Lily's teeth and she released an inhuman growl, surging against his hands, struggling to fully merge their bodies.

Clearly he was not the only one moved to madness. In her right frame of mind—as her proper self—she would never have acted this way. He'd seen that when he'd dropped from the trees and landed at her feet. He'd seen the terror, the revulsion, the wide-eyed stare of a *good* woman. A woman whose careful, controlled life had unraveled. A woman who would never let someone like him touch her. A woman who would have chosen death over a lycan's existence. Knowing her only a night, he knew this much about her. She would never choose to live in the darkness.

No matter what happened, he would lose her.

His most primitive self rose from within him in a hot surge of rage. *But you can have her now. For this night. Take her, take her.*

An answering growl emerged from deep in his chest.

Of all women, this was one he should not touch, yet his hands loosened their hold. The last of his will crumbled. His hands dropped to his sides.

She lifted her hips, impaling herself on him with a satisfied moan.

Buried deep, he groaned at the slick heat of her tightening around him. Not since Danae had he felt *this*. Perhaps not even then. So feral and yet so right. As if she'd been made for him alone, her fit so perfect. He felt the tightening of his face, the telltale pull of his bones, and knew he was losing himself . . . letting the beast come out.

She worked her hips, her nails scoring his chest, oblivious that he was more beast than man in this moment. He gripped the softness of her hips, one hand sliding around to squeeze her plump cheek. Clenching his teeth, he held his passion in check and shoved the beast back into darkness, but hers was on the rise. He watched her in her frenzy, wondering how much she would remember later.

He gripped her face with both hands and brought his head down for a kiss, his lips gentling over hers, tender, thorough, opposite from the beast in him that scraped to be free. Different from the beast in her that struggled into . . . *being*.

He took her . . . her old self dying, the new self emerging. He took her death inside himself, kissing her with his eyes wide open, watching as her pewter eyes drifted shut.

"Look at me," he commanded against her lips. Her lids slid open over those steel eyes, clinging to his gaze. He claimed her lips again as she took her pleasure of him, gyrating and working toward her own release with single-minded intent.

At last she reached it, crying out into his mouth. She stilled. Unfinished, he surged inside her, earning a hot little whimper against his neck. Again and again, he moved. Close now himself, he hooked a thumb beneath each knee and spread her wider for his pleasure. Mewling sounds tore from her lips and she writhed beneath him, roused again.

They cried out together, the sounds sharp and

desperate—as desperate as the painful wringing of his heart. *Too long.* He had been too long without a woman. That had to be it. There could be no other explanation. No reason why it seemed like he would never get enough of this. *Enough of her.*

Suddenly, in that moment, she became everything to him. The one he had been waiting for all these years of hiding, pretending the world did not exist. All his life he had been holding his breath, time propelling him toward this moment, toward her—where he could draw his first breath.

Luc cradled her for a long moment, allowing himself the weakness, allowing a moment during which he could pretend he was normal. Just a man. And she was just a woman he'd asked out on a date, and then another, and another . . . until everything had traveled its natural course, leading up to tonight.

He stroked her spine, running his palm over the sweet arch of it, caressing each and every tiny bump of vertebrae with his fingertips. Danae had not felt so good. So trusting in his arms. There had always been something missing, a rightness that he now felt with Lily.

Sighing, he released her. Lying on his side, he watched her for several moments. She still breathed quickly, chest lifting and falling as if she had jogged a great distance. It would be that way until her transition was complete. He could leave her while she regenerated. She wouldn't rise from this bed for days.

And yet he didn't move. Even as dawn crept upon them, vivid fingers of red and gold clawing through the bedroom toward them, he remained where he was. Beside her.

Chapter Seven

*L*ily opened her eyes quickly, instantly alert, every nerve alive and singing, humming with a vitality she'd never known before. As she sat up, her gaze dropped to the man beside her, who emitted warmth and something else. Something that even while he slept stroked a seductive breath over her.

She pulled the sheets to her chin, her mind racing, tripping over the events of last night. She saw the nightclub . . . *creatures*. Maureen. Then the hunter's ratlike face. *Curtis*. Images swam through her head in an unwelcome blur, cramping her stomach. Then her thoughts crashed on the memory of *him*. Them. Together. Liquid heat swept through her as she remembered every detail, every sensation of his body joined with hers.

Wild, uninhibited sex was not something she

did with any regularity. Not since Adam. And even then it had been gentle, exploratory, their movements always tentative, restrained.

He slept as still as a jungle cat, all long, lean lines, ready to snap and spring at a moment's notice. She sat up, moving as silently, as quickly, as possible. Inching toward the edge of the bed, anxious to flee. She lowered one foot to the floor.

"Where are you going?"

Tightness seized her chest.

He snatched her wrist and rolled her onto her back in one smooth move, the hard press of his naked body a familiar sensation, yet no less shocking.

All her life she'd slept in the same house, in the same room, same bed—her only lover a high school boyfriend, their intimacies stolen moments whenever their parents weren't around. Never had she woken in bed with a large, virile man, her body sated and sore from hours of sex. A five o'clock shadow dusted his face of carved granite—menacing and sexy as hell.

She found her voice, pretending to forget that she was his prisoner before their night together. "I have to go. It's Saturday." As if that made a difference to him. "I have to work—"

"It's not Saturday."

"What?" She blinked.

"It's Monday. You were bitten, infected, on Friday. The change—Initiation—takes a few days. Your body requires that time to regenerate . . . to become lycan."

His words sunk in slowly, unbelievably. *Horribly.*

"See." He nodded to her bare arm.

She glanced down, air hissing from her lips at the sight. The bite, her wound, had miraculously healed. Only smooth skin met her stare—evidence she had no desire to see. She struggled against him, against his words, desperate to leave, to see her mom—

"I can't let you go." The great wall of his body pressed her deeper into the bed, stilling her movements.

"Why not?" she panted against the smooth wall of his chest.

His fingers flexed around her. "You have one month less now."

A month. "And then I'm dead." Her voice rang flat between them. No question, just a simple statement of fact.

His golden eyes drilled into her. "Maybe. Or

maybe your hunter friend will get lucky and find the alpha responsible for your . . . condition."

"How do you know about Curtis?"

"I spoke with him. He was casing the house . . . waiting for you."

Hope swelled in her heart. "And he's going to find my alpha?"

"I explained to him that I'm not who he thought I was and if he wishes to live he can put all his skills and resources into finding the true lycan responsible for your curse."

"And you think he can?"

"It's a long shot. He wasted time assuming I was a lycan and bringing you here when he could have been following leads from the site of attack."

She shook her head. Desperation combined with the suffocating press of his body made it difficult to draw breath. "You don't understand. I can't wait here for a month. I have to go. There's someone—" She stopped herself, hating to mention her mother, to bring her mother into this, hating to taint her with this dark new world from which she might never escape.

His face clouded over. "Someone *who*?"

She shook her head.

He lifted her off the mattress, forcing her face

near his. "A man? A boyfriend?" The light in the center of those amber eyes flickered brighter. "A husband?" His fingers tightened. "You can't go back. Even if we break the curse before moonrise, you think you'll be the same again?" His gaze roamed her bare shoulders. Her breasts tingled against the press of his body.

"Let me go. I need to say good-bye. To my life." *My mom.* "I'll return. I promise."

"Good-bye," he muttered, his gaze crawling over her face, hotly possessive, dipping to where her breasts pressed against his chest. "And how will you explain that? Will you tell him what you are? How becoming a lycan turned you into one hot piece of ass? Will you tell him that you willingly spread your thighs for me? A half-breed lycan?"

Fire erupted in her cheeks, and she beat against his chest and shoulders. "Bastard!"

The light at the centers of his eyes grew, eclipsing the amber. As if he didn't feel her blows at all, his hands moved, skimming down her arms to her waist.

She stilled, feeling herself drowning in those eyes, mesmerized.

He nudged open her thighs with alarming ease

and slid his hardness inside her heat. "You can add that you called me names while you gladly fucked me."

Her mouth opened on a protest, an assurance that there was no one else, but the words never made it past her lips.

Her hands curled into his shoulders. Already she worked her hips beneath him, gasping when he thrust again inside her.

She lifted a leg and locked it around his waist. Her inner muscles squeezed, milking him, racing her toward orgasm with single-minded purpose.

He groaned against the side of her face, one of his hands coiling in her hair. A wild cry ripped from her lips. She shuddered beneath him as he surged inside her several more times, reaching his own climax. Spent, she sank even deeper into the mattress, a boneless puddle beneath him, small ripples of rapture eddying out through her body.

With a groan that sounded part sigh and part curse, he flung himself off her. Pressing her legs together, she scooted as far from him as she could, her fingers digging into her thighs. "You're an animal," she hissed.

He stared at her darkly, one arm tucked behind his head. "So are you, baby. Better get used to it."

"There's no man! No boyfriend. No husband. I just need to go!"

He shrugged as if it didn't matter either way. "Well, I can't let you do that. Look. Let's make the best of the month. I'll show you a good time." He scratched his square jaw. "And given your new condition, you're going to experience urges. Why not experience them with me?"

His words sounded cavalier enough. And simple. But she knew there would be nothing simple about it. In a month's time, she would either shift into a werewolf . . . or die—by his hand.

She had opened her mouth to resume arguing when her stomach rumbled.

"Let's take care of that appetite of yours." He held up a hand to stop her protests. "And then you can keep trying to convince me why I should let you go." His gold eyes fixed on her, hard, probing. "And why I should believe you when you say you'll come back."

"This is beautiful," she murmured, sipping her coffee on a deck overlooking miles of wooded hills. "I don't get to see this in the city." She gazed again at the stretch of countryside. "Doesn't appear that anyone besides you enjoys the view, either." She arched a brow and nodded around them. "No neighbors."

"I like my solitude." He bit down on a buttery croissant, identical to the one she had just consumed.

She reached for another croissant and stared out at the sea of treetops. She couldn't even spot a road. "More like isolation." At the sudden quiet, she glanced across to find him staring intently at her, no longer chewing, no longer moving at all.

"I'm not human," he said succinctly, each word a hard bite on the air. "I have no business being around humans."

She nodded slowly, nibbling her croissant as she studied him, knowing he meant her to take some sort of lesson from those words. Swallowing, she asked, "I suppose you think I should do the same?"

"Yeah. You especially."

"Why me especially?"

He leaned back in his chair. "I'm a dovenatu, a hybrid lycan. I can control my impulses. Can fight the urge to feed at every moonrise. You can't. I shift at will. You can't. Every full moon, you will shift and you will kill—"

"Yeah, Curtis covered this already," she snapped. "I get it."

"Do you? Because you have no business going out into the world until this is . . . rectified. One way or another."

One way or another. She couldn't stop the shiver from trickling down her spine. "So instead I should stay here and keep you company."

His eyes glowed. He idly traced the rim of the glass of juice before him. "The company was good, wasn't it?"

She felt herself blush, the burn crawling all the way to the tips of her ears. She stabbed at a chunk of pineapple and replied quickly, "As you've said, I have a month. I won't hurt anyone until then. I'm going home." Popping the fruit in her mouth, she chewed. It was all bravado. She knew he could chain her downstairs again. Could seduce her with a look or crook of his finger and keep her happily in his bed. But she was hoping he wouldn't. Hoping that whatever impulse had motivated him to free her of that dark basement still held true.

"Very well. You insist on leaving the premises. Fine."

Relief rushed through her. Her words spilled forth in a giddy rush. "I promise I'll come back —"

"I know you will." He cocked his head to the side and relaxed back in his chair. "Because I'm going with you."

Chapter Eight

L uc followed her into the Sun Valley Rest Home and was instantly assailed by the odor of astringents and decaying mankind. He understood how some people could be uncomfortable with the reminder of their own fleeting mortality. It only made him wishful. Wishful to have lived a life wherein he'd . . . *lived*. Instead of merely existing. It made him yearn to age and die in the natural order of man. As God intended, not some witch who'd started the lycan curse over a thousand years ago.

You've lived since Lily crashed into your world—your bed.

He shook his head and watched Lily smile and nod to both the staff and the wizened infirmed trudging down the corridors with their walkers and wheelchairs. She showed no sign of discomfort. She seemed right at home here.

"Where are we—"

"This way. She's in the TV room."

They entered an airy room with several well-worn sofas and armchairs. Three women played cards at a table. Another sat alone on the couch, staring vacantly at the television set.

Lily eased down beside her. Luc hung back, leaning against a bookshelf of paperbacks so old and worn that the titles on the spines could hardly be read.

"Hello," Lily greeted the old woman on the sofa.

The woman looked startled for a moment, blinking warm brown eyes several times. "Hello."

Lily glanced at the television before looking back at the woman. "I like Paula Deen, too."

The woman gave an eager nod. "She doesn't skimp. Fried is fried. Like it should be."

"Absolutely," Lily agreed.

"Do you like to cook?"

"A little bit. My mother's an excellent cook."

The woman patted Lily's hand. "Well, you should get her to teach you."

Lily blinked fiercely and glanced away, the back of one hand swiping at her eyes. And in that moment, Luc knew that the woman with whom she was conversing wasn't a stranger.

"She did teach me how to make a mean turtle cheesecake," Lily offered.

"Hmm, I love turtle cheesecake." Her brow wrinkled in concentration. "I think I might know how to make that."

Lily gave a shaky smile. "I bet you do."

He looked hard at the woman on the sofa, studying her face, the confused gaze, the melting brown eyes—and knew it was Lily's mother.

In that moment, he didn't know what was worse—being alone and not having anyone to love or having someone you loved no longer know you.

"She wasn't always that way."

He flexed a hand on the steering wheel and weaved through traffic. "I'm sure she wasn't."

"I don't want your pity."

He snorted. "Any pity I feel for you has nothing to do with your mother." Only partially true. The stark sorrow, the total loneliness he had seen in Lily's face as she'd sat on that couch, had struck a much-too-familiar chord. It echoed the way he had felt growing up, when he'd endured the hatred of a family that did not want him. When Ivo had fallen to darkness. When Danae had chosen his cousin—and darkness—over Luc.

"So you *do* pity me?"

"What do you expect me to feel for you, Lily? You're in a shitty situation here."

She shook her head. "Couldn't I just lock myself away every full month? Or sedate myself?"

"That's a hell of a burden to carry. If you slip up, innocents die."

She jammed her eyes in one tight blink and rolled her head side-to-side against the headrest with a heavy sigh.

He continued, "You would need one hell of a friend to pull something like that off. Someone to confine you three nights out of every month and then free you. Someone to sedate you if needed. They could never fail. To fail would mean innocents dying."

"Innocents?" she bit out. "Like me."

He nodded. "Like you *were*."

Her face tightened, the smooth features pinching in distaste at the truth of his words. Her new ugly reality. "Yeah. I don't have anyone like that in my life."

Her words resonated deep inside him. Maybe because he didn't have anyone, either.

He glanced to his right. The bright sun struck her hair, bringing out the buried highlights.

"Even if you did find someone you could trust like that, he wouldn't live long enough. Not generations like you. The years pass quickly. Sooner than you think, you would need to replace him with someone else."

"So what I'm looking for is a keeper who's reliable, trustworthy, and immortal?" She crossed her arms over her chest. "Great. Can't be too many of those walking around."

She met his gaze. For a long moment, their stares clung. He knew the precise moment when she realized that *he* was the closest she would ever come to finding that.

A flush crept over her face. Her voice rushed forth then. "Don't think I'm expecting you to do that for me. I don't need you to be my savior."

He looked back to the road, biting back the mad urge to say he *would* do that for her. To put an end to his lonely existence . . . would it be such a sacrifice? As long as he could have her every night. As long as he could keep her with him forever. His hands tightened on the wheel. Impossible. He couldn't keep her. She was a lycan, not a pet. As long as she lived, she was a danger. To the world. To her immortal soul . . . to *him*.

Besides—she didn't want him. She wanted her life back. Her freedom.

"Let's just hope your hunter comes through."

"Yeah," she murmured. "Let's hope."

"You can sleep here."

Lily peered into the guest bedroom, her feet nudging across the threshold. Either he had changed his mind about their enjoying each other for the reminder of the month, or he'd had his fill of her. For some reason, both possibilities made her feel hollow inside.

Something had happened to him during the car drive home. He stared at her as if she were a stranger, the gold fire of his gaze banked, remote. "There's plenty of food downstairs. Help yourself to anything you like."

She strolled into the bedroom, dropping her bag on the center of the bed. They had stopped off at her house and gotten a few things to last the month.

Facing him, she crossed her arms. "No jail cell again?"

"I trust you won't run."

She smiled, but the curve of her mouth felt brittle. "Do you?"

He advanced on her, and she forced herself to hold her ground. "You said you wouldn't. And I don't think you would be foolish enough to try." He stopped directly before her, his eyes at a hard glint. "I would hunt you. And find you."

This close, he flooded her, their breaths mingling hotly. Her skin tingled, every pore vibrating in awareness of him. His eyes dilated, the white flame back again at the centers as he read her desire, the beast in him waking and responding.

She felt him, the attraction deep, primal. Beyond her experience. Heady, euphoric. His earthy male scent filled her nose. She tasted him without touching, the salt of his skin coating her tongue, making her salivate.

Hungry for more, she inhaled, a gaspy sound on the charged air. Then, with a blink, the light vanished from his stare. Without another word, he turned and left. She chafed her hands over her arms, willing the goose bumps from her flesh, willing her heart to still its impossibly fast tempo. Looking around, the room suddenly felt bigger and emptier without him in it. She felt alone, but she was accustomed to that. No reason her heart should ache with an expectation for more.

Basic survival at month's end. She craved nothing more.

But she did. She hungered for more. For life. *For him.*

Silence hummed around her as she stepped into the darkened hall and strode toward the winding stairs. Her feet landed unerringly on each step. She moved with ease, as if it were not dark at all. Her eyes adjusted to the gloom, seeing everything as if midday light poured through the house's many windows. A symptom of her newly altered state, she knew. Even her hunger did not belong to her but to her newly altered self. *Lily, the lycan.*

She'd eaten alone hours ago. No sight of Luc other than his knock at her door and terse words informing her that dinner was downstairs. Alone in her room, little else had occupied her save thoughts of the future . . . and Luc. Luc and the future. Neither of which meshed together . . . but for some wild reason she could not separate the two.

In the foyer, she paused, turning away from the hall leading into the kitchen. Moonlight spilled a wide, irregular circle on the tiled floor. She moved, gazing through the front door's stained glass to the outside world. Turning the lock, she opened the door and stepped outside. The night throbbed all around her. Alive. Pulsing.

She listened, hearing everything in the silence. The wind. The rustle of branches. The scurrying of a small animal nearby. The pulse of the city a half-hour drive from here matched the quick thud of her heart. Closing her eyes, she let herself feel, absorb her new world. Lifting her face skyward, she could see the waning moon even with her eyes closed. Could see it. Sense it. Feel it. Linked, bound to it, she took another step, reveling in the lush, vital world throbbing around her.

Then there was the faintest shift. On the air. In the quickening of her blood. A scent that had not been there before. She whipped around with the speed of a hurricane, the tiny hairs on her arms prickling, telling her she was no longer alone.

One moment nothing was there. Only the whispering night. The next, he was there, unfurling before her like a great wall.

He grabbed her. The biting pressure on her

arm made her cry out. "I told you that you could not escape me," he growled.

"I wasn't—"

"Did you think I wouldn't know?" His eyes glowed, twin torches in the moon-soaked night. "Wouldn't *feel* it the moment you stepped foot from your room?"

Anger swept over her. She wrenched her arm free and growled into his darkly furious face, "I told you I would stay—"

"I don't put a great deal of faith in the word of a woman. Or a lycan." He uttered both *woman* and *lycan* as if they were the foulest epithets.

"What's wrong? Some girl do you wrong?" A muscle in his jaw ticced fiercely, and she knew she'd hit a nerve—the truth. "I'm not her," she hissed, absurdly jealous over any woman who had possessed enough influence in his life to affect him. Unlike *her.* Someone he merely babysat, waiting to see whether he needed to destroy her before the next moonrise.

A long moment passed before he gave a slow nod. "Maybe not, but you can't be trusted any more than I could trust her."

"Yeah? Trust this!" Unaccountably angry, she kicked him hard in the shin and tried to break free. To run, as he'd accused her of doing. Maybe it was his comparing her to another woman, maybe it was the entire hopeless situation.

Or maybe it was just that she was falling for someone she could never have. . . .

He grabbed her again and shook her. "And why should I trust you? She was a dovenatu and *she* couldn't resist the darkness. You're a lycan. How can you fight it?"

"I'm *not* her. I'm Lily. And I wasn't running away. You don't know me at all. I'll face this thing. I wouldn't risk hurting anyone. I would die before I did that."

Their gazes locked, clung. Impossible words filled her heart. A ragged breath lifted her chest, and, unbelievably, she spoke the words her heart battled to deny. "I want to stay here." It was true. She didn't feel that burning need to escape him anymore.

His glittery eyes devoured her. For a moment she feared he would shake her again. Or strike her. That muscle in his jaw ticced wildly. The savage beat of his heart bled into her from where his hands gripped her. She waited, braced and ready.

With a groan, he pulled her into his arms,

crushing her in a hug so tight that she feared he might break one of her ribs.

Then they were kissing, dropping to their knees on the ground in a feverish tangle of limbs and hot, melding mouths. Their clothes fell away. Removed or ripped.

He came over her, seized her hips and entered her, driving hard, deep, pushing her into the unforgiving ground. She wrapped her legs around him, indifferent to the dirt and twigs scraping her back as she met his body's every thrust. Branches swayed above them . . . the silent moon watching through the latticework of leaves.

He cupped her face, snaring her gaze in the glittering gold of his eyes as they moved fiercely together for several moments. Groaning, he shuddered above her. She arched off the ground, crying out and meeting him in his climax.

He collapsed over her, the heavy weight of him thrilling, intoxicating. The sound of their gasping breaths clogged the air. His lips moved against her shoulder, his voice rumbling through her as he spoke. "I won't let it claim you."

His words jerked her back to reality. By *it* he meant the beast, the surrender of her soul. Moisture burned her eyes. She dragged fingers through his hair, stopping at the short ends, clutching them tightly, never wanting to let go. "It might not." Her voice faded on the words — words she could not completely believe. Her life hinged on the slim hope of a *might*.

"I can protect you. Like I talked about in the car. I can keep you safe as long as you're with me —"

She shook her head, knowing what he was offering yet unable to accept. "I won't stay this way." Something so dangerous. An evil creature driven to feed on humans. Like the monster who had devoured Maureen. She had not put her life on hold, caring for her mother for seven years, to lose herself to such a fate. She refused to live that way. She stared hard at Luc, an ache building in her chest at the sight of his too-handsome face. Not even for him. "I won't put such a burden on you."

He stared down at her, his golden eyes intense beneath dark brows. "Let me decide what's a burden."

A grim, vague smile curled her lips. "We'll see."

But she already knew she would not make him spend generations as her keeper. She liked him too much to do that. She winced. *Like*. A pathetic word to describe her feelings for him. But her mind shied away from anything else. She did not believe in love at first sight. Love took time to grow, to build. Whatever she felt for him . . . it was something else. Lust. And she would not give up her mortality for it. She could never stay like this. Somehow she would end the curse. Or die.

Hoping to distract him, she ran a hand down the bristly side of his face. "Let's just make this time we have count." The sound of her voice startled her—all warm female enticement.

The hard glint returned to his eyes. "Oh, we'll have more than this month." His mouth claimed hers again. "We're just starting," he murmured against her lips.

She kissed him back, struggling to ignore the doubt she felt in the hot press of his lips. Like her, he wasn't convinced either.

Chapter Nine

*F*or all the bad that went with being a lycan, Lily could not help appreciating the advantages. Endless hours of sexual gratification. Eating whatever she wanted without weight gain. The heightened senses that made her savor life— *living*—as she never had before. And Luc. They never would have met otherwise.

But through it all, an uneasiness pervaded. The knowledge that it couldn't last. That something approached, encroaching like a foul wind with increasing speed.

She swam beside Luc in his indoor pool, imagining that if mermaids had existed, this must have been what they felt. Gliding so effortlessly beneath the water. After nearly a full minute, she emerged, breaking the water's surface . . . only to get sprayed in the face.

With a squeal, she splashed Luc back. Growling, he grabbed her around the waist and dragged them in a dizzying little circle. Laughing, she dropped her head back, enjoying the cool water swirling through her hair, gliding against her scalp . . . and Luc's hot tongue laving her throat. This, she could learn to love.

You already do.

If Curtis didn't come through, at least she would have had this. More than anything she'd ever had before.

Suddenly, Luc released her.

"What?" she gasped, treading water.

He waved a hand to silence her, scanning the natatorium with a sweep of his gold-brown eyes. As she watched him, the tiny lights at the centers ignited and grew. And she knew. The beast hadn't surfaced in him out of desire. Something else had called it forth.

Chill bumps broke out over her flesh. Evil had arrived. She smelled it like a poison on the air.

"Get out of the pool," he murmured softly.

Lily swam to the edge, Luc close behind her. With a single deft move, he hopped from the water and pulled her up beside him just as a voice rolled over the air.

"Well, you certainly took my instructions to heart."

Lily's head snapped in the direction of the familiar voice. Curtis. He emerged through the archway leading to the spa, his rat face smug. Even less comforting was the gun he clasped in his hand.

"What are you talking about?" she demanded.

"Fucking him."

Luc's hand on her arm tightened, and he shoved her behind him.

"He's not my alpha," she bit out, trying to step around Luc. "You wanted me to kill him for nothing."

"Not for nothing. He's just as bad—a dovenatu." Curtis's eyes glittered with malice. "No one wants his kind around. Not humans. Not even lycans." The hunter's gaze narrowed on Luc. "You don't have anyone, do you, half-breed? Not a pack. No one. Why not just die?"

"I gave you a chance to save your life," Luc replied in an oddly even voice. "Either you give over her alpha, or you're dead."

"Oh, I can do better than that." Curtis paused for dramatic effect. In that time, Lily stopped breathing altogether, the tiny hairs on her arms prickling. "I can introduce you to him. Now."

They emerged then. Two stepped beside Curtis. Another entered through the main doors. She knew them instantly. Knew them. Recognized them as one species knows another. They were *her*. Lycans.

The creatures beside Curtis smiled, looking with avid interest at what could be seen of her wedged behind Luc.

"Lily, isn't it?" one asked, his voice sliding through her like a serpent. "Welcome to the family."

"No," she breathed, digging her fingers into the tight muscled flesh of Luc's shoulder.

"You're a dead man," Luc swore.

"What?" Curtis grinned. "You wanted me to find her alpha. I did. I brought him to you." He nodded. "He's promised to turn me now. It's all I've ever wanted. To be strong. Invincible. To live forever."

The lycan at the natatorium's main doors edged closer to the hunter, and instantly she knew he was her alpha. He patted Curtis on the shoulder, as if he were an overexcited pup. "You did well. And you shall receive all you deserve."

Before Lily could blink, he took Curtis's head between his hands and turned it with a violent snap. Lily screamed. Curtis crumpled. Her stomach pitched and rolled at the ease with which he'd been murdered.

"Lily." The pack leader spoke her name again, his silver eyes intent on her. "You belong with us. Not this half-breed dog." He beckoned her with a flick of a knife he pulled from inside his jacket. "Come."

Here he was. *The key to her freedom.*

The same realization must have occurred to Luc. He faced her. "I hate that you have to see this. Me. But if I don't —" He stopped, dropping his hands from her. "Look out for yourself. Run if you get the chance. Use your speed."

She cocked her head, noticing that his voice had changed, altered as it sometimes did when they made love . . . as though he was on the verge of turning into that thing which he loathed, which he'd spent lifetimes resisting. But he would surrender to it now. For her.

She nodded once in agreement.

Then the Luc she knew was gone. Transformed in a fraction of a second. His face and body shifted, twisted into something horrible in its beauty. Almost feline, with its sleek lines and rippling sinew and muscle. Not swallowed in fur, like the lycans that had attacked Lily and Maureen that first night.

He did this for her. Embraced his beast. All so she could be free. Free of this curse. Free of him. *Free of him?* The thought swiped a bleeding gouge in her heart. She would never be free of him. She never wanted to be.

Her chest ached, and she wondered if anyone had ever cared enough to risk himself for her before. Aside from her mother, who could no longer even remember her, had anyone ever cared for her that much?

Then he was gone, a blur, a flash from her side. He had almost reached the alpha when the two other lycans intercepted him in a smack of bone and muscle. Animal versus animal. Evil versus good.

They fought like beasts. And they were. Bones that would later heal smacked and crunched together. She moved from where she stood, pressing herself to the wall, watching with suspended breath as the two lycans managed to gain the upper hand on Luc.

Wet and snarling, they pinned him to the ground, a grip on each arm.

Then she saw it. Curtis's gun, the weapon innocuous in a shallow puddle of pool water. Silver bullets. A lycan's only fatal weakness. She reached for it, tucking it behind her back as she watched the alpha approach Luc. *Her* alpha.

"A legendary dovenatu, eh?" His glittering silver stare raked Luc. "Disappointing. I thought you would be so much . . . *more*." Snapping his fingers, he motioned to his two comrades. "Finish him."

"No!" Lily surged forward, her palm flexing around the gun's grip behind her back. Her only chance. Luc's only chance.

"Ah, little one." The lycan responsible for what she was—the curse she bore—bestowed a beatific smile on her. "I almost forgot about you." That pewter gaze slid over her curves, and suddenly she wished she were wearing anything but a bikini. His smile slipped, the whiteness of his teeth barely visible as his lips moved. "All heart and sweetness. We'll rid you of that. Come here."

She angled her head, for a moment lost in the mesmerizing pull of those pewter eyes.

"No! Leave her alone!" Luc fought harder. He flung one of his captors over his head into the pool with a splash. With a two-footed kick to the chest, he sent the second lycan flying. He hopped to his feet with the agility of a cat just as a lycan sprang from the pool in a spray of water.

Snapping from her momentary stupor, Lily whipped the gun from behind her and surged forward, her heart a wild, desperate thump in her chest. Squeezing the trigger, she fired at the soaking-wet lycan charging Luc, sending him into the pool again.

The other lycan roared and came at her. Lily jerked back a step, slipping on the wet floor and firing one shot to the ceiling. Luc caught the silver-eyed devil before he fell on her. They crashed to the ground near her, biting and clawing at one another in a wild thrash of limbs.

Lily sat up, trying to focus her aim on the lycan. Luc hurled him off with a vicious kick. Those eerie eyes met hers the precise moment she fired.

"Lily," Luc roared a warning in his thick, guttural voice.

She looked up, finding her alpha practically on top of her.

She swung the gun up, pressing it into his head. He pulled up hard, hands splayed in front of him.

"Easy," he murmured, inching back a step,

easing away from the barrel. His steel-eyed gaze locked with hers and she felt that pull again.

"Shoot him!" Luc shouted.

Shoot him.

Her finger tightened around the trigger. Just the slightest pressure more and it would be over. She would be herself again. Human.

Alone.

The alpha inched back another step. And another.

"Shoot him, Lily! End it now!"

End it. *End them.*

"Save yourself. Break the curse."

His words settled in the pit of her stomach like rocks. In that moment, with her finger tightening on the trigger, she couldn't. She wouldn't. It just felt . . . *wrong.*

Luc snatched the gun from her limp fingers. Her alpha was almost to the doors, his back the perfect target. Luc surged forward, arm outstretched, taking aim.

"No!" She charged Luc, jerking on his arm. A shot fired into the wall.

Like a flash of smoke, the lycan disappeared through the double doors.

"What the hell are you doing?" Luc started to

go after him, but she jumped on his back, arms tight around his shoulders.

"Luc—let him go!"

Luc peeled her off him. He faced her, his fierce face snarling into hers. "What are you doing? You let him get away—"

"I know!" she shouted, tears choking her throat. "Did you mean it? God, please tell me you meant it!"

He grabbed her face with both hands. In a blink, his face transformed into Luc again. *Her* Luc. "What are you talking about?" His thumb roved over her cheeks, rubbing salty tears into her overheated skin.

"You said you would keep me with you. Forever. Did you mean it?"

A long, endless moment passed, the only sound her ragged breaths.

Then Luc dragged her into his arms. Forehead pressed to hers, he pulled them both to their knees. "Lily, Lily, Lily . . ."

She sighed his name.

He pulled back and gave her a small shake, his face tight with a desperation that she felt reverberate deep inside herself. "Don't you understand what you've done?"

She nodded. "Yes." Swallowing past a throat tight with emotion, she answered thickly, "I chose you. An eternity with you."

He stared at her for a hopelessly long moment, and she wondered if he had changed his mind. If he didn't want her . . . the responsibility, the burden. Maybe she wasn't worth it to him.

"Say something." Anything. *Just not that.*

"Lily." He hauled her into his arms, squeezing her breathless. "I do want you—I *love* you. I only hope you don't regret—"

She pulled back to rain kisses on his face. "Never. What I'm getting more than makes up for what I'll lose. Believe that. Don't worry about me regretting this. Instead, think about how we're going to spend the rest of our lives."

He muttered against her lips. "I've already got a couple of ideas."

Chapter Ten

Soft rain pelted the bungalow's window as Lily traced mesmerizing circles over Luc's ridged belly. "Hmm. What now?"

They'd cleared Luc's house of his valuables and left, checking into the Beverly Hills Hotel. Luc didn't want to hang around waiting for more lycans to show up.

"We'll stay here for a while. For your mother."

She sat abruptly, staring down into his shadowed face. When she had asked the question, she had been thinking more along the lines of room service . . . but his answer could not have elated her more. "Really?"

"It's important for you to be with her." He pushed a thick lock of hair behind her ear. "We'll stay. Through the end."

Lowering her head, she kissed him slowly, tenderly, loving him even more in that moment. With their identities now exposed to the world of lycans, she had expected him to insist on their immediate relocation. Staying here for her mother, for her . . . It was more than she had ever hoped. Breaking their kiss, she murmured, "And after that? Then what?"

"Well." A deep breath escaped him. "I want— no, I need to go home."

"Home? Where's that?"

"Ankara."

"Where's that?

"Turkey."

She'd always wanted to see the world. Only her mother's illness had cut short that dream, but there was something in the way he spoke, in the tension of his body beneath her, that made her think a friendly jaunt down memory lane was not what he had in mind. "Why do you want to go back there?"

"I have a cousin there who needs killing. I should have done it a long time ago."

Lily stared down at him with wide eyes. She'd almost lost him. And herself. She did not relish risking life and limb again. Not so soon at least. She shook her head fiercely. "No." Then again, louder. "No."

"He has to be stopped, Lily. You gave me back my life today. Showed me that there are things worth living for. Risks worth taking." His thumb grazed her cheek. "How can I go merrily about life knowing such a threat lurks out there, working its evil? For you . . . for us, I can't do that."

Looking deeply into his intent gaze for several moments, she nodded. He was right, of course. She was not the only one who needed Luc. The world needed him, too. *And the world needed her.* She was a part of this now. She would help.

Swallowing down the tightness in her throat, she gave a single hard nod. She would go anywhere with this man . . . this dovenatu. She'd already determined that with her decision to remain a lycan. "Let's do it, then."

He scowled. "There's no 'us' in this. I won't risk you. You'll be somewhere else. I haven't decided where yet, only that it will be someplace safe. I'll find a way to make sure you're protected during each moonrise—"

Her chin lifted. "You're not leaving me. You signed on for eternity, and that's what you're getting. If there are bad guys out there to vanquish, we're going to do it together."

He opened his mouth, clearly prepared to

argue more, then stopped. Closing his mouth, he smiled crookedly. He brushed the hair back from her neck. "I guess I need to get used to this *us* thing."

"Yeah, you better."

"And a bossy woman."

"That, too."

"And trusting that you can handle all this." He waved a broad hand, his expression sobering. "My world isn't all roses and champagne, Lily."

"It's my world now, too. And the one I want."

He released a heavy sigh and she tensed, prepared for more arguing, anything to convince him that they needed to be together, no matter what. And then his next words penetrated.

"Very well. Guess I should legitimize this and marry you. It does sound as though you're committed to the thick and thin part already . . ."

Her heart squeezed. Despite his teasing tone, he stared at her starkly, his heart in his eyes. Beneath her palm, his chest did not even lift with breath. He held himself tense, waiting.

"Luc." At his growing smile, she cried his name louder. "Luc!" Tossing her arms around his neck, she launched herself against him, sending him back into the bed.

He breathed then, his hard chest expanding as his arms wrapped around her.

And she breathed, too, the air releasing from someplace deep inside of her. Her first breath of life with him. She closed her eyes tightly. The first of many breaths.

The darkness hungers...

Bestselling Paranormal Romance from Pocket Books!

KRESLEY COLE
PLEASURE OF A DARK PRINCE

An *Immortals After Dark* Novel

Her only weakness...is his pleasure.

ALEXIS MORGAN
Defeat the Darkness

A *Paladin* Novel

Can one woman's love bring a warrior's spirit back to life?

And don't miss these sizzling novels
by *New York Times* bestselling author
Jayne Ann Krentz writing as

JAYNE CASTLE
Amaryllis   Zinnia
Orchid

Sometimes love needs a little help from beyond...

Bestselling Paranormal Romance from Pocket Books!

JILL MYLES
SUCCUBI LIKE IT HOT
The Succubus Diaries

Why choose between the bad boy and the nice guy...
when you can have them both?

CARA LOCKWOOD
Can't Teach an Old Demon New Tricks

She's just doing what comes supernaturally....

GWYN CREADY
FLIRTING *with* FOREVER

She tumbled through time...and into his arms.

MELISSA MAYHUE
A Highlander's Homecoming

Faerie Magic took him to the future,
but true love awaits in his Highland past.
